BEAUTIFUL STAR
&
OTHER STORIES

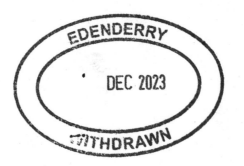

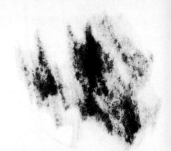

BEAUTIFUL STAR
&
OTHER STORIES

Andrew Swanston

THE
DOME
PRESS

Published by The Dome Press, 2018
Copyright © 2018 Andrew Swanston
The moral right of Andrew Swanston to be recognised as the author
of this work has been asserted in accordance with the
Copyright, Designs and Patents Act 1988.

A CIP catalogue record for this book is available from the British Library

ISBN 978-0-9957510-3-3
[eBook ISBN 978-0-9957510-4-0]

The Dome Press
23 Cecil Court
London WC2N 4EZ

www.thedomepress.com

Printed and bound in Great Britain by Clays, St. Ives PLC

Typeset in Garamond by Elaine Sharples

MIX
Paper from
responsible sources
FSC® C110794

For my family

PREFACE

Each of this collection of seven stories is based on a true historical event and includes real as well as imaginary characters. Other than that the stories are linked only by being, I hope, interesting bits of history.

I learnt about *Beautiful Star* from a newspaper cutting on display in the little church of St Monan on the edge of the Fife village of St Monans. It struck me then as a story that would reward further research. And so it proved. Before the advent of steam, the hardy fishing folk of the East Neuk depended on their skills as boat builders and sailors, on the vagaries of the herring and the capricious North Sea and on each other. Now there is little commercial fishing but the villages and harbours are still there and so is their history. The fate of five fishing Fifies and their crews in the storms of November 1875 is a part of that history. All the main characters, including the well-named minister Mr Foggo, the narrator, Julia Paterson, and her extended family lived in the village at the time of the story.

The story of Eilmer, the Flying Monk, I came across as an historical footnote and felt that it too deserved to be more widely known. Try asking someone in which year the first recorded – by the almost contemporary historian William of Malmesbury – manned flight took place. I doubt that one in fifty will know, any more than I did before visiting Malmesbury. A thousand years ago Malmesbury was a renowned centre of learning – just the sort of environment in which a curious mind like Eilmer's would flourish.

Eilmer was also very unusual for the time in seeing what we call Halley's Comet twice in his lifetime. On both occasions the comet presaged bloodshed – first from the arrival of the Danes and later from that of the Normans.

'A witch and a bitch' was an expression used to describe Jane Wenham, also known as the Witch of Walkern. Her story – a *cause célèbre* at the time – illustrates how beliefs in witchcraft persisted into the eighteenth century and how readily a village could turn against an 'incomer' and use the law against him or her. Jane was poor and unpopular but a witch she was not.

'The Castle' is the story of the gallant defence of Corfe Castle led by Lady Mary Bankes, mother of twelve children and widow of Sir John Bankes, Privy Councillor and close advisor to King Charles, during the War of the Three Kingdoms. There are various historical accounts of the siege and I have selected from them that which best suited my story. If not the origin of the word 'turncoat', it certainly offers a good example of its use.

'The Tree' is based on the best known story of the collection yet is perhaps the most whimsical. William Careless did hide in the oak tree with the king, but the boy… Well, who knows?

The stories of the button seller and the drummer boy, one English the other French, are well documented, although their names remain a mystery. I learnt about them while researching my book *Waterloo: the Bravest Man* and have put them together to form a single story, linked by their presence at the battle. I have given neither of them a name because it seemed more appropriate not to.

Who could not be intrigued by the name Admiral Sir Cloudesley Shovell? His flagship, HMS *Association*, and the three other vessels gave rise to the Longitude Act of 1714 and the later solving of the problem of longitudinal navigation by the brilliant clockmaker, John Harrison. For that alone his is a tale worth telling.

I thank my agent, David Headley of DHH Literary Agency, for encouraging me to put these stories on paper, and my editor, Rebecca Lloyd of The Dome Press, for her expert advice.

CONTENTS

BEAUTIFUL STAR

1875

It was after church one Sunday in January of that year that Father first mentioned the idea. 'I've been thinking about a new boat' he said, 'and I've spoken to Angus Miller. He's going to do some designs. *The Angel*'s fourteen years old now and she's only thirty feet. She looks like a child beside the English boats and she was built for local work, not long voyages. Now we're going south every autumn we need a decked boat and a good deal bigger.'

A new boat made sense. Boats were getting bigger all the time and there was talk of the St Monans harbour being expanded. At least Miller's yard was by the harbour, so the boat would not have to be hauled down the hill on rollers. That was a dangerous business. Our Uncle William had lost two fingers on his left hand that way.

'Can we afford a new boat, James?' asked my mother.

'I've told Angus no more than seventy pounds. And anyway it's not settled yet. I'll decide when I've seen the plans.' We all knew that was a fib. He would never have raised the matter if he had not already made up his mind.

Praying in public and the smell of fish are two things I have always disliked and both still remind me of that time. My mother, Julia Paterson, for whom I was named, claimed that she could tell a fish by its smell. I couldn't. Herring, ling, cod, mackerel – they all smelt the same to me and it was a smell that no amount of soap and water or rubbing with lavender ever quite got off my hands.

As for church, I found the Sunday ritual tedious and embarrassing. Religion should be conducted in private. But off we had to go, all eight of us, to the little St Monans church – men and boys in suits, ties, and 'guid socks', women and girls in bonnets or neepyin' shawls, everyone in clean boots, with hands and faces scrubbed and polished. And all for an hour of singing and praying and half an hour of Mr Foggo. He was well named, the minister. His sermons were impenetrable.

Afterwards there was another half hour of polite gossip outside the church before we were allowed to walk home over the stone bridge, down the hill and along the street by the harbour which we called The Shore. Walk, mind. No running on Sundays.

Churches themselves I quite like when they are empty, and ours was more interesting than most. Built in the thirteenth century and restored six hundred years later, it is so near the sea that on windy days we all had to enter by the back door in case a sudden gust tipped a child or an elderly worshipper on to the rocks below. The story is that King David gave the church to the village after he had been rescued from a shipwreck or nursed back to health after an arrow wound. Or perhaps both.

It is the conformity I find difficult, just as I have always hated having to wear a uniform, wave a flag or belong to a club. Father said I was an awkward child; Mother said I'd grow out of it. I never did. I still avoid herds, flocks and shoals.

Like most fishermen, father tried to be at home on Sundays. That was not possible in early spring when the fleet sailed north in search of the herring shoals or in autumn when they made the long journey south for the 'English fishing', but otherwise he seldom fished on a Sunday. Ours was a God-fearing community, tight-knit, enduring, resilient, and the large Paterson family was at the heart of it.

On fine Sunday afternoons father and mother took a walk around the village and if I was not too busy preparing my lessons for the week, I went with them. By then I had started as a pupil-teacher at Miss Brown's Adventure School. I was lucky to be appointed. A vacancy came up at just the right time and Mr Nevin, the parish school head teacher, had spoken for me. He knew I wanted to teach and he knew I hated fishing. 'You wouldn't be much of a fisherman's wife, Julia,' he told me, 'but I think you might make a teacher.' On the first point at least, Mr Nevin was right. As soon as I had qualified, I planned to find a position in St Andrews or Edinburgh. Or anywhere where there were no fish.

The motto of St Monans is '*Mare Vivimus*', although, apart from Mr Nevin and Mr Foggo, I doubt if there was a person in the village who could read Latin. It was a typical Fife fishing village, built on a steep hillside between the larger villages of Pittenweem and Elie and facing directly out to sea. Returning St Monans fishermen saw the church at the western end of the village and at the eastern end a windmill built to pump seawater to long defunct salt pans. Inland from the salt pans there was once coal mining but that had ended after a fire sixty years ago.

The village was dominated by the harbour and by The Shore which ran around it. The grand houses on The Shore – three storeys high with crow steps at the tops of their gabled walls, grey slate roofs and tall windows, were owned by the fish merchants. The cottages of fishing families like ours had pantiled red roofs, dark windows scanning the sea like so many eyes and whitewashed walls overlapping the roofs to prevent tiles being lifted by the wind. The East Neuk of Fife is a windy place.

Twisting cobbled streets ran up the hill away from the harbour, with drying greens for the nets squeezed between the cottages, and steps cut into the hill – welcome shortcuts for fishermen hauling their kit home to dry, or their wives carrying baskets of fish or children late for school. Mr Nevin's Parish School and Miss Brown's Adventure School were both at the top of the hill.

Except in church, father always wore the traditional fisherman's rig of woven jacket, long inner waistcoat inside the trousers, shorter outer waistcoat buttoned up to the neck, thick woollen trousers and leather boots. It was his uniform and he was proud of it. I cannot now picture him, or my brother Robert, in anything else. Clay pipe in mouth, steely blue eyes, pepper-and-salt side-whiskers, cap at a jaunty angle, skin weathered by sun and sea – the image is as clear as it ever was. And Robert was working at looking just the same.

Our cottage was typical: three rooms downstairs, one for living, cooking and eating, the other two for sleeping; and another room upstairs, partitioned into a storage loft for nets and equipment at one end and my parents' bedroom at the other. At five years old, Alexander was still young enough to share it. When they were first married, it must have been quite spacious but twenty-two years and six children later, it was anything but.

In a village of two thousand souls everyone knew everyone else, even if they could not quite remember how they were related. None of our cottages were big enough for major family gatherings; baptisms and weddings were celebrated in The Anstruther Arms, deaths in the Church Hall.

Towards the end of February, before *The Angel* sailed north in search of the spring herring shoals around Lerwick and Wick, father took four of us – Robert, Margaret, James, and me – down to Miller's yard. He wanted us to see our new boat being built.

It was a short walk along the harbour to the yard, where Angus and Willy Miller were waiting for us. A year older than me, big and bluff, red-haired and blue-eyed, Willy's only interest was boats. He could not have told a daisy from a daffodil and I doubt if he had ever read a book but he had an encyclopaedic knowledge of local boats and was as proud as could be that his great-great-grandfather had started off as a wheelwright and joiner over a hundred years earlier, later turning his hand to building small Fifie yawls. Willy was learning his trade as a boat-builder in his father's yard and while father and Mr Miller disappeared into an office, he insisted on giving us a tour.

The main timber yard was a large rectangle with a blacksmith's forge and a steam kiln for shaping timbers on one side, and a joinery shop, saw pit and timber stores on the other. Behind the yard were offices and storage rooms, with a moulding loft above them. A slipway ran straight down to the harbour from the building berths in the main yard.

As we walked round we saw wood being sawn over the saw pit, nails being hammered into planks, and timbers being moved from the stores to the pit and from the pit to the yard floor. We heard the hiss of cold water on hot iron in the forge and men chattering away in their soft Fife voices.

There were lengths of oak, larch and elm waiting to be sawn and bevelled, some of them twenty or thirty feet long, fifty-foot pine trees destined to become masts, heaps of iron fixings, saws, chisels, adzes, nails of every size and shape, planes, hammers and rope – huge lengths of rope – lying in coils and hanging from hooks. Some of the ropes were as narrow as half an inch in diameter but the thickest, used for mooring, might have been twelve inches. The sweet smells of newly sawn timber mingled with the pungent ones of tar and paint. They were a world apart from the smell of fish.

Laid out on the yard floor were the templates for our new boat. 'We made a half-size model to your father's instructions, as usual, and then laid out a full-size plan,' Willy told us. 'Now we've got the main templates down and we'll start finding timbers for each one. She's a three-quarter-decked Fifie. Her keel length is forty-three feet, so she'll be first class. Her depth is just over seven feet and she has an internal width of sixteen feet.' Willy, of course, knew every measurement and every detail. 'Nearly all the boats we build nowadays are decked but the cabin takes up space. Still, the decked boats are much safer and that's what really matters. She'll carry two lugsails and a jib. And a crew of seven.' There was no stopping Willy in full flight, and he knew the local name of everything on a boat – kaydie, sheeg, cracker, kaymsin – everything.

'What's her tonnage, Willy?' asked James.

'Seventeen and a half. Her frame will be oak and her planking larch. One of the lugs will be fixed, the other dipping.'

'When will she be ready?'

'About ten weeks, so not in time for the Drave, but your father is planning to join the English fishing in the autumn.'

When Father emerged from the office with Mr Miller, he was beaming. 'Well, what do you think? She'll be grand, won't she?'

Robert too was beaming. 'She will, Pa. The finest boat in the fleet, I should think.'

'Will I be coming, Pa?' asked James. 'Willy says you'll be taking her south for the autumn herring.'

'No, James. You're only thirteen and you won't have finished at the cooking school. And it's dangerous enough without the worry of being poisoned.' Poor James. He hated the cooking school, a necessary evil for all young men wanting to join a crew, and was desperate to join Robert on the boat. Father saw the look on his face and softened a little. 'We'll see, James. Perhaps. If there's room.'

Mother had stayed at home with Agnes and Alexander. When we got back, Robert and James bombarded her with descriptions of the boat. She listened quietly until they had finished and then asked, 'And what is she to be called?'

We looked at each other in confusion. None of us had thought to ask what her name would be. Then we looked at Father.

'*Beautiful Star*.' he said, 'She'll be called *Beautiful Star*.'

All through that spring we were in and out of Miller's yard where we watched lengths of timber and lumps of metal being cut and sawn and hammered and shaped into what would be our fine new fishing boat.

The yard was full of wonders and Willy loved telling us all about them. Miller's employed about fifty men, who all had long beards and bushy whiskers and wore filthy old hats. The longer and whiter the beard and whiskers, and the more filthy and ancient the hat, the longer their owner had been working in the yard. They were badges of office.

Mr Miller himself was nearly always there, checking every detail of the boat and sometimes insisting that a timber be replaced by one with a better grain or that a metal fastening be strengthened by the addition of another. When Willy asked for the twentieth time when she would be ready, he was firmly reminded by his father that nothing would be rushed and that every inch of the boat and its equipment would be perfect, because 'brave men's lives depend upon it'.

From timbers which had been cut in the winter from the nearby Balcarres Estate and brought to the yard by teams of enormous cart horses, Father had chosen a suitable length of oak for the keel. 'We have to make sure the grain is good and that it has dried out properly,' he explained. 'Then we'll choose timbers for the stems with grains that will go well with the keel. That'll give her the strength she'll need.'

The keel was laid down on a full-size template that had been drawn out on the moulding-room floor and taken to the yard. Once the keel was down, the stem post was hoisted into place by a pulley rigged to a frame in the shape of a large 'A'. Mother placed a silver coin under the post for luck. I asked Willy why the keel was laid down at right angles to the slipway.

'It's because a ship as big as *Beautiful Star* might otherwise run down the slipway, straight across the harbour and into the wall,' he explained. 'Then she wouldn't be so beautiful, would she?'

We watched the stems being sawn over the saw pit and bevelled into shape, then planed and fitted to the keel. Platforms were erected around the carcass for the men to work on. There was enough good grown oak available for most of *Beautiful Star*'s timbers to be cut into shape, so the steam house was not much needed. While the boat was taking shape in the yard the blacksmith was busy in the forge, fashioning long iron nails, metal knees to reinforce the joints and dogs for clamping the planks. The forge was a hot, noisy, uncomfortable place, and we only ventured in if the timber yard was quiet.

On the other side of the yard, joiners worked with planes and axes on the huge pine logs which would become her masts.

Willy and I saw a lot of each other while *Beautiful Star* was being built. Sometimes I went down to the yard with Margaret or James, sometimes alone. Learning to teach forty small children to read and write and, under Miss Brown's watchful eye, to sew, kept me busy enough but there were Sundays and evenings and a short Easter holiday.

Sewing was an important part of the curriculum for both girls and boys. Squinting over her narrow spectacles, Miss Brown always insisted on precise and appropriate stitches – neat herringbone for hems, slipstitch for folded edges and over-sewing to prevent fraying. 'That's no good at all, Julia,' she once scolded me. 'Your stitches might be all that hold a sail together and keep a fisherman alive. Remember that every time you use a needle.'

When we were not in the yard, Willy and I liked wandering around the village. I told him stories about its history and he told me about the boats in the harbour. He refused, however, flatly refused, to come with me to find flowers to show the children.

'I can't help it, Julia,' he said. 'Blue periwinkle and purple loosestrife are not for me. And anyway what are wild flowers for?'

'Flowers are not wild or tame,' I replied. 'They're just flowers.'

'Perhaps. But they don't do anything. They just happen. Not like a boat. A boat has to be designed and built, and it has a purpose.'

A practical person, Willy. In the sweep of a hull he could see beauty; in fields and hedgerows he could not. He loved to talk about the boats in the harbour, which were nearly all Fifies with upright

9

stems and sterns and long straight keels. The smaller skaffies, rounded at the bow and with steeply angled stern posts, were rarer visitors to St Monans; they were still in common use on the west coast but, on the east coast, only much further north.

Before the building of safe harbours with adequate defences against the sea, fishing boats had to be small and light enough to be hauled up on to a beach or through a gap in the rocks, known as a 'goat'.

'My grandfather fished from an open boat, no more than twenty feet in length and powered by a single sail and oars.' Willy told me proudly.

Willy's grandfather survived to old age but many did not and regular disasters eventually brought changes. When it became possible for boats to tie up safely inside a harbour wall, larger, more powerful designs appeared. Willy, of course, knew all about it.

'Skaffies are less than thirty feet long with a broad beam and shallow draft. They're easier to handle but slower than Fifies. Nowadays, Fifies have partially covered decks, as *Beautiful Star* will have. It's the dipping lugs that give them their speed but watch out when the sails swing round. That can be dangerous. Overall, though, there's no safer boat than a Fifie.'

I got my own back with village history. I had a copy of a book by Mr John Jack, an odd man who ran a private school in the village. It was full of good stories. The village had two spellings, Monans and Monance, both taken from the name of its founder, Monan, an Irish missionary who was supposed to have been killed by Vikings in the ninth century, but its original name was Inverin. There were lots of stories about Monan, such as that he was a hermit who lived in a cave, which may have been true, and that he had the power of healing, which probably was not.

One of the best of Mr Jack's stories concerned the fishermen's hatred of pigs. No St Monans fisherman would put to sea if he had the misfortune to see a pig on the way to his boat because pigs were creatures of the devil and omens of evil. The word 'pig' was seldom used; 'the beast' and 'curly tail' were safer.

In medieval times St Monans was divided into two halves. Overtown, at the top of the hill, was where the farmers lived, and Nethertown, by the sea, where the fishermen lived. The fishermen hated the farmers and their pigs and one day they all set off up the hill with knives and sticks to deal with them once and for all. But the farmers saw them coming and started poking their pigs with pitchforks to make them angry. When they were let out of their pens the pigs charged at the fishermen and chased them back down the hill.

It was not only pigs but ministers whom a fisherman hoped not to meet on a sailing day. If he did, he believed that the minister would meet his body when he returned. No St Monans fisherman would launch a boat on a Friday because St Monan had been killed on a Friday; and the church bell was taken down from its place on a nearby tree when the herring came up the Forth because, if it were accidentally rung, the fish might be frightened away. Thirteen was an unlucky number and if a boat left harbour with a leaky kettle on board there would be a death on the voyage. Fishermen are a superstitious lot.

They also had a reputation for dourness – not surprising considering the life they led. The North Sea is harsh, unforgiving and often terrifying. On their boats they had little time for talk. But, back on land, making repairs, mending their nets, or just sitting smoking their clay pipes on the harbour wall, they made up for it. They all had tales to tell, many of them much embellished.

Father told one about a certain 'Diamond Donald', who was very proud of his earring. Earrings were not uncommon among fishermen but only Donald had one with a diamond in it. At least he claimed it was a diamond. Unfortunately, Donald's earring disappeared while he was out fishing and he convinced himself that it had fallen overboard and been swallowed by a fish. From then on he frequently asked the lassies to look out for his earring when they were gutting the fish. 'If you find a diamond earring,' he told them, 'it'll be mine, for sure.' In some versions of the story the earring was found inside a fish by a lassie who wore it on her wedding day but, in any case, Donald never got it back.

Father loved telling us stories and he never minded our questions. He would sit in his favourite rocking chair by the range, sometimes tying and untying knots in a short length of rope, sometimes examining his prins to make sure the lettering was clear, sometimes just sitting. James was the most persistent questioner. 'How do you know where the fish are, pa?'

'Some say they can smell the oil on the herring, but the birds are the best guides. If solan geese are diving you can be sure of a shoal.' Father spoke with the soft accent of a Fife man, often leaving the final 'g' off the end of a word.

'Why are the herring called "Silver Darlings"?'

'When you see a big shoal feeding near the surface in the moonlight, it looks just like a sheet of silver. And they're our darlings because they're our living. Without the darlings, what would we do?'

'Are you ever afraid?'

'Aye, often.'

'Can you swim, pa?'

'No, James. Few can swim. We'd rather go quick to God if we're in the water.'

'How many kinds of fish are there in the sea, pa?'

'Very many, though only God knows exactly how many. We chase the herring, and there are others who catch the ling and the cod with long lines and hooks. Sometimes we even catch a salmon in our nets but we never use its name on board. The sound of its own name frightens away the salmon. We call it "the red fish". It doesn't mind that.'

I was more interested in places than fish and wanted to know where he had been.

'I've been to Lerwick in the north,' he told me, 'and as far south as Lowestoft. You might see a thousand boats in the harbours there. It's a grand sight. Boys jump across them from one end of the harbour to the other without ever getting their feet wet.'

The walls of our cottage were decorated with reminders of fishing ports up and down the east coast of the country – china plates from Hull, coloured glass from Wick, a small watercolour from Grimsby. Father loved them.

At sea, fishermen look out for each other; in such an environment, they must. But there was rivalry, too, especially between the villages. Disputes between skippers were common, usually to do with lines being cut or not being cut by another boat. Robert liked to tell stories about the men from nearby Cellardyke. 'Daft Dykers' he called them.

'You have to watch out for the Dykers', he said. 'If they think you've a good catch, they'll rub up against your hull to try and steal some of your luck. That James Murray did it to us only last week and the fish disappeared. I'd never do that.' But we knew he would. Rubbing up for luck was a common practice.

By the end of June when all the stems had been fitted to the keel, we could begin to admire the size and sweep of *Beautiful Star*. 'This will be one of our finest boats,' Mr Miller told us, 'and we're very proud to be building her.'

The next step was to fit the planking. While the keel, stems, stern post, frames and beams were oak, the planking was larch. As usual, Willy knew why.

'Larch actually comes from America but there's plenty of it now at Balcarres and it makes the best planking because it has a very long life. Over a hundred years.'

The planks were selected, sawn, fitted to the frame of the boat and riveted together, with their grain following the shape of the mould. Some of the tools used in this process were fascinating. A fearsome-looking maul with a sharp end used to sink nails below the level of the wood reminded me of a tomahawk; there was a strange long-headed mallet for driving in caulking irons and a three-foot drawing bar for pulling out nails. Willy once challenged me to pull out a nail with the bar. It looked easy enough but I soon found out why it was so long. The rectangular tapered nails hammered in across the grain of the wood were almost impossible to move.

Eventually with the frame, stem and stern posts in place, oak beams were fitted crossways and larch planking set over them to form the deck. When bulwarks were built up around her edge, *Beautiful Star* at last looked exactly what her name promised – a beautiful boat.

Another of Willy's pleasures was introducing me to his friends. Mungo Walker was an apprentice in the firm of Macdonald and Smith, sailmakers. Their yard was close to Miller's, so they did most of the repair work that came in and made the sails for new boats. They made the sails for *Beautiful Star*.

The first time Willy took me there to meet Mungo he had a

warning. 'Don't be surprised when you see Mungo. He's a good man and he knows a lot about sail-making.'

When we entered the yard Mungo was sitting on an upturned half-barrel, working on a sail. He had a humped back and a leg that stuck out at an odd angle, but he greeted us with a big smile and a wave. 'Morning, Willy. And who's this? Have you made a friend at last?'

Mungo's hands were the largest and strongest I had ever seen, as if to make up for the strength he lacked in his back and legs. He explained patiently how the cotton canvas was cut to a scale plan and sewn with long needles and a tool called a palm, and how eyelets were cut and sewn into each sail for the ropes, which would attach it to the mast. 'When the sails leave here,' he said, 'they're as white as snow, but after their first season they're boiled in cutch to protect them from the salt water. Cutch comes from the bark of an acacia tree. It turns them brown. I wish they could stay white – they look much finer when they're white.'

He told us that a foresail could be completed by two skilled men in about a week and that the yard was always busy with making new sails and repairing old ones. 'Willy told me about the steam boats up in Aberdeen,' he said, 'but I don't believe him. We'll always need sails. There's nothing to beat a good sailing boat.'

Mungo's disability was no handicap for a sailmaker and like all the craftsmen who served the fishing industry, he took great pride in his work. Mungo's sails, Willy assured me, would never let anyone down.

By contrast to a sailmaker, an expert cooper could make as many as seventy barrels a week, which was just as well because the demand for barrels was enormous. Jock Fraser, whose yard was at the other end of The Shore, had been making them for over forty years. He told us that the best barrels were made from Scandinavian spruce trees. He worked without plans or written measurements of any kind. The spruce trunks were first split into staves and left in the open to dry, which might take two years or more. When they were ready, Jock trimmed the staves and shaped them with a draw knife, dressed each end, fitted them to a frame and put them on an iron hoop. Chippings from the timber yard were used to fuel the fire needed for the shaping, which Mr Fraser did entirely by eye. The top and bottom of the barrel were fitted into grooves in the staves and if there was no leakage when water was poured in, the iron hoop was replaced by permanent wooden ones. It was a complicated process requiring a master's skill, but carried out at speed.

We spent hours in Mr Fraser's yard, watching him at work and savouring the smells of timber and wood smoke.

Although Willy would have nothing to do with the countryside, I did eventually drag him on a short walk along the old coastal path towards Elie. We took a detour to look at the ruins of Ardross Castle, once owned by the Anstruther family, and at Lady's Tower, built in the eighteenth century by Lady Janet Anstruther as a bathing hut. Her Ladyship enjoyed bathing naked in the sea and employed a footman to ring a bell if anyone approached while she was swimming. Foolishly, I told Willy this. I should have known better.

'It's hot enough, Julia. Let's have a swim.' I had no intention of swimming, naked or not, but Willy was serious. 'Then you keep watch and make a noise like a bell if anyone comes, and I'll try the water.' And with that, he went behind the tower, undressed and waded into the sea.

When I looked, he was waist deep. He swam out for twenty yards or so, then turned on his back and waved. I was about to shout at him to swim back when a voice behind me said, 'Good afternoon, Julia. And who is your brave friend?' The minister, Mr Foggo, out for one of his strolls, must have seen us and had crept up silently.

I felt myself blush like a tomato. 'Good afternoon, Mr Foggo. Willy Miller. We were taking a walk when Willy felt like a swim. He's an impulsive fellow, you know.'

'Indeed. And a naked one, I see. How sensible of you not to join him.' Tipping his tall hat, he continued on his way.

Willy, who must have seen Mr Foggo behind me, emerged from the water bent over with laughter. He shook himself like a dog and retrieved his clothes. He was in no hurry to put them on and sat on the grass until he was dry. I tried not to look but he was laughing so much, I had to say something. 'Willy Miller, you must have seen him. Why didn't you shout?'

'Why didn't you make a noise like a bell?'

'Because I didn't see him, you big oaf.'

'Ah, well. Now we're for it. It'll be the Church Elders for us.'

'But we haven't done anything.'

'Try telling old Foggo that. By this evening, every Church Elder will be after our blood.'

The thought of six puritanical old men baying for his blood did not seem to bother Willy. I found it rather alarming. The Elders were a fearsome group who met once a month. Willy's cousin Mabel and her young man had twice been summoned before them, having been found entwined once in a haystack and once among the sand dunes near the windmill. 'Mabel and Donald were terrified,' Willy said. 'The first time was bad enough, but the second time they thought Foggo was going to explode. She said he kept jabbing his finger at them while they had to stand still and listen. "You have sinned against God's

17

laws," he shouted, his eyes bulging with fury, "not once, but twice. You must pray for forgiveness every day and for the strength to resist the temptations of your miserable flesh. This must not happen again." After a good deal more like this, he absolved them from "the sin of pre-marital fornication", so that they could be readmitted to church where they were to do their praying every Sunday. Mabel and Donald were a bit unsteady when they left but I don't think old Foggo's sermon worked. They were just more careful.'

That was the end of our walk. Home we went, Willy in fine good humour, I distinctly apprehensive. I did not relish the thought of having to explain myself to Father. He was rather strict about such things.

Herring are pelagic fish, rising to the surface at night to feed. Pelagic is not a word one might expect children in an Adventure School to know, but ours did. By the time they moved on to the Parish School there was very little they did not know about herring, even the few who did not come from fishing families.

They knew that the great herring shoals could cover as much as four square miles and that the annual journey of the herring took them from their winter grounds off Norway to the seas around the Shetland Isles and the north of Scotland in late winter and spring, and then southwards to the Wash and East Anglia in the autumn.

And they knew that by August the shoals were in and around the Forth, which is when the East Neuk villages were at their busiest. This time was named for the ancient Celtic festival of Lammas, celebrated on the first of August. It was called the Lammas Drave. I hated it.

When the herring arrived in the Forth, the whole village was galvanised. Every spare bed was occupied, every kitchen turned out endless pots of tea and bowls of soup and every spare inch of ground was covered with drying nets. From first light to last, the harbour and The Shore were noisy, crowded, and reeking. Extra men were taken on for the Drave by the skippers, some from the north, others local tradesmen out to earn some extra money.

My cousin David was a shoemaker who shut up his shop during the Drave and went fishing on *The Angel*. As a 'half dealsman', he did not supply his own nets or lines and so took a smaller share of the profits. During the Drave it was still worth his while to put away his cobbler's tools and go to sea.

Almost everyone was involved in one way or another and even I had to help out. The school was closed in August so I had no excuse. Margaret and Agnes did not mind and James loved it. Alexander was too young to do much but he came with Mother and collected scran for the cat. When the boats were being unloaded, there were plenty of scraps to be found.

Our cousins, the Patersons and the Allans, were flat out too. Cousin David's father, Uncle David, had *Quest* which usually came back with *The Angel*, and Uncle William was steersman for father.

At about six o'clock each morning we all went down to the harbour to wait for the fleet to return. As soon as they were secured safely inside the harbour wall, the families were on board, unloading the catch, rolling up nets to be taken away for mending and sluicing down the hold with seawater, ready for the next trip that evening.

By that time cotton had largely replaced hemp and linen. It was much lighter so that more nets could be carried on each boat, but it broke more easily, even when soaked in linseed oil or alum water, and the mesh had to be regularly measured to ensure that it had not shrunk below the legal minimum of one inch square. It all made for more work.

At sea the nets were allowed to drift on the wind, moving in harmony with the boat and the swell. When they returned to harbour at dawn the skippers and their crews made their weary way home only after they had made sure their catches had been unloaded and sold to a merchant. Some boats were tied to one merchant who bought their catch at an agreed price; most skippers looked for the best price they could get.

Willy reckoned he could tell how good a boat's catch had been when he saw it approaching the harbour entrance. A boat making slow progress and riding low in the water held a bigger catch than one riding high. He and James put his eye to the test by making straight for the boats he thought were the most heavily laden and offering, for sixpence each, to help unload the catch. If he was right, and he usually was, the skipper might well be pleased to pay a shilling to have his fish unloaded quickly.

At home, while Father and Robert rested, we made sure their nets were ready, dried their boots and clothes and filled their kit barrels with food for the night. When it was time for them to set off for the fishing grounds again, Mother carried Father on her back out to the boat and Margaret carried Robert. It was a tradition that the men should start their voyage with dry feet, although they seldom stayed dry for long. Luckily, I was not expected to carry more than a kit barrel or two and could nip through the water quickly. It was still cold enough.

Once at the grounds, the fishermen set some of their nets and waited an hour or so before hauling one or two in. If the catch looked promising, they stayed put; if not, they moved on. When all the nets were set they might drift for up to two miles, trapping the fish by their gills.

By the middle of August our hands were rubbed raw from the nets and the salt, and our hands and hair reeked of fish. The Drave seldom failed entirely but daily catches varied. Robert claimed that a poor catch was due to the herring 'having a clear eye' and being able to see the nets. He also complained about 'jigging' – the practice of catching herring with lines and hooks made from knitting wires. 'I don't like jigging,' he said. 'It frightens the fish away. The catch is always smaller when folk are jigging.' At twenty-one, Robert had a habit of pretending to be fifty.

Once the shoals had been located, their size made the fish relatively easy to catch. But their movements varied and their exact location was not always predictable. Father was a typical Fifer, believing that the movements of the shoals were affected by the selling of herring for manure, by catching fish that were too small, by fishing on a Sunday and, above all, the by 'wickedness of the people'. If he was right, the herring must have occasionally got wind of some particularly wicked goings-on because they disappeared altogether. Perhaps they had information from the Church Elders.

The Drave was a constant bustle of men and women at their daily toil and big, pungent smells. The sounds that remind me most of the Drave are those of feeding gulls and the smells not just of fish, but of horses mixed with fish. Flat, two-wheeled carts were pulled by sturdy ponies, chosen for strength rather than beauty, often blinkered, seemingly impervious to the hubbub of the harbour, well fed and producers of large amounts of excellent manure.

And every year in time for the Drave an assortment of itinerant characters arrived in the villages, all of whom Willy seemed to know, and insisted I meet. Among them were Mac the knife-grinder, 'Toy Tommy', who sold toys and puzzles, and a Tyrolean family who played horns and flutes and dressed in leather breeches, braces and felt hats decorated with feathers and flowers.

Willy's favourite was 'Wee George' Macgregor, a cadger who travelled about selling fish door-to-door from his two-wheeled cart. This was known as 'caller fish'. George was a huge man, very tall and very fat, with a black patch over his left eye and not a single hair on his head. He looked terrifying but spoke softly and was as gentle as a kitten. With a glass of whisky in his hand and a willing audience, he had a good store of tales to tell, all of them reflecting well upon himself.

'I lost this at Balaclava,' he told us, lifting the patch to reveal an empty eye socket. 'Now that was a battle. I must have killed a dozen Russians before they took my eye.'

He also claimed to have been a champion prize-fighter in Edinburgh and to be descended from Rob Roy Macgregor. If beauty is in the eye of the beholder, a story is in the ear of the listener. My mother dismissed him as a scapegrace, saying that there was less to him than met the eye and advising me to stay clear of him.

'He's always cheerful, Mother,' I pointed out.

'I daresay he is but you never hear a cadger cry "stinkin' fish".' It was an old saying.

Miss Farthing, known to all as Penny Farthing, was another regular. Penny was no more than five feet high and looked frail, but she must have been a tough old soul. Her face reminded me of a walnut. She had been in service with a wealthy family in Dundee but cheerfully admitted that she had lost her position when she stole six silver teaspoons, intending to sell them to raise money for her sick mother. Without a job and with no hope of a reference, Penny had been forced to eke a living as best she could. She did this as a travelling mender.

Like the fisher lassies, Penny followed the fishing, not gutting and packing as they did, but mending nets. She worked outside in all weathers, mending the nets with astonishing speed, a clay pipe clenched between her teeth. She used a thin wooden mending shuttle with a bone tongue to hold the cotton and took the pipe out of her mouth only for talking, eating and scratching. She did a lot of scratching.

'I've got the swithers again,' she often complained. 'They're driving me mad, little beggars. I suppose I'll have to take a bath.' Hot water might have got rid of the invisible mites which made net menders' eyes red and their skin itchy but Penny showed no sign of ever putting it to the test. She smelt like a rotten haddock.

After her experience in service, Penny did not much care for those she called 'the ships', her contraction of Lordship and Ladyship, and used for anyone she thought of as at all grand.

'I asked the ships for a little money for my ma,' she said. 'I told them she was sick but they didn't care. They said it wasn't their concern. So I stole the spoons, only a handful mind, and would have sold them for a few shillings. Well, wouldn't you? But Ma never got the money. They put me out on the street and Ma died soon after. The ships told me to be thankful I wasn't in prison. Still, I don't regret it. Following the fishing's more fun than scrubbing floors and you meet proper people, not ships. Mean as old mutton, they were.'

George and Penny were harmless enough, which was more than could be said for some. The gangrels, who begged for rags, sold pegs and sometimes played tattered old sets of pipes, were rough types. They too came and went with the seasons, setting up their makeshift camps in the trees outside the village; we never understood quite how they survived or where they spent the winters. They were travellers, feared by some for being different, but apparently content with their precarious way of life. We saw them, and heard them speaking their strange, guttural dialect, but were under strict instructions never to approach them.

Mr Foggo, true to form, was among the most vociferous opponents of the gangrels and he based one of his fiercest sermons on them. 'These ungodly people are a threat to our property and the safety of our children,' he thundered, 'and should be removed at once.' At home that evening, we discussed this. 'It is a view neither charitable nor Christian,' said my father, and as an afterthought, 'nor practical. Who is going to remove them, I wonder, and where will they go?'

Mr Foggo could be alarmingly unchristian. I never understood why he went into the church.

The merchants who set the prices for cured herring, bought it and transported it to market, were never short of customers. Many of them became very rich. Mr Nevin, our school teacher and an admirer of Charles Dickens, had a habit of giving Dickensian names to local people. There was a Uriah Heep in the Town Hall, an Oliver Twist and a Little Nell at school and a butcher known as Micawber. The prosperous merchants had names like Pickwick and Scrooge.

Before the merchants could take the fish to market, it had to be cured and packed. This was done by the fisher lassies, though some were hardly lassies. They started as young as fifteen and often went on beyond sixty.

It was an extraordinary life and the lassies were extraordinary people. Many of them came from the northern fishing communities of Wick and Lerwick, travelling in groups around the coast from Shetland in early summer to East Anglia in autumn, following the fishermen and the fish as they travelled south. Their train fares were paid by the curers whose livelihoods depended upon their skilled labour. Very few of them ever set foot on a boat, although they did help the fishermen's wives carry the men out to the boats on their backs. Even when a lassie married a local man and settled down in one of the villages, she seldom gave up the fishing altogether. The draw of the lassies' life was as much social as survival. Willy thought they were wonderful.

When the lassies arrived that year, Willy gleefully introduced me to Effie and Annie, cousins, both in their twenties, who had been sorting and packing herring since they were younger than I was. They had big, open faces, toothy smiles and fishy hair.

'Stand up straight, now, Willy,' they said when he took me to meet them, 'and let's look at you properly. A year's growth on you. That's good. You look well. And handsome too.' And, with a glance at me, 'No wonder the girls have noticed you.' I must have blushed but her flattery was ignored in favour of more pressing matters.

'How are the fish, Effie? Better than last year? How many crans have you done?'

'Now Willy, it's only August. The Drave and the winter herring are still to come. But it's been good so far. Just you look at my hands.' She held them up for inspection.

Like all the fisher lassies, when she was gutting the fish Effie protected her fingers with linen cloots tied on with strips of rag. But still her hands were red-raw and cut. The gutting knife and the salt were cruel workmates. 'They're not like this till November, most years.' she said, laughing. 'They would hurt terrible but the shillin's in my pocket make them better.'

When they were working, the lassies wore long skirts and leather aprons, linen or woollen shirts rolled up at the elbows and a neepyin shawl on the head. At the end of a working day of anything up to fifteen hours, the aprons and shawls came off. They were cheerful, gregarious women and, working outdoors in all weathers, were as tough as their short leather boots.

Once a sample of the catch had been inspected by the auctioneer or merchant, the baskets of herring were carried by labourers from the boats to the farlans where the lassies worked. They worked in teams of three – two gutting and sorting, one packing. My sister Margaret and cousins Agnes and Jane made up a team at the busiest times. The fish were tipped into the troughs and mixed with large amounts of salt by the coopers, then the lassies gutted, sorted and packed them into barrels. Every catch was made up of fish of different weights, so the herring had to be sorted into one of the approved sizes – matties, full, and spent – then carefully packed with brine into the barrels, which were sealed and left for several days to settle and soak. Finally, the excess brine was tipped out, the barrel topped up with fish, resealed, and branded by the local agent with the official Fishery Board mark. Only then was it sent off to market by carriage or train. The fish guts were sold for fertiliser.

As many as a hundred thousand crans of herring were landed in the East Neuk each year. The curing process, known as 'The Scotch Cure', called for skill and stamina and the lassies were vital to it. Herring are fatty fish and have to be cured quickly to prevent their rotting, as well as being sorted into the right barrels. So the lassies were paid bonuses on top of an hourly rate and worked very fast, each team aiming to fill over fifty barrels a day with up to a thousand fish each. Their wages were never very high but at the end of the season they took welcome money back to their families.

On warm evenings, they sat outside their lodgings, chatting and knitting. Knitting was as regular as church-going on Sunday. They knitted even while going for an evening stroll and were astonishingly adept at it. They knitted ganseys, drawers, sea-boot stockings, mittens, scarves and 'guid socks' for Sunday wear, with a bewildering variety of needles and wools. Designs were copied as they went from port to port and some could even copy a pattern they had only seen worn by someone in the street. The patterns all had seafaring names like anchor, flag, and herringbone.

The village did come alive during the Drave and every family depended on it. Without it, we would have had little to live on. But still I dreaded it. A month of unloading fish, cleaning and mending nets and even, sometimes, gutting and sorting the catch, was more than enough for me. When term started again at the end of August I breathed a sigh of relief, offered up a silent prayer of thanks to Mr Nevin and Miss Brown and left the others to it.

As expected, *Beautiful Star* was not finished for the start of the Drave and her launch was set for the first Saturday in September which, all being well, would see her ready for the English fishing.

The launch day of a new boat was a big occasion and that morning the piers and The Shore steadily filled with onlookers. Both Paterson families, ours and Uncle William's, were there in force – eight of us and eight of them. So too were the Allans, ten more of them, including Uncle Andrew who sailed with Thomas Fyall, skipper of *Thane*. Uncle David's boat, *Quest*, had been launched the year before. Of the twenty-seven family members present, ten would be sailing south with the fleet.

As soon as the Drave had finished, the visiting boats had departed and our own would soon follow. The harbour, which during August had been packed, would be deserted, and wives and children would have to wait patiently for the fleet to return from the south. But on *Beautiful Star*'s launch day we were all excited. We had come to see a grand new boat making her entrance.

Father took Robert, Uncle William and his son, also Robert (in our two families, there were two Jameses, two Roberts, two Julias, two Margarets, two Agneses, two Alexanders and two Janets – it could get very confusing) to join the crew in the yard where *Beautiful Star* was waiting. Willy stood with us among the knots of spectators who had found good vantage points on the piers and, at ten o'clock exactly, *Beautiful Star*, her registration mark KY1298 newly painted on her bow and flags strung between her masts, was ready. When the wedges holding her were knocked out by the joiners and she began to accelerate down the slipway, a huge cheer went up. No-one cheered louder than Willy.

On board, Father waved proudly to the crowd and, with a graceful dip as if taking a bow, she hit the water and immediately righted herself. The crowd cheered even louder, bottles were opened and flags were waved.

Once afloat, she was pulled swiftly in to the fitting berth where the crew would spend the rest of the day carefully checking her planking and fittings, before her masts, rigging and sails were fitted. An enormous frame, shaped like the letter 'A', would be used to raise the pine masts on pulleys and drop them carefully into place. Finally, with nets and equipment loaded, she would be ready for her first voyage.

As the crowd dispersed, Willy had a surprise for me. 'I asked Father if I could go out on *Beautiful Star* before she starts the fishing,' he said. 'He spoke to your father, who said he would take me as long as the weather is good. We're going to sail round the Isle of May next week. James is coming and Robert, of course. I wondered if you'd come too?'

'Willy, you know I don't like boats. I'd probably be sick.'

'Nonsense. *Beautiful Star*'s brand new. Not a hint of fish about her. You'll enjoy it.'

I was unconvinced. 'I'll think about it.' I said, not intending to.

Surprisingly, it was Father who persuaded me to go. 'It's a short trip,' he said, 'and it'll be your only chance to sail on *Beautiful Star*. Once we start fishing, we'll be much too busy to take passengers. It's a long time since anyone went round the Isle of May, thirty years or more. New boats always did it but there was an accident. Some children drowned and the tradition died out. It was called a Dance on the May. I'd like *Beautiful Star* to start it up again.'

'There's an old monastery on the island and a lighthouse. Will we be going ashore?' I asked.

'No. It's too rocky. We'll anchor offshore. You'll be able to see the lighthouse. There's not much monastery left since the Vikings got to it. Robert and James are coming, and Willy Miller.' Father wanted me to go, so I agreed.

At eight o'clock sharp on the following Tuesday, James and I presented ourselves at the harbour, dressed for the short voyage to the Isle of May and back. Father and Robert had left earlier to prepare the boat. Willy was already there, complete with kit barrel filled with enough homemade lemonade, apples, cheese, slices of cake and hard boat's biscuits for all of us. He seemed to be expecting to be marooned on the island.

29

'Stow your kit,' said Father, 'and we'll be off. It's a grand day for a trip and we'll see how she goes.' Preparations on board did not take long and soon we were off. With the jib set and two men on the oars, Uncle William steered us out of the harbour. As soon as we were clear, Father called for the foresail and mizzen to be hoisted. For this, we were sent below. It was a dangerous time when sails were raised or lowered and the boom came round. Accidents were common. Besides, the last thing the crew needed were three spectators getting in the way.

The cabin was small, with four narrow bunks set into the sides of the boat and an iron stove in the middle. A table would have taken up too much room but there were two chairs nailed to the hull. We tried the bunks and found them awkward to get in and out of, but tired fishermen would have been thankful for anything.

Back on deck, the same warm sou'wester that had brought the good weather filled our sails and sent us speeding away across the Firth. Although it was simply a trial run and no net fishing would be done, Father and all six of his crew were on board, keen to get the feel of their new boat.

Like all Fifies, *Beautiful Star*'s long straight keel gave her speed and we were soon close enough to the island to see the lighthouse. I tried to interest Willy in it, but got only as far as Stevenson and the refractor light before he made a face and went to talk to Robert, who ordered us below again while the sails were lowered. When we came on deck, the boat was at anchor two hundred yards from the island's rocky cliffs, where gulls, kittiwakes and razorbills had formed colonies.

'Don't tell me puffins nest on the other side, Julia,' said Willy, 'because I know that.' I ignored him.

We stayed there for an hour or so tucking into the contents of Willy's kit barrel, while Father, Willy and the crew discussed the boat.

Back we went below while the sails were set for the return journey and then we were off again. It took longer back into the breeze, but I did not mind. In fact the sun, the gentle wind and the salt spray were exhilarating. Despite myself, I enjoyed it.

Mr Miller was waiting for us as we entered the harbour and hurried along the pier to where we tied up. 'Well, James,' he called out, 'how did she go?'

'She's as fast as any, George, and easier to handle than some. We'll have good fishing with her.' And, turning to Willy, my father continued, 'And what did you think of her, Willy?'

'She's the finest boat in Fife,' replied Willy, beaming.

'Yes, she is,' I agreed. 'And she'll find the fish, too.'

Father laughed. 'I hope so. We'll be sailing south soon and we'll need good catches. And how about you, James? What did you think?'

'I think I should be going with you, that's what I think.'

Father shook his head. 'No, James, not this time. We've a full crew. You can join us in the spring.'

On a bright afternoon in early October, *Beautiful Star* was among thirty boats from St Monans, together with forty-three from Cellardyke and nine from Pittenweem, to set sail in convoys towards the rich fishing grounds off East Anglia. There they hoped for good fishing before returning home until the new year, when they would head north to Shetland and Caithness.

The 'English fishing' had been popular for about a dozen years. It could be very profitable but involved a long journey and six weeks or more away from home. Fishing families had mixed feelings about it and some boats preferred to go north to catch ling and haddock with long lines.

The boats made a grand sight as they left harbour, the tide and their powerful lug sails quickly sweeping them out to sea and far away from the crowded pier. *Beautiful Star* stood out as one of the larger boats and easily the newest. Her tarring and sails were as light and white as could be.

Settling in the middle of the convoy as if being protected by older relatives, she sped away over the horizon. Mother had insisted that we all go down to wave *Beautiful Star* off. *Thane* and *Quest* were in the same convoy, so the piers were full of Patersons and Allans. Apart from a few tearful children, the mood was cheerful. The last voyage of the year, the hope of good reward from the English herring, and the prospect of husbands and fathers at home over Christmas.

There would be nets to be mended, ropes to be tarred, old clothes to be repaired, new ones to be sewn or knitted. The boats would be hauled up and prepared for the new season, the fishermen would gather at the harbour to talk boats and fishing or just to pass the time of day, there would be visits to friends in Elie, Pittenweem and Anstruther and perhaps an outing or two to St Andrews or Cupar. Even with a break from the fishing, it would be a busy time.

We watched *Beautiful Star* until she was out of sight, by which time it was well into the afternoon and the autumn light was beginning to fail. Deciding that we might catch one last glimpse of the convoy, Willy and I set off up the hill towards the church. From there we did see the last sails dipping below the horizon, although it was too dark to see which were *Beautiful Star*'s.

We also saw the tall figure of Mr Foggo in the graveyard near the rocks. Dressed, as always, in black, and standing motionless as he gazed out to sea, he must have been watching the boats. As a minister, he would not have been welcome at the harbour on the day of a sailing, but it crossed my mind that he could possibly have been seen from one of the boats. I hoped not because that would have greatly alarmed the fishermen. Theirs was not a superstition I shared, yet there was something unsettling about seeing him. Willy and I looked at each other but said nothing, then walked quickly home together down the hill.

At this time, before the age of steam ships, in favourable conditions the voyage from the waters of Fife to those of East Anglia took about forty-eight hours. On the voyage, it was usual for the steersman and one crew member to keep watch on deck, while the others rested below. The time spent was usually well invested, given the size and quality of the expected catches, and the Fife fishermen were welcomed and respected for their steadiness and skill. So much so that the *Yarmouth Independent* that year carried a report which was reprinted in the *East of Fife Record*. The report compared the 'Scotch fishermen' favourably to their East Anglian counterparts and ventured the wish that the visitors would have a beneficial effect upon them. The Scots, it seemed, were 'sober, reliable, canny men' who seldom missed church on a Sunday. The local men, by contrast, 'earnt their money like horses, and spent it like asses'.

Mother enjoyed reading the piece out to us. She told us we were lucky to have been born in Scotland and not among the drunken savages down south. She did not tell us, although we knew, that our uncles William Paterson and David Allan were quite capable of holding their own in any Yarmouth inn.

Respectability and sobriety were not the only differences between the men of Yarmouth and their 'Scotch brethren'. When East Neuk boats first started making the journey to the 'English fishing', they were thought absurdly small and vulnerable by comparison with the local two- and three-masted, fully-decked English luggers up to seventy feet in length. The same newspaper report expressed some concern over their ability to withstand heavy weather. But the skill of the Scottish skippers and their crews made an impression, and they were soon accepted as at least the equals of the local men.

Two days after he left we received a telegram from Father to tell us that they had arrived safely in Yarmouth; some men also wrote letters and sent back messages with other boats that were returning home. Hardy though they were, all but the youngest of the fishermen had families and, during long nights on the boats, wives and children must have seemed far away. Nights ashore were not much better for some. Each man took his own bedding but not all found beds. The youngest had to sleep on the floor of their lodging house if there were not enough beds to go round.

Father was conscientious at sending letters and telegrams home. The telegrams did little more than tell us about the fishing. This was known locally as 'the word'. If you wanted to know how good the fishing in the south had been, you asked what 'the word' was. The letters, however, were long and detailed. They were written on Sundays after church, and told us about his lodgings, his English friends and about *Beautiful Star*. He said that she was much admired, so much so that 'half the men in Yarmouth have been aboard to inspect her. If I'd charged them a guinea each, I could give up the fishing and come home.' We wished he would.

Of the forty children in the Adventure School, twenty-seven had fathers and brothers away with the fleet. It was a difficult time for all of us. Concentration was harder and tempers shorter. One day, however, a large brown parcel arrived at school from Mr Smith's bookshop in St Andrews. In front of all the children, Miss Brown untied the string and carefully removed the brown paper. Inside was a brand new edition of *The Atlas of the World*.

'Now children,' she said, holding it up for all to see, 'this is what we need.'

The atlas had one hundred and fifty pages of coloured maps and a further seventy-four devoted to an index of countries and place names. The maps were wonderfully detailed, especially those of Great Britain and Europe, and the atlas immediately became a favourite with the children. All through that autumn, it was taken down from the shelf and the pages carefully turned until somewhere or something of interest caught our eye. Knowing what would hold the children's attention most readily, we started with maps of the east coasts of Scotland and England. We worked our way down from Lerwick, past Wick, Fraserburgh, Peterhead and Arbroath, to Eyemouth and Berwick, each of them busy fishing communities. We considered the size of each place and its likely population, and discussed historical events – the Battle of Culloden, the Highland Clearances, the Moray Firth disaster – but we only strayed inland occasionally.

The Grampians, Glasgow and Edinburgh were speedily dispatched as we sped southwards. Pausing briefly at the important harbour towns of Yorkshire and Lincolnshire, we arrived at Great Yarmouth. This was our destination because this was where our fathers and brothers were to be found, the men of Cellardyke, Pittenweem and St Monans, braving discomfort and danger, steadfast against all that the North Sea could hurl at them, bringing home much needed money for their families and soon, we hoped, to embark on the return journey. Everyone loved the atlas.

While the fleet was away, Willy went with his father on a trip to Aberdeen and Lossiemouth to see for themselves what was going on in the yards there. Steam-driven boats were appearing along the coast and there was talk of a new design.

When they returned, Willy could hardly wait to tell us all about it. 'We went to Stonehaven first, then Peterhead, then Lossiemouth,' he told us breathlessly. 'The railway goes right round the coast up to Wick, but we didn't go that far north.

'We saw decked Fifies being built at Stonehaven and Peterhead, but Lossiemouth was the most interesting. One of the yards there is working on a new design which is a mixture of Fifie and skaffie. We saw some drawings and a scale model. It was fully decked and had a straight stem like a Fifie, but an angled stern like a skaffie. The idea is that it will have a Fifie's speed but be easier to handle because of its shorter keel length. Two masts, it'll have, up to sixty feet, fore and mizzen sails and a jib. They plan to try out the design before building a full-size boat. It'll be well over seventy feet, nearer eighty probably. And they're even talking about a steam-driven capstan.'

When Willy stopped briefly to draw breath, James had a question. 'Will that mean they'll carry more nets?'

'It will. The hauling in will be much, much easier. And it'll also be used to raise the sails, so they'll be bigger. More sail, more speed.'

'When do you think we might see one?' I asked.

'A year or so, perhaps. They'll want to test it thoroughly before sailing this far.'

'And what's the design to be called, Willy?' Mother asked politely. I think she feared more outlay on another new boat.

Willy looked puzzled. 'Now that's odd, Mrs Paterson. They're calling it a Zulu of all things.'

'A Zulu? Why?'

'It's in support of the Zulus the English are fighting in Africa. The Highlanders think the Zulus are being treated much as they were during the clearances.'

'It's a funny name for a boat, but I suppose it's their boat so they can call it what they like. What would you call it, Willy?'

'It's being made in Lossiemouth, so I'd call it a Lossie.'

'So would I,' she said, 'unless we're fighting people called Lossies somewhere.'

Willie ignored the joke. 'Here's something that will interest you, Julia. In Peterhead I met a man named Storm. I thought it was an unusual name for a Highlander, so I asked him about it. He told me that he was descended from a baby who had been washed up in a wooden box at Nairn about two hundred years ago. From the markings on the box they thought the baby must be German and had been put in the box when the ship it was on was sinking. The fishing family who brought him up named him Storm and there are now quite a few Storms in the area.'

And he had a wooden box under his arm. 'I've got something to give you, Julia,' he said, opening the box. 'Well, it's for everyone really. I made it for you.' He took out a model of *Beautiful Star*, about twelve inches long, with a wooden hull, tiny iron fixings and canvas sails secured by plaited cotton ropes. The planking was clinkered and it had a three-quarter deck.

I was astonished. 'Did you really make it, Willy?'

'I did,' he replied sharply, frowning at my tone. 'It took me two months. I worked from plans in the yard. Everything's to scale and it's made of pine and elm.' Adding with a smile, 'Father did help a bit'.

It was beautifully made. We examined it minutely and agreed that it stood comparison with anything to be found in the shops in St Andrews or Cupar. 'It's lovely, Willy,' I said.

He was delighted. 'Look, Julia. Here are the hatches and that's the kaymsin. I made these hooks and toggles from scraps of iron. Do you know what they're called?' I did not. 'That's the breist hook at the stern for a reefed sail, and that's the teck hook for a fully reefed sail.' He pointed them out.

Having told me the names and functions of all the boat's features, he asked me to paint on the name. 'You're much better at writing than me,' he said. 'I've brought paint and a brush.'

'Of course I will, if you're sure.'

When I had carefully painted on the name with Willy's fine brush, we put *Beautiful Star* on the mantelpiece above the range. Father and Robert would love it.

The first boats to return to St Monans arrived on the Wednesday after All Hallow's Eve and three or four more followed every day that week. Some of the Cellardyke and Pittenweem boats had also returned safely and, by the end of the following week, less than half the fleet were still in the south. Several weeks of hard fishing and the demanding journey north were exhausting, but their families were always there to welcome them and the men came ashore smiling, delighted to be home. The weather throughout October had been stormy and strong winds had dispersed the herring shoals, resulting in only mixed catches and many broken nets, but the trip had still been profitable for them. A few boats brought home as much as five hundred pounds to be shared among the crew.

At school I could tell which fathers had returned just by looking at the children's faces. The strain of absent fathers and brothers told even on the six-year-olds and, when they returned, the joy was visible. The boys talked about little else, comparing reports of the fishing and stories from the south. They talked of storms and seas and sails, of boats and crews and catches. I could just imagine each of them sitting at a father's knee, listening to his report to a much-relieved wife and soaking it all up effortlessly. The girls said less but their smiles told us everything. Each morning there were more of them.

It was at the end of that week that the first autumn storms hit the east coast. Very high winds and drenching rain lashed the villages and we were among many families who left the comfort of their houses only to attend Sunday service. We had to enter the church by the back door, the front door on the seaward side remaining firmly closed against the wind and a tide which swept over the rocks and threatened to reach the south wall. It would have been easier by far to have stayed at home but, particularly with men still away at the fishing, attendance was a solemn duty. Prayers were said for the safe return of all; Mr Foggo delivered one of his lengthy sermons and 'Eternal Father', Mr Whiting's poem set to music, was sung with extra vigour. Afterwards there was none of the usual standing about. Heads down and backs bent, we all struggled home as quickly as we could.

For three days, up and down the coast, boats in harbours were hurled about, slates flew off roofs, chimney bricks came down, debris swirled dangerously about in the streets and windows and doors stayed firmly shut. Most cottages in the village were protected from further damage by their thick stone walls, but outside it was dangerous and frightening. In Cellardyke the storm and a very high tide beat down the sea walk at the Golden Strand, exposing the herring boats wintering there to the sea. Even on the Sabbath, everyone, including the Kirk Elders, turned out to rebuild it before the next tide.

Telegrams from the south reassured us that all was well with the fleet and the winds gradually, very gradually, abated over the next two days. On Tuesday, the Cellardyke harbour master received a wire informing him that two more boats had left Grimsby that day, believing it safe enough to start the journey. This was followed by wires the following day to say that most of the remaining thirty-one boats, encouraged by forecasts of calmer weather, had also left.

Father's message, telling us that weather permitting he would leave in a convoy on Friday afternoon, arrived on Thursday. It was a relief that the skippers now felt able to set sail and that all should soon be safely home, but the winds were still more than blustery in the north. We could only hope that their journey would be quick and safe.

On Friday the two boats that had left on Tuesday arrived safely in Cellardyke. They reported strong winds but an otherwise uneventful journey. My mother, whose quiet calm had been rather shaken by the ferocity of the storms, was visibly relieved.

'Thank God for their safe arrival,' she said. 'It's an anxious enough time when the boats are far away and we all know what an autumn sea can be like. Let's pray we see the others home tomorrow.'

'Of course we will,' said James testily. 'They're fine boats with the best skippers and crews there are. We'll see the first ones tomorrow morning, I shouldn't be surprised.'

The winds now being no more than moderate and the skies clear of rain, James was surely right. The storms had passed, and the passage home should be good. We went to bed that night in good spirits.

But in the early hours of Saturday morning I was abruptly woken.

Screeching and furious, the wind had risen again. Even more powerful than before, it crashed against the cottage as if trying to rip out our front door and smash through our windows. It woke us all. Shocked at its sudden ferocity, we knew that a storm of that strength would not be narrowly confined and was probably lashing the coast from Wick to Lowestoft. Worse, it would be at its most destructive out at sea, where as far as we knew, thirty-one boats, including *Beautiful Star*, were trying to get home to Fife.

There was no improvement during that long, sleepless night. We sat silently together, listening to the storm and waiting anxiously for dawn. When it came at last, we dressed in our warmest clothes. There would be no school that day and we might be spending much of it outside.

By the time we had eaten, the wind was noticeably less fierce and in mid-morning Mother suggested we might venture out to see what damage there was and to offer whatever help we could. 'Agnes, please stay here with Alexander. The rest of us will go down to the harbour,' she said, 'to see if any boats are back.' *Beautiful Star* would not yet be back, having only left Yarmouth the day before. Father would have ridden the storm out at sea, then made for a safe harbour. He would send word from there.

We made our way cautiously to the harbour over cobbles made dangerous by rain and debris. There we found the piers crowded with family groups huddled together against the east wind and an icy spray. All heads were turned to the sea and all eyes searched intently for a hint of sail on the horizon. Mr Gourlay, the harbour master, had received a telegram confirming that the remaining boats had put to sea on Friday morning and that the storm in the south had been the worst anyone could remember. Half- or three-quarter decked Fifies of forty feet or so would have been tossed about like corks. We could only guess at what it must have been like for their crews but when the boats which had left Yarmouth on Wednesday arrived safely, we would all feel better. The others should soon follow.

The reading on at the mercury barometer, which had been installed by the town council on the gable end of Mr Robinson's house in the square, was almost as low as it could be. We walked out along the central pier where we found our aunts Janet Paterson and her sister Jessie Allan. They told us that *Quest* had left Yarmouth on Friday in convoy with *Beautiful Star* and *Thane*. Jessie's nephew, Andrew Allan, was on *Thane*. Her sons, Robert and William, were on *Quest*. Janet's son Robert was with his father William on *Beautiful Star*.

The boats carried neither compass nor navigation lights and depended for their survival solely on fortune and the skill of their crews. God willing, all would be safe, but at sea in such a storm it would be a miracle if there were no loss of nets or equipment. All that morning we stood together on the pier. At midday Mother sent us home. She stayed at the harbour with Janet and Jessie. When at last she did come home, shivering with cold, no boats had arrived, no sails had been sighted and no telegrams had been received.

We sat around the range, six of us, saying little. Margaret and I took turns with Alexander. He knew something was wrong. The afternoon light was fading when there was an urgent knocking at the door. Mother rushed to open it. It was Willy.

'Mrs Paterson, all the line fishers in the north are safe, four boats from the south have just arrived and they say two more went to Cellardyke. All are damaged and some Cellardyke men are lost. I ran to tell you.'

Mother shepherded Willy into the parlour. 'Thank you, Willy, I'm glad you did. Sit here and tell us the news.'

'I don't know much more, Mrs Paterson. Only that one of the McRuvies is missing and someone from another boat. Lots of nets are lost.'

The McRuvies were a Cellardyke family, but well known in St Monans where they had relatives. The loss of nets was a serious blow to a fisherman. They were expensive and would have to be replaced out of his own pocket.

'Where did you hear this, Willy?' I asked.

'Mr Jamieson was talking to Mr Gourlay. I heard them, but not everything. Then I came here.'

'Anything else, Willy?' I asked.

'Nothing else yet. But the rest of the fleet will be back soon. *Beautiful Star* should be home tomorrow.'

Willy did not stay long. When he had left, Margaret and James went out to see if any more news had arrived, while Mother and I prepared supper. She seldom asked for help with cooking, but we both needed to be occupied. As it was a Friday, we made oatmeal herring. The routine helped.

The food had not been in the oven long when Margaret and James returned. They did not need to speak for us to know that the news was bad. Both were ashen. Margaret spoke first.

'Two men are lost. Alexander McRuvie was swept overboard from the *Excelsior*, which was trying to get back to Grimsby when it happened. Just seventeen, and his poor father could only watch him drown. The other was also a Cellardyke man, John Watson. He was young too. Lost when his boat turned back for Yarmouth. They say the wind suddenly shifted from north-west to north-east and may well have driven the fleet towards land. Any boats near the Wash will have been in the most danger.'

Mother shut her eyes and clasped her hands in silent prayer. None of us spoke. There had been no news at all of the three boats carrying ten members of our family. That night, Mother did not even try to sleep. She sat silently by the range. We took turns to sit with her.

On Sunday morning we were down at the harbour by six o'clock. Church, for once, would be missed. It was still stormy and a good deal colder than the day before, yet the piers were crowded even at that hour. Every boat and every man would be welcomed back. No-one would walk home alone. There was no sense of panic, no sounds of distress. Everyone waited and watched in silence, shoulders hunched, hats and bonnets pulled down, boots stomping for warmth on the stones of the pier. Not knowing how long they might be there, everyone wore their thickest hooded coats, woollen gloves and scarves.

Mr Nevin was there. He went from one group to another before walking back along the pier towards East Shore. Returning ten minutes later, he said, 'Julia, I've been to Mrs Cook's house. She's boiling kettles for tea. Please go round and tell everyone.'

Mr Cook was one of the fish merchants who lived close by the harbour. Sarah Cook was a pupil of mine and I knew their house. I did as I was asked, glad to have something useful to do and oddly pleased that many made their way there. Most families left at least one member on the pier while they went for the tea, not wanting to desert their vigil entirely.

Before long, Willy appeared and came over when he saw me. 'Have you had tea, Willy?' I asked. 'There's some at Mrs Cook's if you want it.'

'No thanks, Julia. I came to watch for the boats but I can't stay long. Ma wants to go to church.' He put his arm around me and hugged me tightly; I rested my head on his shoulder.

'Mother is terrified,' I whispered. 'And so am I. Please, please, let *Beautiful Star* come home safely. She will, won't she, Willy?'

'Of course she will. I'm sure of it. She's the best boat we've ever built and your father's a fine skipper.'

It was about midday when the first shout went up. Sails had been glimpsed on the horizon and all eyes immediately strained to try and identify them. As they approached we could see that there were three boats, apparently undamaged, and making good progress towards the harbour. The leading boat soon entered the outer pier, followed immediately by the other two. By then all three boats had been identified and their families had run round the pier to greet them. The crews had barely stepped off their boats when they were engulfed by women and children. But the tears and kisses did not last long. There were others still waiting, others whose kisses might never be bestowed. The overwhelming joy of the moment was quickly restrained.

All the men except one went straight home. Thomas Smith, skipper of *The Haven*, reported to Mr Gourlay. He said that three Cellardyke boats had joined up with them on the way back and would by now be safely home. The storm had been the fiercest ever experienced by any of them; some boats had probably put into harbour wherever they could, and there would certainly be a great deal of damage to boats and equipment. But, worse by far, the storm had arisen so suddenly and had been so unremittingly ferocious that there were fears that some boats might have been driven ashore or even have gone down. Any boat near the Wash when the wind changed direction would have been in the gravest danger because the banks and shallows in those waters could be perilous even in calm conditions.

We had no way of knowing if any boats had been caught in the area of the Wash. All we knew was that of thirty-one that had left Grimsby and Yarmouth by Friday, nineteen were still awaited. That number was soon reduced to seventeen when Mr Gourlay received another wire to say that two boats, one from each village, had managed to put back into Grimsby that morning and were safe. But by nightfall, one hundred and eight men were still not accounted for.

The knots of watchers on the pier gradually dispersed as early darkness fell. There was no point in our remaining there through the night – no skipper would attempt the harbour entry in the pitch black – and many of us had been there all day. We had to eat and rest and allowed ourselves to be taken home. Having barely slept for three days, Mother was exhausted. Margaret and I put her to bed as soon as we got home. She did sleep that night but we did not. It was our turn to wait for news.

By morning none had come, so James and I went again to the harbour. Margaret and Agnes stayed with Mother and Alexander. We found Willy among the watchers and our aunts and cousins. Willy had been to Cellardyke after church the day before. He said that the mood there was just as it was in St Monans – anxious, fearful and desperate for news. Telegrams had been sent to Lowestoft and Yarmouth but the replies told us only that nothing more was known about the missing boats.

During the course of that day twelve more boats returned, four to Cellardyke and eight to St Monans. All were damaged, some badly. Eighteen nets had been torn to pieces, eight boats had sails cast off, and planking and masts would have to be replaced. There were grim reports from all the skippers, some of whom spoke of miraculous escapes. David Ballingsall, skipper of *The Welcome*, could scarcely believe that he and his crew had survived. He had felt the boat touch bottom more than once and had expected to be holed at any moment. But, as he said, by the grace of God, they had been swept away from the shore in time and had just been able to ride out the storm at sea.

Five boats had managed to get to Holy Island where their crews were well taken care of and two had got under the lee of Farne Island so close that they could shout to the lighthouse keeper, although they could not get ashore. One skipper threw into the sea a bottle containing a message asking the finder to contact his wife to let her know they were safe. We heard later that the bottle washed up at Cullercoats but not before the boats had returned safely.

Another, *The Brothers*, skippered by James Stevenson, sailing in convoy with three others on Wednesday evening, had been saved from being wrecked on Dowsing Lighthouse by a damaged fishing smack from Grimsby which led her into Wytham harbour. From there they had managed to send a telegram home. But when they set off again, they were blown into Scarborough, where they had to be hauled into the harbour by twenty men on the pier. Twice more they tried unsuccessfully to return before eventually taking advantage of what they called a 'prosperous breeze' which took them home.

One of the Cellardyke boats carried a seriously injured man. Robert Brown had been struck on the head by the foreyard. The crew were too occupied trying to save the boat to help him; they got him home but he was not expected to live. Another, skippered by John Wood, had also been caught near the Farnes on Friday night. He and several others had cast their nets and made sail for home. Among them was *Janet Anderson*, a new boat skippered by James Murray, the man whom Robert had accused of 'rubbing up' for luck. It had last been seen in grave difficulty and there was little hope of its survival.

As each boat limped into harbour the watchers on the pier became fewer, the joy of each arrival tempered by the misery of those still waiting. It was harder by the hour to believe that any boat that had set off on Friday would not have made it safely home by Monday or sent a message, unless it had met with disaster. By that evening, three St Monans boats and twenty-one men were missing, as were two boats from Cellardyke with thirteen men. Among these were the uncle and cousin of Alexander McRuvie, who had earlier been lost overboard. The boats for which we still waited were *Janet Anderson* and *Vigilant* from Cellardyke and from St Monans, *Quest*, *Thane*, and *Beautiful Star*.

Miss Brown had announced that she would not re-open the school until the fate of all the men was known. 'No-one will be able to concentrate on a lesson,' she said, 'least of all me. Fifteen of our children are still waiting for their fathers to return. They should stay at home with their families.'

After another dreadful night we went again to the harbour. The families of all the men on the three boats were there but, in truth, we had given up hope. Perhaps we felt it our duty to be there, perhaps we simply did not know what else to do. Wives, fathers, sons, brothers and sisters, we stood together, many weeping, all desolate and struggling to grasp the terrible reality of what had happened.

In mid-morning Sir Robert and Lady Anstruther of Balcaskie arrived in their carriage. The Anstruther family was one of the most distinguished, and by then one of the most respected, families in Fife. In the seventeenth and eighteenth centuries they had treated their tenants cruelly, even throwing them out of their own homes for little reason, but Sir Robert's father, Sir Ralph, was admired in the area for his courtesy and kindness, especially to the poor, and Sir Robert himself, as a Member of Parliament, landowner and philanthropist, did much to help those in need. They walked out on to the pier to speak to those of us still there, gently encouraging us to go home. The pier gradually emptied until just a few men were left to keep watch. That night, five boats and thirty-four men were still missing. They had not been heard from for four days.

The next news came on Wednesday. It was brief and dreadful. Mr Gourlay received a telegram from King's Lynn to say that the previous day *Quest* had been sighted keel up off Wells and had been driven ashore that morning at Blakeney, on the Norfolk coast. There was no sign of any of the crew.

Mr Gourlay had the terrible task of informing Jessie Allan and her family. In addition to our Uncle David and his sons Robert and William, Alexander Irvine, father of seven, Alexander Hutt, Alexander Latto and David Easton were lost. Seven men were presumed dead, leaving three widows and eighteen children. The whole village grieved but worse was to come. When more news arrived, it was terrible, stark and final.

On Friday, the *Sea Nymph*, skippered by a Captain Samuel Farr, was on its way from Hull to Lynn. Six miles east of Trusthorpe, she came upon a flooded and dismasted fishing boat, which was towed into Lynn and laid in the Boal Fleet. As the tide fell, Captain Farr's son made out the head of a man under water in the cabin.

Next morning, the police were called and the water was baled out of the wreck. They found not one but five men in the cabin, one on his knees with his arms resting on a sleeping berth, another lying in a bunk and a third, thought to be the skipper, lying on the floor with a fractured skull with two men lying over him. All were dressed in sea boots and oilskins and had money in their pockets. The skipper was found to have a letter dated 31 October in his jacket. It had been rendered largely illegible by the water, but began 'Dear Father and Brother' and was signed 'Your loving son and daughter'. James and I had written that letter. The skipper was our father. The boat was *Beautiful Star*.

Another telegram was despatched to Mr Gourlay, who again had the task of taking the news to the families. We knew when he knocked on our door that it would be terrible. It did not take long. He told us what had happened, offered his sympathy and left quickly. We sat together and wept.

As the bodies had to be formally identified, the Lynn police had requested that someone able to do this travel there without delay. David Duncan, who knew all the crew of *Beautiful Star*, had volunteered to make the journey. He left by train on Monday evening.

On his arrival in Lynn the next day, Mr Duncan confirmed to the coroner that the five bodies were those of my father, James Paterson, his brother and nephew, William and Robert Paterson, David Allan the shoemaker and David Davidson. It was assumed that my brother Robert, and David Allan's son James, must have been washed overboard. Our father was dead, our brother was dead and every one of the crew on our trip to the Isle of May was dead. Between them, they left three widows and sixteen children.

It was thought by the coroner that the crew had exhausted themselves in their battle against the storm and had left a watch of two on deck. While the boat drifted towards the Wash, the sea unshipped the mast, which wedged itself against the cabin door trapping the five men inside. The two missing men must have been swept overboard. Strangely, the recovered bodies were described as untouched by the sea and looking peaceful in death.

The dead were not brought home but, like soldiers, buried where they fell. Their funerals took place on Wednesday. We were told later that, on learning that three of them had been members of the Order of Good Templars, the Lynn lodge took responsibility for arranging and paying for the funerals. The bodies were taken in five hearses to Hardwick Cemetery where they were buried with due ceremony in the Presbyterian section of the graveyard. The procession was followed by the Royal Naval Reserve, a large number of Good Templars and several thousand local people. The manner of the men's deaths had evinced such a wave of sympathy among the fishing communities of Norfolk that the Lynn Templars announced that they would organise a public subscription to pay for a suitable memorial.

A few days later the third St Monans boat *Thane*, which had left Yarmouth with *Beautiful Star*, was found stranded on the Boston Deeps. She was keel up, her port side buried in the sand with eight planks stove in, suggesting that she might have been run down. She was first sighted by some dredgers who had to wait for an ebb tide to get to her. In the forecastle they found three bodies, which they took to Lynn. These were identified as Thomas Fyall, Alexander Duncan and Thomas Lowrie. The skipper, also Thomas Fyall, Lawrence Fyall, David Fyall and Andrew Alan were presumed to have been swept overboard. Five more St Monans women were widows and eleven more children were fatherless. Again the people of Lynn turned out in their thousands to bury the dead.

In the storms of the 19th and 20th of November 1875, St Monans lost twenty-one men, who left eleven widows and forty-five children. My mother lost her husband, her son, two brothers, three nephews, a brother-in-law and a cousin, and her mother lost two sons, two nephews, a son-in-law and two grandsons.

The following week, wreckage of *Janet Anderson* was washed ashore at Cullercoats and the next day, *Vigilant* was found by a Trinity House cruiser, sunk in six fathoms on the Inner Dowsing. Both boats were little over a year old. There was no trace of either of the two skippers, James Murray and Robert Stewart, nor of any of the eleven members of their crews. Like St Monans, Cellardyke had suffered grievously. Eight more women were widowed and twenty-seven more children made fatherless. In addition, Robert Stewart's widow was expecting her fifth child.

The people of both villages had endured the agony of not knowing what had happened to their missing men, followed by the certainty of their deaths. For some there came the release of a proper burial, but for most there did not. The sea had taken them. The *Fife Herald* reported that, 'Every face is clouded with sorrow and everywhere you hear the wail of broken-hearted mothers and children weeping in despair.'

The small group that made the journey by train to Lynn for the funerals included no member of the bereaved families. We did not even consider it. There was barely time, it was too far and not one of us would have been capable of it. My mother hardly spoke for a week, sitting staring at Willy's model on the mantelpiece and surviving on bites of food and sips of water that we put beside her. If we had let her, I think she would have quite happily drifted away.

We had three visitors. Mr Foggo came and said something about God's will and praying for us. With difficulty I refrained from telling him that loaves and fishes would have been more helpful. Lady Anstruther called, as she did on every bereaved family, and on

Christmas Eve Willy knocked on the door. He asked if there was anything he could do, wrapped me up in a huge hug, which only made me cry, and left quietly. Otherwise, we were left to our grief. For three weeks, Margaret and I took turns to go out to buy food, returning as quickly as we could. Neither of us could face talking to anyone and not even church got us out of the house.

Even before all the wrecks were found an appeal had been launched for the bereaved families, and this letter from Sir Robert Anstruther appeared in most of the leading national newspapers, including *The Times* which published it on 29th November 1875:

> *Sir,*
>
> *I do not think I need apologise for asking some assistance from the public through your columns for the many among the fishing population in our immediate neighbourhood who have suffered from the late storms. We have lost two boats belonging to Cellardyke and three belonging to St Monance, with the whole of their crews; and the sorrow, misery, and want in those towns are of a kind that I cannot attempt to describe.*
>
> *Such a catastrophe, under any circumstances sufficiently dreadful, is in these cases rendered still more calamitous by the fact that many of the boats' crews are closely related to each other by family ties.*
>
> *In the town of St Monance, one unfortunate woman, Mrs Paterson, has lost at one blow her husband, her son, two brothers, three nephews, a brother-in-law, and a cousin; another, Mrs Allan, about seventy years of age, has lost her two sons, her two nephews, her son-in-law, and two grandsons.*
>
> *A public meeting will be convened by the Provost of Anstruther on Monday, the 6th day of December, in order to obtain aid for the sufferers;*

and I am authorised to say that subscriptions will be gladly received for them by the Rev. David L. Foggo, the Manse, Abercrombie, St Monance; Mr Thomas Nicol, Chief Magistrate, St Monance; the Rev. Dr Christie, the Manse, Kilrenny, Anstruther; Mr Martin, Provost, Kilrenny; Mr Tosh, Provost of Pittenweem; and W.R. Ketchen Esq of Elie.

The above two small towns have lost at one blow 37 of the flower of their sea-going men; 19 women are left widows; and 72 children are made orphans; besides, several aged persons dependent upon the deceased men have been deprived of their support.'

I am, &c,

Robt. Anstruther

The letter had an immediate effect. The loss of thirty-seven men, leaving nineteen widows and seventy-two fatherless children, was, as Sir Robert said, a catastrophe. They included all ten of the Paterson and Allan family members who had sailed south with the fleet. It was also a catastrophe all the more poignant for being just a few weeks before Christmas, a time when fishing families looked forward to being together.

The *Fife Herald* spoke of the wail of mothers and children weeping but it was the silence which descended upon the village that was most eloquent of its pain. Men and women had still to go about their business but the daily hustle and bustle were muted by the knowledge that, behind so many doors, women and children were grieving for husbands and fathers they would never see again. And those who had not lost a relative had lost a neighbour or friend. Not a person in St Monans was left untouched by what had happened. There were no street games, no peevers on the sea shore, no hornie up and down the cobbled lanes, none of the usual hubbub by the harbour; even the carters' ponies, seeming to sense the mood, hung their heads. It was a time of misery, tears and despair.

School had not reopened for what would have been the final week of the term. 'I can't bring myself to open the doors,' Miss Brown said, 'and if I did, I doubt that many would come. The Education Board will just have to show some compassion for once.' Her pupil-teacher would certainly not have come. She would have been worse than useless.

Meanwhile we were aware that contributions to Sir Robert's appeal were arriving from all over the country and that the people of Fife had lost no time in getting organised. Meetings were held, committees formed in each village and The St Monance and Cellardyke Shipwrecked Fishermen's Fund was established. The Fund committee included Mr Nicol, the Chief Magistrate, and two Bailies, Mr Macfarlane and Mr Robertson. Between them, they knew almost everyone of consequence in the area and would spare no effort in raising money.

The response from all sorts of people was extraordinary. At a meeting in Anstruther, for example, Sir Robert reported good progress, substantial donations having already been received from several distinguished gentlemen, including the Secretary of State for War, Mr Gathorne-Hardy, and the London banker Sir Coutts Lindsay. While donations received by Mr Foggo included one pound from an elderly man in Dundee, who wrote that he 'had sent his all'. Public sympathy knew no boundaries.

A meeting in St Andrews was not well attended, but the *Scotsman* reported that the mood was one of determination to help in any practical way possible. The Pastor, Dr Boyd, normally a forbidding and aloof man, had spoken with typical directness. 'The calamity has come near to our own doors,' he said, 'and nothing can move the heart so much as the contemplation of so many children made fatherless and so many wives widows at one blow. It is a rough gauge of human feeling how much a man will give and I trust all will give liberally.'

They did, and a variety of local money-raising events were hastily organised. A Grand Bazaar organised by Lady Anstruther in Colinsburgh raised £346-6s-81/2d.

At the bazaar she sold copies of a lament she had written. They were printed in copperplate style on thick cards with black and gold borders:

Their rest is calm and deep
No tempest now can wake
The silence of their sleep.
Above them storms may break,
And billows rage, and winds blow high,
And brave hearts sink, and brave hearts die,
In waters cold they sleep,
While wives and children weep,
They sleep, they sleep.

Hark! How the wild waves roar,
See how the white foam lies
On bleak St Monan's shore,
Beneath the wintry skies.
No fishers may return today,
Oh no! They lie far far away;
In waters cold they sleep,
While wives and children weep,
They sleep, they sleep.

Fundraising went on well into the New Year. Among the events arranged was an exhibition and sale in Edinburgh of paintings by several distinguished members of the Scottish Royal Academy. Even in the city the plight of the bereaved families was such that everyone wanted to help in whatever way they could.

Contributions to the fund continued to arrive daily and, aware of the material hardship the disaster had caused, the trustees met urgently to make an immediate distribution and to decide on the fairest basis for allocations in the future. When their calculations were made public, we learnt that they had determined 'as a rule' to make weekly payments of 4s to each widow, 1s/6d to each child under sixteen and 3s to each other dependent relative. £450 was divided among those who lost boats with a further £320 for nets and equipment. They also made a special payment of £5 to Robert Brown who had been struck on the head by the foreyard. Faced with the difficult task of estimating how much income the capital would produce and for how long it would be needed, they calculated that these allocations would amount to £585 in the first year. This meant that mother received a single payment of £154 and weekly payments of 8/6d. As Margaret and I were working, we were better off than most.

The final amount raised of £7,206-15-3d was so large that it caused some resentment on the part of others in need. Ironically, the generosity of some was resented by others. It was not as if anyone was worse off than they had been. And it was not so much when you consider how many people it had to help. But the terms of the Trust Fund did not allow for allocations to anyone other than the families and dependents of those who had perished in the November storms, so widows and orphans, and there were many, of Fife fishermen who had lost their lives at other times and in other places could not be helped. Some had even been forced to resort to their Parochial Boards for help from the Poor Roll, from which they might get a shilling or two a week.

Most villages did have Sea Box Societies, some of the smaller ones joining together to save costs. Sea Box Societies are an ancient idea. Ours, formed in 1784 to help 'widows, orphans and fisher folk fallen on hard times', made a contribution of £5 to the appeal.

On the first Sunday after Christmas – a Christmas that went unremarked in the villages – mother said that she would like us all to go to church. On a grey morning, we trudged together up the hill and over the stone bridge. We walked over the ground on which the monastery and the nunnery had once stood – Robert had always insisted that there had been a secret tunnel between them – and entered from the main door on the seaward side.

After a mercifully brief service, we gathered outside with our aunts and cousins and walked back with them. Without knowing it, we were taking the first steps on a long road to recovery.

Seven years have now passed since that terrible time. For nineteen widows and seventy-two children life has never been the same, nor can it ever be, yet in the villages much is unchanged. The rhythms of life are still dictated by the seasons and the annual journey of the herring shoals around the coast. Our fishermen still go north in spring and south in autumn and the Lammas Drave still breathes energy into our communities. I have qualified and teach at the Adventure School, James is a fisherman, Margaret is married to one, Agnes and Alexander are at school and mother mends nets and makes clothes. Father's prins – those that were not lost with him – sit on the mantelpiece, and so does Willy's model.

Mr Foggo has gone, although the Church Elders have not, and Mr Nevin still runs the Parish School. The improvements to the harbour foreseen by my father have been carried out. A breakwater to protect the harbour entrance and new middle and west piers were designed by Thomas Stevenson, the son of Robert Stevenson, designer of the lighthouse on the Isle of May.

One afternoon in May, two years after the disaster, Willy asked me to marry him. I was not surprised. I thought he was going to. I told him that he would have my answer when I returned from the trip to Lynn that Margaret and I were planning. We wanted to see the memorial to the lost men erected by the people of Lynn.

In July, before the Drave started, we made the long journey by train. We spent our first night in a small lodging house in the town, and next morning walked down the Hardwick Road to the cemetery. As we approached the memorial we could see that it was in the form of a Fifie, with straight stem and stern, but without masts, rudder, or bowsprit. That was how the wrecked *Beautiful Star* had been found by Captain Farr of the *Sea Nymph* on his way from Hull to Lynn in November 1875. It was bigger than I expected, constructed from a white, flecked stone and standing on a stepped, immensely heavy-looking pedestal.

Hand in hand, we walked slowly around the memorial, admiring the fine workmanship and reading the inscriptions. On the boat itself had been carved BEAUTIFUL STAR and KY1298 ST MONANCE. On the upper face of the pedestal were the names of the men buried in the graveyard.

On the port side: JAMES PATERSON BORN 18 JULY 1826; DAVID DAVIDSON BORN 1 FEBRUARY 1852; WILLIAM PATERSON BORN 18 JANUARY 1836; SON ROBERT

PATERSON BORN 31 OCTOBER 1857. And on the starboard side: DAVID ALLAN BORN 28 AUGUST 1827; ALEXANDER DUNCAN BORN 7 JUNE 1829; THOMAS LOWRIE BORN 3 OCTOBER 1854; THOMAS FYALL BORN 27 JUNE 1851.

There were other inscriptions on the lower faces of the pedestal. At the stem: THIS MONUMENT ERECTED BY PUBLIC SUBSCRIPTION TO THE MEMORY OF EIGHT SCOTCH FISHERMEN DROWNED ON THE NORFOLK COAST IN THE NOVEMBER GALE 1875. At the stern: LIFE, HOW SHORT! ETERNITY, HOW LONG? On the port side: WHILE WE LINGER ON THE SHORE OF LIFE, A WAVE WAFTS US TO ETERNITY. And on the starboard side: WHEN THE SHORE IS WON AT LAST, WHO WILL COUNT THE BILLOWS PAST?

That evening a Mr Finney called at our lodging house. He had heard that we had travelled from Fife and wanted to pay his respects. He was a small, weatherbeaten man with the shoulders and arms of a sailor. Mr Finney remembered the storms well and told us more about the memorial. It was made of Kenton stone, brought down especially from Newcastle for the local masons to work on.

'If I remember rightly,' he said, 'the whole thing, memorial and pedestal, weighs about seven tons. As you probably know, it's modelled on the Grace Darling memorial at Bamburgh. It took the best part of a year to complete. There were two funerals because *Thane* was found later near Boston Deeps. Both were attended by several thousand mourners who followed the procession down the Hardwick Road. It was an extraordinary sight and one that spoke of the high esteem in which the men were held. The first boat found was *Quest*, at Blakeney, but there were no men on board her. The other two were found the following week, one of them up at the Farne Islands. They were *Vigilant* and *Janet Anderson*.'

'And the second boat was *Beautiful Star*,' I interrupted. 'She was brand new and on her first voyage south.'

'I know, and if ever a boat was well named, she was. She stood out in the harbour even among the larger boats we build down here. Everyone admired her.'

'Her skipper was my father, Mr Finney. That's why we're here.'

'Ah, James Paterson. And Robert must have been your brother. I knew them well. They were good men and your father was one of the finest skippers I ever met. I'm sorry for your loss. It must have been a terrible time for you all. It's St Monans you come from, isn't it?'

'It is. The boats came from St Monans and Cellardyke. Have you ever been to Fife?'

'I fear not but I've heard a good deal about the East Neuk and its villages from your fishermen. Very devoted family men they all are.' He laughed lightly. 'The English fishing, you call it, don't you?'

'Yes, we do, and it's made quite a difference to us. My father always said, 'The herring won't come to us, so we must go to them.'

'Still, it's a long journey and it takes brave and skilful men to make it. We were astonished when the first boats came down from Scotland – they were tiny compared to ours and some weren't even decked. It must have been a cruel voyage. But we soon found out how good they were in the right hands. There are no better fishermen than the Scots.'

'Thank you, Mr Finney.'

'No at all, my dear. I counted your father and brother as friends and it was one of the saddest times we have ever known in Lynn when the men were lost. You had other relatives on the boats too, if I recall?'

'We did. Ten members of our family died in the storms. Mr Finney,

I never understood how my father and four of the crew came to be found in the cabin as they were. Were they trapped?'

Mr Finney looked surprised. 'Are you sure you want me to talk about this, my dear?'

'Quite sure.'

'Very well. They weren't trapped. The cabin had a sliding door, the mast wasn't blocking it. James Allan had a fractured skull and two men were already lost overboard, remember, one of them Robert. The other four must have been worn out and when the cabin became waterlogged, they hadn't the strength to escape. That storm was the worst any of us could remember. It was ferocious beyond words and it seemed to go on and on. The waves would have been enormous. It was a miracle any of the boats survived. And what's more, the wind swung round to the north-west. Any boat near the Wash when that happened was doomed and there were only four able men left on *Beautiful Star*. They could not have saved her. Most of the boats which got home were further north when the storm struck and a few were close enough to Yarmouth or Grimsby to make harbour. Your father was not so lucky.'

He went on, 'If I may, there is one more thing. I am a man of the sea but I have always loved poetry. May I read you two verses I wrote at the time?'

'Of course you may.'

Mr Finney produced from his jacket pocket a single sheet of paper, cleared his throat, and read.

> *Twas bleak November and the nineteenth day,*
> *They left the port their season's labour done,*
> *Brilliant with hope that they again should see,*

Those friends they loved so dear, their friends at home.
Swiftly she glides across the raging main,
The Beautiful Star, *with all her manly crew,*
Destined, alas, that they should never gain
Those shores for which they steer and billows plough.

Mr Finney must have been a better sailor than poet but he meant it kindly. And he had one more surprise for us. 'Your father and his crew perished in the storm, my dear, but *Beautiful Star* survived and in a way still survives, and so, as a matter of fact, does *Thane*.'

'How is that, Mr Finney?'

'Both boats were salvaged and, under the law of salvage, sold by their finders. *Thane* is moored on the river and *Beautiful Star* is in the stream we call Heacham Harbour. Her name has been changed to *Jacobina*. They are used in the shingle trade. Would you like to see them?'

We looked at each other and shook our heads. 'Thank you, no, Mr Finney,' I replied. 'But there is someone who will be pleased to know that *Beautiful Star* has survived. I will tell him when we get home.'

I accepted Willy's proposal, and we were married in the church of St Monan on the first of June 1878. We live in a small cottage on East Shore from which I often watch the fishing boats putting out to sea and, God willing, returning safely the next morning. Willy is usually to be found in the boatyard where they are now building steam-driven Zulus, but I have persuaded him to venture from time to time into the countryside. We have walked along the coastal paths to Anstruther and Elie and inland to Kilconquar. He now knows a kestrel when he sees one and, on a good day, can even tell a celandine from a crowfoot.

63

It was Willy's suggestion that I write this account. He says it is a story that our family should remember. Our first child is due in the spring. We hope that he or she will one day pass it on to our grandchildren.

Author's Note

The St Monans families were:
James Paterson = Julia (nee Allan)
x Robert, Margaret, Julia, James, Agnes, Alexander

William Paterson = Janet (nee Gowans)
x Agnes, Alexander, Jane, Margaret, Robert, John

David Allan = Jessie (nee Gowans)
x Agnes, David, Helen, James, Jean, John

The lost boats and their crews were:

Beautiful Star: KY 1298
Port: St Monans
Owner & Skipper: James Paterson
Description: Decked, two masts, two lugsails, one jib.
Tonnage: 17.5 tons. Keel Length: 43 feet
Crew: William Paterson, Robert Paterson, David Allan, James Allan, David Davidson, Robert Paterson.

Thane: KY 1071
Port: St Monans
Owner & Skipper: Thomas Fyall
Description: Decked, two masts, two lugsails, one jib.
Tonnage: 17 tons. Keel Length: 41 feet
Crew: David Lowrie, Lawrence Fyall, Thomas Lowrie, Thomas Fyall, Andrew Allan, Alexander Duncan.

Quest: KY 221
Port: St Monans
Owner & Skipper: David Allan
Description: Decked, two masts, two lugsails, one jib.
Tonnage: 15 tons. Keel Length: 39 feet
Crew: Robert Allan, William Allan, Alexander Irvine, Alexander Hutt, Alexander Latto, David Easton

Janet Anderson: KY 1176
Port: Cellardyke
Owner & Skipper: James Murray
Description: Half-decked, two masts, two lugsails.
Tonnage: 17 tons. Keel Length: 41 feet
Crew: Andrew Stewart, William Bridges, James Walker, Alexander Lothian, Hugh Mackay, William Mackay.

Vigilant: KY 1214
Port: Cellardyke
Owner & Skipper: Robert Stewart
Description: Decked, two masts, two lugsails, one jib
Tonnage: 17 tons. Keel Length: 43 feet
Crew: William Stewart, James McRuvie Snr, James McRuvie Jnr, Alexander Doig, Leslie Brown.

By the stark measurement of men and boats lost, the events of the 19th and 20th of November 1875 were by no means the worst nineteenth-century Scottish fishing disaster. The final tally of five boats and their crews was much lower, for example, than in the 1848 Moray Firth disaster in which 124 boats were lost, and in 'The Great

Storm' of 1881 when 189 men, the majority from Eyemouth, perished. But for two very small villages which depended for their livelihood almost entirely on fishing, the loss of thirty-seven men was devastating.

Although it is not part of this story, both *Jacobina* and *Thane* were swept away by the storms which hit the east coast in the winter of 1953.

THE FLYING MONK

1002 AD

Just as he did almost every evening, Eilmer stood alone outside the west wall of the abbey. He was a slight figure, with brown hair and brown eyes and wearing the tonsure of the order of St Benedict. He looked less than his twenty years.

After work in the garden or in the library Eilmer nearly always found a little time to himself before Vespers at six o'clock. Shading his eyes against the low September sun, he gazed up at a flock of daws circling overhead. He watched them soar and swoop, then soar again before gliding down to their nests high up in the abbey towers.

Of all the birds which lived in and around the abbey, it was the daws which Eilmer loved the most. Daws were talkative birds, forever calling to each other in their squeaky voices, and striking in their shiny black feathers interwoven with silvery threads. In flight their wings beat hard and fast unless they were riding the winds which carried them out over the fields and the river in search of the insects and rodents upon which they lived. Not that they were above stealing an egg from a thrush's nest or a crust of bread from the abbey kitchen. Daws were clever birds.

As he watched, a pair launched themselves from the top of the wall and, with powerful beats of their wings, rose high into the sky. When they found a friendly current they floated down towards the river, gradually losing height until they flapped their wings again and returned to the safety of their nest. It was as if they had decided to take a final flight before the sun set, just for the pleasure of it.

The evening was still warm and it was not yet time for Vespers, so Eilmer smoothed down his habit and sat on the grass with his back to the wall. There was comfort in the feel of the ancient stones, their age and solidity reinforcing the strength of his faith.

To the west, he could see fields and open pasture leading down to the River Avon which curled around to join the River Ingleburre, together providing a formidable defence for the town. To the south was Malmesbury itself – capital of England and immensely wealthy in possessions and land. The wool merchants and farmers of Malmesbury grew prosperous and ensured their places in Heaven by endowing the abbey with gold, jewels and precious artefacts, each one, to the delight of the abbot, trying to outdo the others. The abbey coffers were overflowing and St Benedict would surely have rejoiced to see such prosperity.

The bell for Vespers rang and Eilmer got to his feet. The rule of St Benedict called for immediate and absolute obedience and it would not do to be late. Abbot Beorhtold was every bit as strict about adherence to the rules as Abbot Beorhtelm had been. He hurried through the abbey gate and across the yard to the Church of St Mary where evening prayers were said. His brother monks were assembling and he joined the line entering the church. No-one spoke – their order did not demand a vow of silence but discouraged unnecessary speech and encouraged periods of silent contemplation.

Eilmer nodded to his friend Orvin. During their periods of work together in the abbey garden, they had risked the displeasure of the abbot and talked quietly about Eilmer's ideas. Orvin was interested and encouraging. In the ten years since Eilmer had entered the abbey as an oblate, he and Orvin had become friends.

The Benedictine horarium was unchanging and demanding, the monks living by a daily routine of work and prayer. Matins were said at midnight, followed by Lauds at three. Sleep was allowed until Prime, after which the whole community came together for the abbot to give them their instructions for the day and for abbey business to be attended to. After this and a brief period of private prayer, they said Terce and then High Mass. Sext was at noon, followed by None at three, Vespers at six and Compline at nine. All work was done between None and Vespers.

Eilmer had come to the abbey illiterate and ignorant. Now he could read and write in English, French and Latin and had studied not only the gospels and the rule of St Benedict but also the ancient philosophers and mathematicians, including Aristotle, Plato, Pythagoras, Euclid and Archimedes. Malmesbury was, above all, a seat of learning, and Eilmer loved learning.

After Vespers Eilmer made his way to the library. Successive abbots from the time of Aldhelm had added to the abbey's wonderful collection of books and King Athelstan, himself a scholar, had donated more. Eilmer loved to sit by the window with one of the illuminated manuscripts and wonder at the skill and craftsmanship of the scribes and artists who had created such a beautiful object.

Eilmer took down a book of classical legends from its place on a shelf and carried it to the window. It was a large volume, written in Latin and generously illustrated. He sat on a low chair with the book on his knees and opened it at the story of the Athenian architect, Daedalus. It was a story that he had read so often that he could recite it word for word, although that did not stop him reading it again.

Daedalus, it was said, had made wings for himself and his son Icarus, with which to escape from the island of Crete, where they were being held prisoner by King Minos. They made the wings from feathers glued together with wax, which worked well until the wax melted when Icarus, contrary to his father's advice, flew too near the sun and fell into the sea. According to the story they had flown halfway across the Hellespont when this happened.

Eilmer gazed at an illustration of the two men. Daedalus, long white beard flowing in the wind and winged arms outstretched in flight, looked down in horror as his son plummeted towards the waves, his broken wings trailing behind him.

The library door opened and Orvin came in. Seeing Eilmer, he too set a chair by the window. When he saw the page Eilmer was looking at, he sighed and shook his head in resignation. Strictly speaking no conversation was allowed in the library, but they were alone and Orvin could not help himself.

'Eilmer,' he whispered, 'do you read nothing else? Whenever I come in here, you are reading this same story.'

Eilmer pretended to be put out. 'You know very well that I read all sorts of books, Orvin. And I am thinking of writing one myself – about the birds I see around the abbey. You know that.'

'Indeed I do,' replied Orvin, not wishing to upset his friend. 'And you are becoming a fine scholar. I only pray that you are not still dreaming of trying to be a bird yourself. After all, look what happened to Icarus.'

'Icarus flew too near the sun. If he had done as Daedalus had told him, they would both have survived.'

Orvin's voice rose above a whisper. 'Eilmer, it's a legend, a fable. Surely you don't still believe it really happened.'

'I believe it could have happened.' Eilmer paused, 'And it could happen again.'

Orvin clapped his friend on the back. 'Well, Brother, if you are determined to kill yourself, I cannot stop you, but do not expect me to join you.'

'Of course not. And anyway I shall need the abbot's permission, and I doubt he'd grant it.'

'Thank the good Lord for that. You might yet live to see thirty.'

Eilmer rose from his chair and returned the book to its place on the shelf. From another shelf he took down a smaller volume and brought it over to the window. 'Have I shown you this?' he asked Orvin, opening the book.

Orvin peered at the open page. There was just enough light to make out the words. 'And who is this Abbas Ibn Firnas?' he asked. 'He sounds like another madman.'

'He was anything but,' said Eilmer. 'He was an Andalucian scientist and poet who lived to be seventy-seven. He died little more than a hundred years ago. Among other things, he invented a water clock and a means of making clear glass. He also studied astronomy and engineering. I am surprised you do not know of him.'

Orvin laughed. 'Don't tell me he flew to Andalucia from Mecca.'

'No, but he did fly. Look. This report says that he made a pair of wings, jumped off a high place and flew in a wide circle, eventually landing back where he had started.'

'And what happened when he landed?'

'He damaged his back.'

'And no doubt never tried again. Enough, Eilmer. I am going to rest before Compline. You should do the same.'

Back in his tiny room, however, Eilmer was not in the mood for resting. He sat on his bed and thought about Daedalus and Ibn Firnas. Even if the story of Daedalus and Icarus was no more than a fable, the man who made it up must have thought that flying across the Hellespont was possible and the people who heard him tell the story must have thought so, too. If not, he would have been laughed at and his story would not have been passed from generation to generation for over a thousand years. As for Abbas Ibn Firnas, the account of his flight was well-documented. There was no reason to doubt it.

Eilmer thought, too, of the dream he often had. In the dream he saw himself in a crowd near a river, unable to see whatever the people around him were looking at. He pushed down with his feet and rose smoothly into the air until he could float over their heads. It was as if he could fly just by believing he could. Before going to sleep, Eilmer always offered a prayer that the dream would come to him. Like all dreams, it had no clear ending, but when he awoke, he felt a sense of elation. He could fly if he believed that he could.

Eilmer had been fascinated by birds for as long as he could remember, although, had it not been for the Danes, he might never have had the chance to observe them and learn about their ways.

It had been eleven years earlier, when he was a boy. He had been collecting firewood with his parents, Leofric and Ayleth, when a party of fugitives from the east arrived in the village. They said that Danish warriors had come in their longships, armed with swords and spears and carrying their round shields of iron and leather, and were cutting a brutal swathe of death across the country. The Danes were raping women, slaughtering their fathers, husbands and brothers, and plundering the Christian churches they despised. Lacking weapons, training, and, above all, a strong leader, the English had little means of defending themselves and many were fleeing westwards. For fifty years there had been peace. Now there was bloodshed and destruction again.

The arrival of the Danes came as no surprise to Leofric. Although the invaders had been defeated by King Athelstan half a century earlier, the previous autumn he had watched a fiery comet cross the night sky and had feared the worst. 'It is a sign from God,' he told Eilmer and Ayleth, 'He is telling us to be prepared.'

'Prepared for what?' asked Eilmer, more curious than frightened.

'For whatever he sends us.' Although Leofric knew in his heart what God would be sending. His own father had told him stories of the men who had first come from across the sea two hundred years earlier. Merciless butchers, he had called them, butchers who drank the blood of their victims. And he had warned that one day they would come again.

Had it not been for Eilmer, Leofric and Ayleth might have trusted in God and remained in the village, where they owned a hide of good land on which they grew wheat and grazed their sheep and goats. 'What is the point of hiding from these Godless men,' asked Leofric, 'if we know they will steal our animals and burn our houses? We will simply starve to death. We should stay and fight.'

Some of the villagers agreed with him, but Ayleth could not bear the thought of her nine-year-old son being slaughtered like a lamb or carted off in chains as a slave. She insisted that they leave their land

and their animals and seek refuge in the forest. The Danes would not trust their gods to protect them among the ancient oaks and elms that grew so densely up the sides of the hills, and were unlikely to come looking for women and gold there. 'Even if we return to find everything destroyed,' said Ayleth, 'Eilmer will be alive and that is what matters.'

So Leofric, Ayleth and Eilmer did what previous generations had done and went with the other villagers into the forest. They carried with them clothes and blankets, an axe, a knife and a saw, a side of salted pork and six chickens in a wooden cage. The sheep and goats they left behind. With the tools the others brought, they would be able to build shelters, trap wild pigs, rabbits and deer, and collect the berries and fungi that thrived in and around the forest. It would be better than facing the Danes.

Eilmer had listened to the men of the village telling stories about the bloodthirsty Danes and understood the danger they were all in. But secretly he was excited about living in the forest. Although Ayleth had told him never to go there alone, he had often sneaked out of the village while Leofric was with the animals and climbed up the hill to the edge of the trees. At first he had been too frightened to do more than peer into the gloom and wonder what he might find there. He imagined strange beasts with claws like pitchforks, snakes as long as the rope his father used to tether a goat and spiders the size of his hand.

One summer day, however, he found the courage to take his first steps into the trees. He ventured no more than a few yards, moving carefully from oak to oak and peering round each trunk before going on. His courage did not last long. When he heard a twig snap, he turned and ran, stumbling and rolling down the slope in his haste to get home.

It was several weeks before he tried again. This time he carried a stout stick cut from a blackthorn bush and made his way deep into the forest. He saw neither beasts nor snakes nor spiders. Just squirrels, a rabbit or two, and pigeons.

After that first cautious try, Eilmer made many trips into the forest, each time finding things he had not noticed before. He found a badger's set and a fox's den, rabbit warrens and a place where wild pigs snuffled about in search of acorns. Over the course of a summer, he lost all fear of the forest and went there whenever he could. He found that he liked being alone and he loved watching the animals and the birds.

It was early April when the villagers left their homes and entered the forest. The trees were coming into leaf and the birds were building their nests. Not that the villagers noticed. Their only concern was finding a safe hiding place. They chose a clearing deep within the forest, not far from a shallow stream which meandered down towards the village. They built rough shelters in a circle around a communal fire on which the women cooked whatever the men caught in their traps or shot with their bows.

Each day a look-out was posted at the place where they had entered the forest, ready to run back and warn them of approaching Danes. At nine years old Eilmer had to take his turn on look-out duty, although he spent most of the time looking out for birds and animals. Once his daily chores were done – finding wood for the fire or mushrooms for the pot, cutting branches to plug holes in the roofs of their shelters, or feeding the chickens and collecting their eggs – he spent hours watching rabbits and squirrels, pigeons and woodpeckers, even spiders and beetles. He learnt what each creature ate and where they found their food, where and how they built their homes, and how they protected themselves against danger. Although he was small for his age, Eilmer was strong enough to hold his own against the other village children, but he joined in their wrestling matches and archery contests only when he had to. He much preferred to be alone with the birds and animals.

On a moonlit night, he sometimes crept out of the shelter where his parents were sleeping and made his way quietly to a small clearing where he had recognised the signs of foxes and badgers. He sat at the edge of the clearing with his back to a tree, and waited for the creatures of the night to appear. Often they did. Badger cubs played in the clearing while the sow snuffled about in the earth for grubs and berries, and foxes sloped off into the trees in search of burrows and nests where a meal might be found, usually returning with a pigeon or a rabbit in their jaws.

A colony of bats had found a hole high in a birch at the edge of the clearing, much too high to be reached by climbing the trunk. When they returned from hunting just before dawn, Eilmer knew it was time for him to sneak back to the shelter. Better to be pretending to be asleep when his mother woke, than to tell a lie about having to relieve himself.

The bats fascinated Eilmer. He knew when they were returning from the swoosh of their wings and their strange clicking sounds, and he knew, because his father had told him, that they spent the hours of daylight hanging upside down. He did not know how they found their way around in the dark, nor what they ate. In fact, he had never seen more than their outlines against the sky. He had never touched a bat or had the chance to examine one. To Eilmer, a creature which could fly but which was not a bird or an insect was a source of wonder and mystery, the more so as it flew at night.

Eilmer wanted to know why it was hot in summer and cold in winter; why two sticks rubbed together made a flame; why oak wood was stronger and heavier than elm or birch; why some trees shed their leaves in autumn but others did not; and why foxes and badgers appeared at night. He asked so many questions that Leofric eventually lost patience and told him he could ask only one a day.

It was the birds which interested Eilmer most. In amongst the trees he could not watch flights of geese and ducks in majestic flight or starlings swooping and swirling at dusk, but he could watch pigeons and robins and woodpeckers bringing food back to feed their young and he could listen to them calling out to each other. He climbed trees to look at the pigeons' nests, taking care not to disturb the chicks, and he peered into holes in the trunks of the trees where he thought there might be a woodpecker's nest.

One morning after he had collected wood for the fire, Eilmer slipped off to the clearing – his favourite and most secret place – and sat quietly by an old oak. There was a pigeons' nest high up in the branches of another oak opposite him and he knew there were chicks in the nest. He had watched their mother bringing them insects and worms and had heard them calling for her.

As he watched, one of the chicks emerged from the nest and stood uncertainly on a branch. The pigeon must have seen the chick because she flew across the clearing and landed beside it. The chick watched her take off again and, after hesitating briefly, followed her. It flapped its wings, dropped alarmingly towards the ground, flapped harder and rose to join its mother across the clearing. Then it flew back to the nest.

Eilmer sat fascinated. What gave the bird the courage to jump off the branch and try to fly? Did it know what would happen if it did not fly? How did it know that it could fly? Was it just copying its mother or was there something in a bird that told it to fly? And, most importantly, what enabled it to fly? Was it having feathers? No, because bees and bats did not have feathers and they could fly. Was it because birds were light? No, a goose was a heavy bird and so was a swan.

It could only be the wings. Flying creatures had wings, other creatures did not. But if, say, a mouse had wings, would it be able to fly? Or a goat? Now that would be something – a flying goat. There were flying beetles and flying ants, and perhaps somewhere in the world God had created other flying animals.

When he returned to the circle of huts, Eilmer asked his daily question. He asked Leofric if he knew of any creatures that could fly but did not have wings or of any creatures which had wings but could not fly. Leofric shook his head.

'Others might have seen such things, Eilmer, but I have not. Even a chicken can fly a little. And where have you been? We need more wood for the fire.'

'Yes, Father.' Eilmer hurried off to find wood. He did not want to be drawn on where he had been. The little clearing was his secret.

Only once during the summer was there any sign of Danes. One warm afternoon after a sudden shower, the look-out ran back to say that he had seen a war party marching towards the forest. What was more, they had appeared suddenly from under a rainbow. The terrified man had not waited to see which way the Danes had gone, but had turned and fled back to the huts. The villagers gathered up a few possessions, left their huts and went deeper into the forest. Better to spend a night in the trees than be found by Danes.

Eilmer did not sleep that night. He lay awake listening for the sound of a fox or a badger and wondering why the owl's voice was so different from that of other birds. He thought too about wings – about their shape and strength and about the ways in which birds used them. The sparrow and the robin – small birds – flapped their wings hard, while the goose and the duck – large birds – seemed to glide through the air. Eilmer wondered why that was.

The next morning they returned to their huts, where they found that the only intruder had been a fox which had killed three chickens. Cursing the look-out who had sounded the alarm, they cooked the remains of the chickens and vowed not to leave the huts unattended again.

Spring turned into summer and by August all the villagers were desperate to leave the forest and go home. They wanted a proper roof over their heads and they wanted to get back to their land and their animals. Wheat would need cutting and grain must be stored for the winter. Pigs and cows, if there were any left, would have to be slaughtered and their meat salted. Ditches would need digging and hedges repairing. If they waited much longer, said Leofric, there would be nothing left to go home to. But no-one wanted to return to a village full of Danes.

After much argument around the fire, it was agreed that one of the men would venture out of the forest on the seventh day after they felt the first chill of autumn. If he reported back that the Danes had gone, they would all go home. If not, they might have to face winter in the forest. With luck, the Danes would have taken their plunder and gone back to their ships. They too would want to spend the winter at home.

The only person who would have been happy to stay in the forest was Eilmer. When the scout was sent out, Eilmer hoped that he would return with the news that the Danes were still about. Not that he wished ill upon anyone; it was just that birds and bats were more interesting than cows and goats.

When the scout returned it was with unexpected news. The Danes had visited their village and helped themselves to the livestock and anything of value that they could carry away, but they had gone. Not because they had been defeated in battle, nor because they wanted to go home, but because they had signed a treaty with King Aethelred. In return for the payment of an annual tribute, they had withdrawn to the eastern side of the country where there had been Danish settlers since the first invasions two hundred years earlier, and promised not to launch any more attacks. Time would tell whether the Danes would keep their word, but for the present there was peace. The villagers collected up their tools and weapons, their clothes and blankets, and the few chickens that were still alive, and went back to their homes.

The scout was right. Leofric and Ayleth's stone cottage was still standing, but inside it the Danes had left no more than a few sticks of furniture and the narrow cots on which they slept. Everything else had gone. Eilmer looked at his parents' faces and wondered how they would cope over the coming winter. They had a bare cottage and that was all. They had no meat, no grain and only one miserable chicken.

As it was much the same for all the villagers, Leofric called a meeting to discuss what they should do, although in truth they had little choice. It was agreed that they would contact all the neighbouring villages with a view to sharing their resources and thus somehow struggle through the winter. There was no point in moving anywhere else. The Danes would have been there too.

Not all the villages had suffered as much as theirs, and they were able to scrape together enough for most to survive – a few pigs and sheep, a little wheat and barley, apples, nuts and berries. Some of the old and infirm died, but then they died every winter.

Eilmer wanted to know why God had made the world as he had and why it worked as it did. It never crossed his mind to question God's purpose; he just wanted to know what that purpose was. And since they had returned from the forest, his mind was such a jumble of thoughts and questions that he worried it might burst like an over-filled sack of grain.

Most days, Eilmer was sent out to trap rabbits and hedgehogs and to collect herbs and fungi. Although he did not like killing animals, he was skilled at it and seldom came home with an empty bag. As the winter went on, he withdrew more and more into himself. When he thought about the future, he saw only a life of toiling on the land, eking out a meagre living as his parents did, and hoping the Danes kept their promise. He was ten years old. For all he knew, he had fifty more years of this to look forward to. Even to Leofric and Ayleth he spoke only when he had to, he ate less than his share and became thinner and weaker each day. He did not know why he felt as he did, or what would make him feel differently, only that he could do nothing about it.

By the spring Leofric and Ayleth were worried. Eilmer's cheeks were hollow and his arms and legs like sticks. He could not work and did not eat. Worse, he had almost stopped speaking altogether. He answered their questions with nods and grunts and, whenever he could, hid himself away on his own.

It was Ayleth who decided that something had to be done about the boy. 'What was the point of our protecting him from the Danes, if he is going to starve himself to death?' she asked Leofric. 'What are we going to do about him?'

'We must find a way to make the boy talk to us,' replied Leofric. 'We must find out what thoughts are in his head. Then we might be able to help him.'

That evening, the three of them sat, as usual, in front of their hearth. 'Eilmer,' said Leofric gently, 'can you tell us what is troubling you?'

Eilmer shook his head and stared at the fire. 'We are your parents,' said Ayleth. 'It is disrespectful not to speak to us.' Still Eilmer said nothing. 'We have survived the Danes and we have survived the winter. Can you not be happy now that spring is here?'

Eilmer could not be happy because the life he had to look forward to was not the life he wanted. But he lacked the words to say so without giving offence. So he remained silent. Ayleth's patience had run out. 'For the love of God, child,' she shouted at him, 'be thankful for what you have. It is more than most.'

Eilmer knew that. But a man's thirst is not slaked by being told that another man's thirst is greater. He rose from his chair and went outside. Although it was dark, he made his way slowly to an old oak at the edge of the village. He sat under the tree and tried to make sense of his feelings. For an hour he sat there, then another hour, before returning to the cottage. He had made little progress. He knew what he did not want, but not what he did want.

Two days later, Leofric spoke to Eilmer again. 'Your mother and I have been talking. We would like to take you to the abbey at Malmesbury.'

In Eilmer's mind, something stirred, and he managed to speak. 'Why, Father?'

'Now that the threat from the Danes has receded and you are old enough, the abbot might be willing to take you as an oblate.'

'What is an oblate?'

'He is a young man who joins the abbey to learn its ways and to receive an education.'

Suddenly Eilmer knew what he wanted. He wanted to learn. He wanted to acquire knowledge. He wanted to read and write. He wanted to be a scholar.

'When shall we go?'

'If you wish it, tomorrow.'

'So soon.' It was a big step. Eilmer knew very little about the abbey or the monks who lived there. His enthusiasm was tempered by a fear of the unknown.

'You cannot stay here as you are. You are no help to us, nor we to you. We shall pray that the monks can help you. Your mother and I will take you to Malmesbury tomorrow.'

They set off at dawn and despite walking slowly, were outside Malmesbury before midday. It was a fine, clear day and the road was dry. They passed through the town gate and climbed the hill upon which the three abbey churches had been built. They were old churches, built by Aldhelm three hundred years before, and now restored for the use of the monks who lived by the rules of St Benedict. The abbey was also surrounded by a wall. Leofric and Eilmer left Ayleth sitting on a grassy bank outside it, and made their way to the abbey gate. A monk answered Leofric's knock and, on being told their business, let them into the abbey grounds. The monk introduced himself as Halig.

Eilmer stood in the middle of a cobbled courtyard and looked around in amazement. He had never imagined such buildings. Three separate churches, each a rectangle of solid stone, and each with a high tower at its western end; monks' quarters around the courtyard and, at the eastern end, an archway through which he could see part of a garden.

They were led by Halig around the Church of St Michael to the abbot's quarters. 'Abbot Beorthelm will be preparing for the office of Sext,' Halig told them. 'After that he will eat and rest until None. I will ask him if he will see you after he has eaten.'

The monk knocked on the abbot's door – a narrow piece of dark oak with sturdy iron fixings – and entered. Eilmer and his father waited nervously outside. If the abbot could not see them or if he would not take Eilmer in as an oblate, they would have had a wasted trip and the problem of Eilmer's future would remain unresolved. If they had to return home with their son, Ayleth, with a mother's intuition, doubted if he would be alive to see another spring. Eilmer himself, during a sleepless night, had realised with absolute certainty that a life in the Abbey of Malmesbury was exactly the life he wanted. He could not bear the thought of returning, disappointed and without hope, to the village.

Halig soon appeared again. 'The abbot will see you after he has eaten. Until then you are welcome to walk or sit in our garden,' he said, pointing through the arch. 'Have you eaten today?'

'We have not,' replied Leofric. 'Nor has my wife. She waits outside the abbey gate.'

'In that case, I will arrange for food to be brought to you and taken to her and I will find you when the abbot is ready to see you. Now I too must go to Sext.' He nodded to them and went to join a line of brother monks entering the Church of St Michael.

Leofric put his arm around Eilmer's shoulders and led him through the arch into the garden. As it was a time of prayer, the garden was deserted, but Eilmer was enthralled by it. A carefully tended bed of lavender and sage ran the length of the garden, and alongside it another of garlic and thyme. Apple and pear trees had been trained against the wall on their left which faced the midday sun, while on their right stood a line of wooden beehives. In the corner of the far wall was a dovecot on a tall pole. There were more beds, some home to hard-pruned roses not yet showing their new shoots, others packed with herbs and flowers that Eilmer did not recognise.

After they walked slowly around the garden, admiring its order and variety, they sat on a thick log, set just inside the archway for that purpose. 'Would you be happy here, Eilmer?' asked Leofric.

Eilmer turned to him and smiled. 'I would.' He could think of nothing more to say.

They ate the bread and cheese brought to them by a young man dressed in the black habit of the Benedictines, but without a monk's tonsure, and waited to be summoned to meet the abbot.

After about an hour, Halig appeared and told them the abbot was ready to see them. He took them back to the narrow door, knocked and led them into a small, plain room, furnished only by a single chair, a writing table with ink, quills and parchment, and a simple altar on which stood a silver cross. An elderly man, tonsured and wearing the black habit, his hands clasped at his chest, rose stiffly from the chair to greet them.

'I am Abbot Beorthelm,' he said in a deep, musical voice. 'Brother Halig tells me that you wish to speak to me.'

'I am Leofric,' replied Eilmer's father. 'I wish to speak to you about my son becoming an oblate.'

The abbot peered doubtfully at Eilmer. 'How old is the boy?'

'He is ten, father,' replied Leofric.

'He is small for his age. Has he been sick?'

'We have all suffered since the Danes came. He will grow strong again.'

The abbot cleared his throat. 'The life of a monk in this abbey is one of work and prayer. It is the same for an oblate, even one of this boy's age. It is not a life for the weak or infirm. What is your name, boy?'

'Eilmer, Father.'

'And why do you wish to join our order, Eilmer?'

'I want to study, Father. I want to read and write and to learn from books.'

Beorthelm smiled. 'That is good. Since it was founded more than three hundred years ago, our community has embraced the study of science and nature as well as that of the Gospels and the Rule of St Benedict. Malmesbury Abbey is now a noted seat of learning. And thanks to King Athelstan our library contains many beautiful and sacred books. Is there anything in particular that you wish to study?'

'I would like to study birds, Father.'

'Birds? How unusual. I do hope you will not be trying to fly.' Eilmer said nothing, sensing that this was not the moment to speak of such a thing. 'Do you have any Latin, Eilmer?'

'No, Father.'

'Then you will not know that oblate is a Latin word. It means "bring before" or "offer one's services to". If you were to join our order as an oblate you would be offering yourself to God. Do you understand that?'

'Yes, Father.'

'We are a God-fearing family, Father,' said Leofric. 'Eilmer has been brought up as a good Christian.'

'Indeed. I am pleased to hear it.' The abbot stroked his chin. 'We already have two young oblates residing in the abbey. I do not know if we should take in another one.' Again he peered at Eilmer. 'Especially one as young and frail as Eilmer. Are you sure that he is ten? We cannot take him if he is not.'

'Quite sure, Father.'

'In that case, please wait in the garden while I consider the matter. I will find you when I have made my decision.'

In the garden, they sat on the log and watched a monk at work on the beehives and another hoeing the bed of lavender and sage. Both men worked steadily, neither rushing nor resting. Eilmer wondered if one day he would be collecting honey or cutting lavender in this garden. When Abbot Beorthelm came into the garden, he had beside him the young man who had brought their food earlier. He introduced the young man as Orvin.

'I have asked for guidance,' said the abbot, 'and believe that our community would benefit from having Eilmer as one of its members. Are you still sure that this is what you want, Eilmer?'

Eilmer beamed. 'Quite sure, Father.'

'I thought so. In that case, say farewell to your father. Orvin will show you where you will sleep and pray and will teach you our ways. He too is an oblate.' He turned to Leofric. 'While Eilmer is an oblate, he may leave us at any time if he wishes and, except during Lent, you may visit him as often as you like. We do not admit visitors while we are fasting.'

'My wife Ayleth is outside,' said Leofric. 'May Eilmer say goodbye to her?'

'Of course.'

They found Ayleth still sitting on the bank and told her what the abbot had said. Eilmer kissed her and hugged his father. Then Orvin led him back into the abbey.

Very early one morning in June, when Eilmer had been at the abbey for eleven years, before the office of Prime, Eilmer and Orvin climbed the spiral stairs which led to the top of the tower on the south-west corner of the abbey church. In one hand Eilmer carried a bunch of feathers collected from the dovecot and the ground under the daws' nests.

As the abbey stood on a steep hill overlooking Malmesbury, the top of the tower was the highest point for miles around. From there, they could see the rivers circling the town, the town itself and for several miles in every direction. To the south lay St Aldhelm's Meadow and, to the west, the road to the small town of Bristol.

On top of the tower there was only just enough room for the two of them. They held on to each other to steady themselves against the blustery wind which could easily blow a man off balance and over the low parapet which was all that protected them from a long drop to the ground. 'This is an uncomfortable place, Eilmer,' said Orvin, gripping Eilmer's arm. 'I would rather be asleep in my bed. What exactly are we going to do?'

'We are going to observe the flight of these feathers,' replied Eilmer. 'I want to know how the wind affects them and where they fall to ground.'

Orvin sighed. 'I need hardly ask why, but please do not try following the feathers while I am up here. I do not wish to see you fall on your head.'

'Do not concern yourself, my friend. I shall not be flying today. There is more to learn before I do that. Now, take these feathers and throw them as high as you can into the air.' Eilmer handed Orvin three feathers, which he launched off the tower with a flick of his wrist. At first the feathers swirled about above their heads, blown this way and that as if not quite sure in which direction they should be going. But when a gust of wind met the hill upon which the abbey stood, it rose sharply upwards and sent the feathers soaring into the sky. The two monks watched as they climbed higher and higher before disappearing into the distance.

'There. Just like the daws. It's the wind which the birds use to soar along the hill. It comes up the valley from the south-west, meets the hill and the tower, rises up and carries the daws with it. The daws use their wings to ride the wind in the direction they want to go.'

As if they had been listening, half-a-dozen daws left their nests in the tower and rose effortlessly on the wind before swooping down towards the river. With no more than tiny movements of their wings, they adjusted the direction of their flight along the ridge of the hill before turning back over the town towards the abbey.

'It is wonderful to watch God's creatures,' said Orvin, 'but I am not sure that I want to watch you trying to copy them, Eilmer. Even you are much heavier than a bird. Won't you simply plummet to the ground and kill yourself?'

'I might. But when a bird leaves its nest for the first time does it not have the same fear? Yet a bird must learn to fly and that means overcoming its fear. One day a man will learn to fly like a bird, just as he has learnt to swim like a fish. Why should it not be me?'

For some time Orvin stood looking out over the town. Then he said, 'You will need help.'

'I shall. Will you help me?'

'Yes,' replied Orvin. 'As long as I do not have to fly too.'

Eilmer laughed. 'Have no fear, Orvin. I will do the flying.'

The monks had very little time to themselves between saying the nine daily offices and their work in the abbey or among the poor and sick of the town. What free time they had they were expected to spend in sleep or prayer. For nearly twelve months Eilmer and Orvin snatched whatever minutes they could to work on a design for the wings Eilmer would need for his flight. Eilmer had begged parchment and ink from the scribes in the library and together they pored over their drawings, often by no more than the light of a single, evil-smelling tallow candle.

They agreed that the wings should be as long and as wide as possible, given that they would have to be carried up the narrow stairs to the top of the tower before being attached to Eilmer. As there was no protection from the wind up there, fixing the wings would be difficult and dangerous. If they were too large to be easily managed, they might lose control of them and be blown off the tower. They also agreed that they should make the wings out of the lightest materials they could find. At first Eilmer suggested parchment, fixed to frames of ash. But they soon realised that parchment would not be strong enough and might tear, and turned instead to linen. And the ash was replaced by willow, which grew abundantly around the town and which they found to be lighter and more flexible. It was Orvin's idea to make a model. 'You will have to seek the abbot's permission,' he told Eilmer, 'and that will be easier if you can show him how you plan to do it.'

They cut thin strips of willow which they fashioned to make the frames of two wings shaped like those of a bat, and sewed pieces of linen over the frames. Then they attached leather straps to the underside of the wings. Eilmer would hold on to the straps and flap the wings with his arms. Each wing of the model was two feet long – about a quarter of the size the real wings would be.

When Abbot Beorthelm had died five years earlier, Abbot Beorhtwold had taken his place. One day in the summer of 1003, after the meeting which followed the saying of Prime, Eilmer and Orwin approached the abbot and requested permission to speak to him. Although this was unusual, the abbot agreed and told them to come to his quarters after the office of Sext at noon.

Beorhtwold was not a man who often smiled. His long face was invariably cast in the sternest of frowns, his forehead creased and his gaze fixed somewhere in the distance as if he were contemplating some difficult theological problem. When Eilmer and Orvin entered his room, each bearing a model wing, the frown deepened and his eyes narrowed suspiciously. 'And what is this that you bring me?' he asked them.

They held up the wings for the abbot to see. 'These are models of a pair of wings that we seek your permission to make and try,' replied Eilmer.

'Wings, Brother Eilmer? How exactly do you propose to try them, and why?'

'I have studied the flights of the daws which nest in the church tower, Father, and I believe that, with the right design of wings, a man might copy them. I wish to put my theory to the test.'

Beorhtwold's expression did not change. 'And you, Brother Orvin, what part do you play in this?'

'I shall assist Eilmer in the construction of the wings, Father, and in fitting them to him at the top of the tower.'

'So you will jump from the tower, Eilmer? And how far do you expect to fly?'

'I aim to land in St Aldhelm's Meadow, Father.'

'That is a considerable distance. A thousand yards or more. What if you do not reach the meadow?'

'Then we shall at least have learnt that my ideas are wrong. A small but valuable contribution to the abbey's store of knowledge.'

The abbot's frown returned. 'And a high price to pay for it if you lose your life. Please show me a wing.'

Eilmer handed him a wing and together he and Orvin explained how it was made and how it would work.

'I have no idea if these will work as you think,' said the abbot when they had finished, 'and I need time to consider the matter. The Lord will guide my thoughts, as he always does. I will let you know when I have made my decision.'

'Thank you, Father.' said Eilmer and Orvin together. They took the wings, bowed their heads and left.

Outside, Orvin asked Eilmer how he thought it had gone. 'Better than I had feared,' said Eilmer. 'He listened and he did not refuse us. Let us hope that he does not take too long to decide.'

For seven days Eilmer went about his business, attending the offices, working in the garden and tending the abbey's chickens. He tried to concentrate on his prayers and on his work. Worrying about it would not change Beorhtwold's decision or make him reach it any the sooner. But it was a long seven days. He sat in his room and held the model wings in his hands. They would work. He knew it. A man could fly and he would prove it. He just needed the chance.

After Prime on the eighth day after he and Orvin had been to see him, Beorhtwold sent for them. When they entered his room, he was on his knees in prayer. He rose stiffly and turned to face them. 'I have prayed for guidance and I have discussed your request with some of the older monks. It is true that our abbey is a noted seat of learning and that we value knowledge above everything but our faith, but I cannot grant you permission to do as you wish. It is too dangerous and I would be at fault if you were killed or injured. That is my decision.'

Eilmer felt his face redden. 'But, Father...'

Beorhtwold held up his hands. 'That is my decision, Brother Eilmer. Let there be no more talk of the matter. It is not God's purpose that we should fly. Destroy the wings and return to your duties. I shall pray that your minds are swiftly turned to more godly things.'

There was nothing for it but to accept the abbot's decision. Eilmer and Orvin bowed their heads and left. This time they did not stop to speak outside but walked in silence straight to Eilmer's room. There Eilmer handed the model wings to Orvin. 'Please destroy them as the abbot instructed,' he said. 'I will dispose of everything else.' Orvin took the wings and Eilmer gathered up the strips of wood, linen, needles, thread and leather that lay about his room. He carried them to a place just inside the north wall of the abbey where a large hole for rubbish had been dug. He threw them in and returned to his room.

There would be no flight. Eilmer would just have to make do with his dreams.

Try as he might, Eilmer could never quite put the idea of flying out of his mind. He spoke to no-one about it, not even Orvin, and lived strictly by the rule of St Benedict. He spent the little free time he had in the library and in the garden where he studied the plants and animals, and sitting by the abbey walls gazing up at the swooping daws. If he could not fly himself, at least he could watch the daws.

In the autumn of the year 1009, Abbot Beorhtwold had died. His replacement, Eadric, was a scholarly man, a mathematician and linguist, who had studied in Rome and Paris. Eadric immediately set about adding to the abbey's library and encouraging scientific research of all kinds. He asked the gardeners, Eilmer among them, to experiment with different plants, the beekeepers to study more closely the behaviour of their charges and the almoners to try new remedies such as mandrake roots and arnica when they visited the sick of the town. Eadric was a man who embraced new ideas and wanted to enhance the abbey's reputation as a seat of learning.

Eilmer was hoeing a vegetable bed when he saw Abbot Eadric approaching. Despite the winter cold, he wore only his habit and sandals – the monks of Malmesbury were expected to bear all seasons alike. Eilmer bowed his head to the abbot and continued his work. It would not do to speak to the abbot unless he was invited to. Eadric stood and watched Eilmer working away at the soil, worrying out the weeds, and putting them in his basket ready to be added to the heap of garden and kitchen refuse which he would dig into the soil the following autumn.

'What will you plant here?' asked Eadric

'Leeks and carrots, Father,' replied Eilmer.

Eadric nodded. 'God is bountiful.'

'He is, Father.'

Eadric bent to pull out a weed and dropped it in the basket. 'St Benedict recognised that although idle coversation is to be avoided, there are times when it is necessary to talk, Brother Eilmer, and it is my duty as Abbot to know about my fellow monks in the abbey. Please tell me how you came to Malmesbury.'

Eilmer put down his hoe and turned to face the abbot. The request had taken him by surprise and he thought for a minute before answering. He told Eadric about his parents and about the arrival of the Danes in the village and their hiding in the forest, and how he had come to realise that life on a farm was not what he wanted. He explained how, when Leofric had suggested he come to Malmesbury, he had known what sort of life he did want. He had joined as an oblate and had been content in the abbey for nearly twenty years.

'And what was it about our life that made you think it was what you wanted?' asked Eadric.

'The order and discipline of the abbey, Father, and also the opportunity to learn. In our village I would have learnt how to survive and little else.'

'And what have you learnt here, Brother Eilmer?'

'I have learnt to read and write and about the rule of St Benedict, Father, and also about this garden and the animals we keep. Most of all, I have studied the birds,' replied Eilmer, thinking that he might have said too much.

'That is good.' Eadric smiled and wandered off down the garden, leaving Eilmer to his hoeing.

That evening, Eilmer did something he had not done for many years. He climbed the stairs to the top of the tower and looked out on the countryside below. The sun was low over green pastures, the river glinted as it twisted its way around the town and the chattering daws circled above him. He thought of the fledgling pigeon that day in the forest. It had watched its mother, hesitated a while, then launched itself off the branch and into the air. It was that, more than anything, which had brought Eilmer to the abbey.

Orvin was feeding the chickens when Eilmer approached him. He told his friend about his brief conversation with the abbot and about climbing the tower. Orvin looked up in surprise.

'Are you thinking of trying again, Eilmer?' he asked.

'Perhaps. I think Abbot Eadric might be more amenable to the idea than Beorhtwold.'

'What makes you think that?'

'Just a feeling.'

Orvin scattered the last of his scraps around the chicken run and, together, they walked back down the garden to the abbey. 'Come with me, Eilmer,' he said. 'I have something for you.'

Eilmer followed Orvin to his room. Inside, Orvin reached under his narrow cot and pulled out something wrapped in an ancient piece of cloth. He handed it to Eilmer.

'There. You might need this.' Eilmer carefully unwrapped the cloth. Inside were the model wings they had made to show to Beorhtwold. Orvin had not destroyed them, as Eilmer had asked him to, and they were quite intact.

'I knew you would need them again one day.' said Orvin with a grin.

Eilmer gripped his arm. 'Thank you, Orvin. This is the sign I needed. I shall speak to the abbot tomorrow after Prime.'

'And how long do you intend to make these wings?' inquired Eadric with a twinkle in his eye. If he had been surprised by the arrival at his door of Eilmer bearing two objects in the shape of wings made of willow, linen and leather, he had not shown it. 'They will have to be strong enough to support you.'

'Yes, Father. I plan to make each one eight feet long.'

'Eight feet? Surely that would make them too heavy for you to flap like a bird. And how do you propose to steer?'

'As the daws do, Father. I shall tilt the wings according to the direction I wish to go in.'

'And how will you land?'

'In the same way. The daws tilt their wings to slow their flight and lose height. I shall do the same.'

Eadric looked doubtful. 'Have you any evidence that this will work or are you just guessing?'

'I have studied the way in which the daws use the winds around the abbey and I have read about the flight of the Andalucian, Ibn Firnas, Father, and I believe my design closely follows his.'

Eadric nodded. 'I know of this man, but did he not damage himself on landing?'

'He did, but he survived.'

'As, if I permit this, I trust you will.'

'I shall, Father.'

'Hmm,' Eadric hesitated. 'Please leave these here. I would like to seek the advice of Brother Wregan. He has a scientific turn of mind and I would value his opinion.'

Eilmer did not know whether to be encouraged or disappointed by the meeting. The abbot had not laughed at him or rejected his idea out of hand, but neither had he been very enthusiastic. 'He thinks the wings are too long,' he told Orvin, 'and he wondered how I would land without injuring myself.'

'I too wonder about that,' replied Orvin, 'unless you manage to land on a haystack. If you land in the river you might drown and if you land on the ground you might break all the bones in your body.'

'That is why I shall fly towards St Aldhelm's Meadow. The ground there is soft. It will be much like landing on a haystack.'

'Eilmer, it will be nothing of the kind, as you know perfectly well. Wherever you land it will be dangerous. Are you sure you still want to do this?'

'Quite sure. I shall pray that the abbot allows me to. If he does, shall I ask if you may assist me?'

'Yes, as long as I do not have to jump off the tower with you.'

When Eilmer was summoned to the abbot's room, he found Wregan already there. He and Eadric were examining the model wings.

'Wregan and I have discussed your request, Eilmer,' said Eadric, 'As it stands, I cannot agree to it.' Eilmer's heart sank. Another rebuff. He tried not to show his disappointment. 'But we think that with some alterations to your design, such an attempt might be successful.'

'And we won't know unless we try,' added Wregan.

So sudden was Eilmer's change of mood that he wondered if he had heard right.

'So, Father, if we make the alterations, I will be permitted to attempt the flight?'

'As long as you are able to satisfy Wregan and myself that everything else has been properly taken into account. The required wind strength and direction, for instance, and how you can be sure of landing safely in the meadow, which is, after all, surrounded by the river.'

'I have thought of all that, Father. The tower is…'

Eadric held up his hands. 'Not now, Eilmer. Tomorrow at this time we will begin work.'

'Yes, Father. And may I bring Orvin? He helped me make these wings.'

'You may. We may need a younger pair of hands.'

'Thank you, Father.'

The next day, Eilmer and Orvin presented themselves at the abbot's room. As before, Wregan was already there.

'Before we begin,' said the abbot sternly, 'I want to stress that this matter is to be kept confidential between us. I do not want our daily worship and work affected by foolish thoughts or idle gossip, nor do we want the townsfolk hearing about it. If they do, rumours will spread and our peace will be shattered. Let us take care not to speak of it outside this room.'

Eilmer and Orvin nodded. 'We understand, Father.'

'Good. Then let us begin by examining the wings. Wregan and I believe that you will not be able to manage wings of eight feet in length. They will simply be too big and heavy.'

'But I shall need wings big enough to lift me on the wind, Father, and even I am heavier than a daw.'

'Indeed you are. But you must be able to control the wings, not they you.'

'I suggest that we make wings of six feet in length,' added Wregan. 'We will use linen and willow for the frames as you have done. Silk would be better than linen but it is very scarce and expensive. Then we'll be able to see whether you can manage them.'

It was clear that if he was to be permitted to carry out his experiment, Eilmer would have to agree to Wregan and the abbot's ideas or offer a very good reason for not doing so. For an hour they discussed the shape of the wings and the design of the frame. The less wood used the lighter they would be, but the frame must be strong enough. They discussed, too, the best way to attach the linen to the frame, deciding that silk thread should be used, and how best to fix the leather handles for Eilmer's hands and arms.

When Eilmer and Orvin left the abbot's room to prepare for Terce, they had a clear picture in their heads of how the wings would look. Each would be six feet long, in the shape of a daw's wings, widest in the middle and tapering to a point at the end. They would be made of linen and willow with leather straps. And they would start collecting the materials the next day.

It was hopeless trying to keep it secret. By the time Eilmer had cut willow branches and carried them from the river to the abbey, and Orvin had bought linen and leather in the market, there was not a monk who did not know that something unusual was afoot. At the next weekly meeting of the monks, Abbot Eadric was forced to make the matter public and to instruct them not to discuss it outside the abbey. This was to be a scientific experiment. They did not want the town full of gawping visitors.

Eilmer and Orvin did all the work entailed in making the wings. They more or less took over the carpenter's workshop and between them cut the willow into the right lengths, bent it to the shapes they wanted, tied the pieces together with leather and cut and stretched the linen over the frames. Finally, they attached the straps.

They agreed that the courtyard would be the best place for Eilmer to try on the wings. When he and Orvin carried them there from the workshop very early one morning, they found that all the monks had already assembled there. When Eadric arrived, they stood in silence all around the yard watching Orvin lift each wing and hold it up behind Eilmer. One at a time, Eilmer slipped his arms and hands through the leather straps, stood for a moment to feel the weight of the wings and to get his balance, then gently moved his arms to flap the wings – and immediately fell on his face. There were a few stifled laughs but, undeterred, Eilmer allowed Orvin to help him to his feet to try again.

He flapped again and immediately fell over again. Lying face down on the ground he struggled out of the straps, got up, ignored the whispers of the grinning onlookers and approached Eadric. 'The wings are too long and cumbersome, Father.' he said quietly. 'We must think of another way.'

The abbot spoke equally quietly. 'It is you who must think of another way, Eilmer. I have more important matters to attend to, and so does Wregan. You may have one week to come up with a better design or that will be the end of the matter. God will not look kindly upon us if we ignore our duties for the sake of a hare-brained scheme.' And with that, he turned on his heel and returned to his room.

All the monks dispersed, leaving Eilmer and Orvin alone. One week. Not very long and they had no idea of a better design. They picked up the wings and carried them back to the workshop. Perhaps the frames and linen could be reused in a different way.

The carpenter, however, a wiry little man named Magan, had been less than pleased at his workshop being taken over and had observed their antics in the yard. 'It isn't going to work,' he told them, 'and I need my workshop. You'll have to find somewhere else.' So they carried the wings to a quiet spot near the west wall and left them there while they went to pray.

It was not until after None at three that afternoon that Eilmer and

Orvin were able to meet in the garden to discuss what to do. By that time, Eilmer had come to the conclusion that he would never be able to flap wings of sufficient length to keep him in the air so they would have to approach the problem from a different angle. 'The daws glide on the wind,' he told Orvin, 'and so shall I. We will build one large wing, with a frame in the shape of a cross and linen stretched over it. I will attach my ankles to the frame with rope and hold on to another rope tied across the wing. So the wing will be rigid. No flapping.'

Orvin looked doubtful. 'How will you steer?'

'As before, by tilting the wing, but with both hands and both feet. It should be easy. Look.' Eilmer picked up a stick and scratched a shape in the earth. 'From top to tail, we will make it ten feet long, and from side-to-side eight feet.'

'That is much more wing area than we had before. Are you sure you will be able to manage it?'

'Quite sure. The balance will be different and there will be no need for flapping.'

'So you will be tied on to the wing, jump off the tower and trust in the wind to carry you down to the meadow, where you will land as gently as a butterfly.'

'Exactly. We know the tower is eighty feet high and the meadow might be another sixty feet lower than its base. So I shall have a drop of one hundred and forty feet in which to glide about twelve hundred feet. If I descend at a rate of one foot for every eight and a half feet travelled, I shall land in the meadow. If necessary, I shall adjust my speed and direction by tipping the wing up and down or from side to side. I don't know why I ever thought I would need two wings. This is much simpler.'

'If you say so, Eilmer. But will the abbot agree?'

'We shall have to persuade him.'

That evening after Vespers, Eilmer went to the library where he sat at the scribes' writing table with a duck-feather quill and a pot of oak-apple ink. Very carefully, he drew his design on a sheet of parchment. When he was satisfied with the drawing, he dried it with sand and took it back to his room. He and Orvin would show it to the abbot the next day. That night Eilmer prayed as hard as he had ever prayed. If Eadric did not give his permission the next day, he would never fly. It was his last chance.

When they knocked nervously on Eadric's door, the drawing under Eilmer's arm, they found the abbot in a surprisingly receptive mood. He seemed to have got over the fiasco in the courtyard and studied the new design with interest.

'I can see how this might work, Eilmer,' he said, 'as long as you choose a day when the wind is just right.'

'Yes, Father. This is the time of the year for a northerly wind. I will wait for one which is strong enough to carry me.'

The abbot turned to Orvin. 'And you, Orvin, what part will you play in this?'

'I shall help Eilmer construct the wing and will tie him to it at the top of the tower, Father.' He grinned, 'I shall make sure he is tied securely.'

'That would be sensible. Very well, you have my permission to make this wing. Inform me when it is ready so that I may inspect it. And do try not to disrupt our community; I do not want a repeat of the last episode.'

Eilmer and Orvin were able to reuse some of the willow and leather from the wings they had put by the wall, but they had to acquire new linen. When Orvin returned from the market with it, he looked shaken. 'I don't know how, but everyone in Malmesbury seems to know about the flight. They are even wagering on the outcome.'

Eilmer laughed. 'How far do they think I shall get?'

'About ten feet along and eighty feet down. They think you are mad.'

'Then we must show them how wrong they are.'

'And hope that the abbot does not hear of it. He might change his mind if he does.'

'We'd better get on with it, then.'

Over the next two days, they used every minute they could to finish the wing. When they had, it was just as Eilmer had drawn it – eight feet across and ten feet from tip to tail, in the shape of a cross. They tested the leather straps and silk stitching and found them to be sound and they practised tying Eilmer into place. On the third day, Eadric inspected it and gave them his blessing. He instructed them to inform him when the day came so that he might assemble the monks and ask for God to smile upon their endeavour. To Eilmer's relief, he made no mention of spectators or gamblers.

They did not have to wait long. On the third day after Eadric had given his permission, a good stiff wind was blowing from the north as they made their way to Prime.

'God has sent us our wind,' whispered Eilmer. Orvin smiled. Today Eilmer would fly.

Eadric must also have realised that the day had come because at the end of the daily meeting he looked inquiringly at Eilmer, who smiled and nodded. 'Today, Brothers,' he announced, 'Eilmer will attempt his flight from the tower. We will assemble now in the courtyard to pray for his safety and for the success of his experiment.'

Eilmer sensed a mood of excitement among the monks. At last he would show them that a man's flight was possible.

After prayers had been said, Eilmer and Orvin carried the wing to the base of the tower and attached to it a light rope with which to haul it up to the top. Knowing the wing was too big to be manhandled up the narrow stairs, they had procured the rope and tied it to the parapet as soon as Eadric had consented to the flight. They left Wregan in charge of it while they climbed the stairs, and then heaved the wing up. Although it was light, the wind by now was blowing strongly and they had to take care not to damage it against the tower. Watched by their brother monks, they pulled the rope as smoothly as they could, lifted the wing over the parapet, and checked that it was undamaged.

In the narrow confines of the top of the tower, tying Eilmer into the wing was the most difficult part of the operation. While Orvin held the wing up, struggling to keep it steady, Eilmer backed into it and held on to the ropes. Then Orvin squeezed around him and knelt down to secure his ankles and to loop a rope attached to the cross-piece around his stomach. The north wind had strengthened further and more than once Eilmer thought he might be blown off the tower before he was ready. Holding an eight-foot-wide wing up there was a different matter from holding it on the ground.

Eilmer looked up. The daws were circling above as if they too had come to watch, floating on the wind and rising high when they caught an upward draught. Exactly what he hoped to do. Orvin touched him on the shoulder and pointed in the direction of the town. A crowd of spectators had gathered below the King's Wall and along the east bank of the river. There must have been five hundred or more. The moment had come.

Eilmer stepped on to the parapet, wobbled, and jumped. The wind immediately caught the wing and sent him flying over the heads of the watching monks and towards the abbey wall. When he felt himself falling, he pushed his hands back and his feet forwards until he was almost vertical. The wind lifted him again and he sailed over the wall in the direction of the meadow. Eilmer laughed out loud. By the grace of God, he was flying.

He shook his head to clear the tears from his eyes. To his left he saw the streets and houses of the town, to his right the river and the trees and fields that stretched away towards the west. It was a view seen every day by the daws but never before by a man. He was right. Man could fly.

Eilmer was about forty feet above the ground and could hear the cheers of the townsfolk as he flew over them when there was a slight change in the direction of the wind and he veered to the west, away from the King's Wall and over a place where the ground sloped sharply down to the river. He tried to counteract the wind by tipping the wing back to the east. It made no difference. The wind dropped and he quickly lost height. He tried to rise by tipping the wing upwards. That too made no difference. He was falling and there was nothing he could do but hang on and hope. In a matter of seconds he hit the ground. The wing frame snapped and he tumbled down the slope, coming to a halt a few yards from the river.

Eilmer knew at once that his legs were broken. Both of them were twisted unnaturally below the knee and the pain was fierce. He sat on the ground and waited for help. The nearest townsfolk were with him very quickly, followed by a handful of monks, including the almoner, who ordered him to be carried gently to the abbey.

By the time he was laid on a cot in the infirmary, Eilmer had passed out. The almoner moved fast. While two oblates held Eilmer down by the shoulders, the almoner straightened his left leg and bound it tightly with a linen bandage. Eimer briefly opened his eyes before closing them tight against the pain and silently mouthing a prayer. Then the almoner did the same with his right leg. When the legs were set, he helped Eilmer sip a cup of water mixed with St John's wort and valerian root and told him to lie quite still. Eilmer knew he had been lucky. Such a fall might easily have killed him, and, although there was still a risk of fatal infection, he had flown and lived to tell the tale.

When Eilmer next opened his eyes, Orvin was sitting beside the bed. He took Eilmer's hand and squeezed it. 'I am much relieved to see you alive, my friend,' he said, 'and have prayed for your recovery.'

Eilmer smiled weakly. 'I am in God's hands. How far did I fly?'

'We think it was about six hundred feet. Was it the wind that turned you towards the river?'

'It was. I could not fight it. We should have fashioned a tail. Next time, I'll have a tail to help me steer.'

'Eilmer, even if you live to be a hundred, there must be no next time. You have flown. Whether you live or die now, let that be enough.'

Eilmer closed his eyes and slept.

1066 AD

The monk stood in the abbey garden and watched the comet crossing the night sky. He was frail and old – more than eighty years old – and lame; he used two stout sticks when he walked. He had lived in the abbey for almost all of his long life and had known six abbots and more monks than he could remember. He was revered in the community for his age and wisdom and for his feat of daring over fifty years earlier. Everyone in and around Malmesbury knew him as the monk Eilmer, who had leapt from the abbey tower and flown like a bird.

Eilmer was the only man in Malmesbury who had seen the comet before. When he was a small boy, he had stood outside his parents' cottage and watched it. Leofric, his father, had feared then that it foretold impending disaster, and had been proved right the following year when Danes appeared from the east and laid waste the countryside, plundering villages, killing the men and raping their women. Now the comet had come again and Eilmer feared that England was once more in danger.

'Thou art come!' he cried, gazing at the comet. 'A matter of lamentation to many a mother art thou; I have seen thee long since; but I now behold thee much more terrible, threatening to hurl destruction on this country.' He turned to the young oblates around him. 'It is a sign from God. Mark it well and be prepared. England's enemies will come soon.' He spoke quietly, as was his way, but with the force of conviction. 'Once before it was the Danes. This time, who knows?'

The outline of the abbey tower was visible against the sky. With an effort, Eilmer lifted one of his sticks and pointed at it. 'And note this. One day, a man will fly. Not, as I did, for a matter of feet, but for miles. He will fly over land and sea and think little of it. Just as man learnt to build a boat which would carry him on water, so he will learn to build wings which will carry him through the air. I am sure of it.'

HMS *ASSOCIATION*

1708

A true account of the final voyage of HMS Association
by Daniel Jones, pressed man.

In setting this down, I know that the wrong eyes may see it, but when I'm gone there should be at least one true account of that voyage, there having been neither inquiry nor inquest. Only twelve months have passed, yet already there are stories – fanciful, foolish stories – of the kind that men of the sea have ever been fond of telling. And in the villages of Cornwall and in the islands there are many men of the sea happy to spin a tale for the price of a pot of ale. The more pots of ale, the finer the tale. So this, from one better placed than any to know the truth of it, is what occurred. First, however, I should explain how I came to be on board HMS *Association*.

The greater part of the fleet had set sail from Portsmouth in July and had put in to Falmouth to take on food and water. Ships of the line crammed the harbour and lay at anchor just outside it. War with the French dragging on, ships in need of crews – every man in the town knew that the press would be about and all but the most foolish kept themselves out of harm's way. Against the law or not, the press would think nothing of taking men from inns and taverns, from fishing boats and shipyards, even from fields and farms, caring little if their 'catches' were men of the sea or of the land. It was bodies they needed, nothing more. I was one of the most foolish and, on my birth day, for the sake of ale and a woman, I took the risk. And regretted it.

The press burst in to the Mermaid Inn – six of them, with short swords and cudgels – looked about, saw only one able-bodied man and ordered me, in the name of the Queen, to come quietly. That I did not, but laid out two of them before I was knocked senseless and carted off to serve in Her Majesty's navy.

When I came to, I was deep in the hold of a ship among the cack and the rats and bound at the wrists. There were four of us, all taken that night and all wishing we had stayed in our homes. We said little, but lay without food or water until the ship weighed anchor and we felt the sea's swell under us. When, eventually, bruised and sick, we were released and ordered on deck, we were a mile or more from shore. Even I, a strong swimmer from playing for hours in the river as a boy, was not going to risk the water, especially among those treacherous currents. Every fisherman in Cornwall knows to beware of them. An only son to my widowed father, my mother having died at my birth, I was a fisherman, as he was, working at the drifting and the seining to catch pilchards. Hard labour it was to be sure, but we had a decent enough living, which many, in these harsh days, do not. And we knew full well about the fickle Cornish seas.

While we stood huddled together around the main mast, trying to come to terms with the misfortune we had brought upon ourselves but ignored by the rest of the crew who had doubtless seen enough newly pressed men not to care much about us, a sharp-faced youth, barely old enough to have need of a razor, barked at us that he was Midshipman Alexander, and that we were on HMS *Association*, a second-rate, ninety guns, with seven hundred men on board, Edmund Loades Captain and, he added proudly, flagship of Admiral Sir Cloudesley Shovell, Commander-in-Chief of the Mediterranean fleet.

Behind us fourteen other warships followed in line astern. It was off to war for us and we had best set to or we would not live long enough to see a Frenchie, never mind kill one. I looked at one of my new shipmates and saw misery in his eyes. He might have seen the same in mine. I cursed myself for an idiot and wondered if I would ever see Falmouth again.

There can have been barely a man of the sea who did not know of Sir Cloudesley Shovell, a tarpaulin who had worked his way from cabin boy to his present rank and whose reputation for bravery and leadership was unmatched in the navy. At that time I could not have told you anything more about the man – but I was to learn.

At first the four of us were given simple tasks – hauling ropes, swabbing decks, working the pumps – and were watched over by Alexander or another of the callow midshipmen. We had all taken immediately against the boy and on land I would have cheerfully given him a bloody nose just for being a smug little toad, but here there was no gain to be had from causing trouble, only the knotted end of a rope on a man's back. So I held my tongue and did as I was told. We all did.

By the time we reached the island of Ushant at the southern end of the channel – as far from England as I had ever been – we had been joined by twenty more vessels: fourteen warships, four fireships, a sloop and a yacht. Thirty-five ships in all, under Admiral Sir Cloudesley Shovell. A formidable force which would not have been assembled without good cause. The word was that we were bound for the port of Toulon where much of the French fleet was anchored. Had the French known we were coming, I daresay they would have put to sea to avoid being trapped like fish in a net. Whether that was the reason we were not told our destination, I could not say, but as the days passed it became accepted among the crew that Toulon was where we were headed and that the admiral and captains of all the ships in our fleet were hopeful of a good reward in the form of prize money. If we could capture a vessel or two and take them back to England, there would be money in it for all, even the pressed men, and treasure for the captain and officers. That was what we thought.

There were three gun decks on *Association*. When not in use, the guns were secured with ropes so that they did not slide about. A loose cannon could maim or kill as easily as enemy fire. Our hammocks were slung between them. On our passage through Biscay, when gunnery practice was ordered for three days on end, we stowed the hammocks before each practice and hauled the guns into position at the gun ports. I was put to a gun crew and shown how to swab out the barrel to extinguish stray embers left from the previous firing. After the cannon had been charged with powder, loaded with its shot, packed and rammed, we all heaved on the tackles to position it correctly and stood well back while our gun captain lit the priming powder. We did it again and again until we could carry it out in our sleep.

Salt pork, hard, maggoty biscuit, even beer as thin as piss, I got used to. So too sleeping in a hammock no more than fourteen inches wide, and hard up against snoring, grunting neighbours on either side. But the smoke and the crash of the guns of twenty-nine warships I never did become accustomed to and nor, I think, ever would. At times, the deck seemed to shake under our feet; at others, the gun-thunder echoed around us, bombarding our ears and rattling our skulls. It was no wonder so many who served on a warship were deaf.

Our captain, Captain Loades, was the nephew of the admiral's wife, Lady Shovell, whose two sons by Sir John Narborough were also among the officers on board. This much we learnt from an ancient member of the carpenter's crew, a gawky tittle-tattle with a lop-sided face and a cast in one eye. Plank was his name – apt enough for a carpenter – and he knew, or claimed to know, more or less everything about the ship and its officers.

From Plank I learnt that Sir Cloudesley's rise, not by preferment or the advantages of birth but from cabin boy through the ranks of midshipman, master's mate, captain and rear admiral was by no means unheard of. But no man could reach such a rank who had not distinguished himself in battle, which Sir Cloudesley certainly had, having been in actions against the Dutch and the Spanish and having won a gold medal, awarded by the late king, for destroying a pirate fleet anchored at Tripoli on the African coast. It was said of him that he never ordered a junior officer to carry out a task that he himself was not willing to carry out.

There was no doubting our admiral's courage or skill and we were pleased to know it. Our fate was in Sir Cloudesley's hands more than any other. On a warship, as on a fishing boat, a man must have confidence in his leader. Setting nets to catch pilchards or sails to catch the wind, feeling your boat, knowing the tides, being sure of where you are – the skills of the mariner vary little. True, we seldom lost sight of land when we went out after the fish, but then our boats were small and vulnerable. In the waters off the Lizard or the Scillies, a sudden storm can swallow a fishing boat. By comparison, *Association*, carrying over seven hundred crew and marines, was a castle.

It was on the second day of gunnery practice that I first set eyes on the admiral. When it was over and the guns had been secured again, we were called up from the gun decks to take a few welcome breaths of sea air. There was no mistaking Sir Cloudesley Shovell. He was a large man with an unusually big, round head, not unlike one of the thirty-two pound balls we had been firing from the demi-cannons. He wore a full wig and a blue woollen coat edged in gold braid to his knees. I remember shafts of sunlight reflecting from his gold buttons. Strangely, he held on a lead a small greyhound.

Beside the admiral on the poop deck stood Captain Loades and below them on the quarter deck half-a-dozen lieutenants and midshipmen. They seemed to be inspecting us, as if we were creatures brought up from the depths for their amusement. One scarred old salt danced a little jig for them, but they took no notice of him.

The biscuit we ate was maggoty, as I have said, and the meat perforce salted. But there was plenty of it, as well as fish, cheese, rice, peas and flour. Never believe a seaman who tells you he had not enough to eat. Nor did we lack for drink. A gallon of the watery beer or two pints of wine or half a pint of brandy or rum was issued to each man every day. Having never had a taste for wine or brandy, I made do with beer and was content enough.

Plank told us that Captain Loades was not a 'flogging man' and only once on the outward voyage did I witness such a punishment. The wretch had saved up his rum ration for a week, drunk it all one evening and could not get out of his hammock the next morning. He was tied to a grating and given fifty lashes while those of us not engaged in other duties were made to watch. He survived, just, perhaps thanks to the rum in his blood helping to deaden the pain, but he could do no work for a week.

On the twentieth day of July we turned east and followed the line of the distant Spanish coast, past the island of Gibraltar and into the calmer waters of the Mediterranean. Three days later, we were in *la grande rade,* the big natural harbour of the French city of Toulon. There we anchored, outside the range of French cannon, to await the arrival of those ships of the fleet that had fallen behind. To the delight of our officers, the French ships at anchor in the inner harbour had not put to sea and were trapped. On *Association* we had lost just one man fallen from the topmast and two from sickness. Rubbing his hands in anticipation, Plank told us it had been a 'good' voyage which boded well for the fighting ahead and that we could expect to capture 'a fine few' Frenchies.

I have mentioned Midshipman Alexander and there were others of his kind; as there were others like me – pressed into the service of the navy – and wishing only to be able to return to their homes and families. Having no family, I was perhaps less affected by our condition than some, but still I thought of little but Falmouth when I was not at work on the ship and I avoided close conversation with my fellows. I did what I was told and no more. Captain Loades and his lieutenants we viewed from afar or at least from the distance between the main deck and the quarter deck. I confess to having formed no strong impression of any of them.

On the occasions that he appeared, the admiral, however, caught my attention, not only for his size and the extravagance of his dress but also for his presence. It was a presence that few men have and is all the more remarkable for that. Scrubbing the deck or heaving on a rope, I sometimes sensed eyes on my back and, turning, found that the admiral was staring down at us. Not at me particularly but on all of us. More often than not, he had the little greyhound with him, sometimes on a lead, sometimes under his arm. It was a strange sight on a warship.

Once, when the admiral descended to the quarter deck, I noticed that he wore two large rings – one on the third finger of each hand. On the right, a thick band of gold, on the left a large green stone, which I took to be an emerald. The rings, the greyhound, his wig, his dress and demeanour, his unusual presence and his climb from the lowest rung to the very pinnacle of the service – it seemed to me that Admiral Sir Cloudesley Shovell was far from your ordinary seaman. I wondered if he ever addressed a man at a station almost as lowly as his own once was and, if so, what he might say. I saw him speaking to Captain Loades but could not hear their words.

Stories, true and false, spread on ships as they do in villages. We were never directly informed of our purpose but as our fleet assembled we came to understand that we would be bombarding the port of Toulon while our allies, the Dutch and the Austrians, launched an attack from the land. Without thinking much on it, we simply accepted this. It took Plank to point out that if we bombarded the town while our allies were attacking it we would be as likely to kill friend as foe, unless they stayed out of range in the hills above the town, which indeed is what they did.

I cannot with certainty state exactly what events took place at this time or in what order because of the confusion of battle and of my own station on the lowest gun deck, from which I could see very little. Here I thus rely in part upon the reports of others.

A party of about six hundred marines led by Rear Admiral Sir John Norris were put ashore and attacked the enemy fortifications before withdrawing back to the fleet. What they achieved I do not know. While our allies, led by the Duke of Savoy, fired down from the hills, we fired across the harbour, both sets of guns trained on the town. We bombarded it with every cannon in the fleet, and watched towers of smoke and flames rise into the sky as we unleashed their full fury. On *Association* we loaded and reloaded our guns and fired round shot and case shot in thundering salvos. We suffered a little damage from French cannon but the most danger we were in was from accidents and fires on board. With these the surgeon was kept busy. And we took great care, under threat of a lashing, not to let our shot fall short and land among the French ships. There was no prize money to be had from a sunken vessel.

For three weeks we kept the bombardment up, each day expecting to be told that it was over and that our allies had taken the town. At least once each day a barge would arrive and a message would be delivered to the admiral but still our guns kept firing. Only when we were running low on shot, a fireship was sent in among the French fleet and we were ordered to lower our aim from the town to the harbour, did we realise that the Dutch and the Austrians had failed to take it. Later we learnt that they had abandoned their attack and retreated, leaving the hills in French hands.

The fireship did no damage that we could see, but our cannon did sink several French vessels. We need not have wasted the powder and shot because, before our eyes, the French set about scuppering their own ships. Within two days, fourteen of them lay with only their upper deck above the water. We stood and watched and bellowed insults which were carried away on the wind.

On *Association*, this was a time when petty squabbles, often fuelled by drink, arose to fill the empty hours of inactivity and the frustration of seeing our prize money going up in smoke or down to a watery grave. Tempers flared, false accusations were made, fights broke out and three men were tied to the grating and put to the lash for drunken brawling. At sea or in battle, a warship is like a nest of ants – scurrying, carrying, pulling, pushing – always busy and with a purpose. At anchor with its guns silent it is more like an idle, ill-tempered bulldog. And the mood was made worse by our failure to take Toulon. A victory of sorts possibly, the French having scuppered their own ships, but no prize money for us. Punishments became harsher and more frequent – rations cut, the rope knotted, the gauntlet run.

Plank the carpenter told us that it was too late in the year to attempt another action and that we would be home before winter storms made the voyage perilous. From that we took some comfort.

The cloud hanging over us was not lifted, however, until we hauled anchor and set sail for Gibraltar. There we left thirteen of our fleet for the winter, the remaining twenty-one vessels (one fireship having been used at Toulon) included *Royal Ann*, flagship of Sir George Byng, and *Torbay*, flagship of Sir John Norris. I recall wishing that winter in that island at the mouth of the Mediterranean had appealed to Sir Cloudesley Shovell and that *Association* had been among the ships left there. From Gibraltar, a man might quite easily have made his escape. Of course no such thing was possible, the admiral bearing the responsibility of bringing the fleet safely home, not to mention the prospect of his receiving yet more glory for the destruction of the French ships and, in early October, we left the calm waters of the Mediterranean and turned north into the stormy Atlantic.

If I have dealt too briefly with life on board *Association* and with our bombardment of Toulon, it is because my purpose is not to recount those matters in detail but rather to tell the story of our fateful voyage home. There are many others better placed than I to describe what occurred to this point but none, I think, more able to recount what befell us thereafter.

Entering Biscay we were met almost at once by the first of the autumn storms for which that long stretch of water is known and feared by all who have sailed it. With the storms came a great change in our lives. No longer becalmed by inactivity, we were occupied day and night in trimming our sails to keep her on a steady course and securing anything that moved with double lengths of rope. It was hard labour and no time to do other than sleep, eat and carry out our orders. This we did with a will, fearful of the consequences if we did not.

On our passage Captain Loades and Admiral Shovell were to be seen more often on the poop deck or the quarter deck, although without the little greyhound. Too stormy for dogs it was, yet not too stormy for us to be sent aloft to cast off the topsails, haul down the mizzen sail, bring down the yards or a dozen other things that must be done in rough weather. Even I, a novice at such work – and dangerous work it was with the ship tacking and being buffeted by wind and waves – had to take my turn on the lines high above the deck with little to hold on to and yards as wet and slippery as eels. This was, for me, more frightening by far than any French cannon.

For several days – I cannot recall quite how many – we were tossed about by the storms before there came a lull. Somehow, the fleet had kept together and we were able to count all twenty-one vessels. On

Association we were put to replacing torn canvas, securing our guns and pumping out the hold and lower decks.

Our spirits at this time had been battered as the ship had been battered and the more our spirits fell, the more frequent were the punishments. Clumsiness, slowness, simple mistakes – none went unremarked and unpunished, the sharp-faced Midshipman Alexander, most especially, being ever watchful. And the more the punishments we suffered, the lower our spirits fell. There was talk of the admiral and his officers having very little notion of where we were and of our having been blown far out into the Atlantic. Older voices cautioned discretion lest these doubts be taken as evidence of insurrection among us, while Plank took pleasure in exciting the cabin boys with tales of huge sea monsters lying in wait in the deep ocean for ships that had lost their way. I knew only that I would be happy when I saw land again.

After two days the storms returned and the daily wheel turned again. We trimmed the sails, worked the pumps and the capstans and made fast that which moved. If the admiral had known where we were before, he surely did not then. The wind rose and fell, shifted one way and then the next, and threw up waves that crashed over our main deck and through the ports on the gun decks. It was all we could do to keep her afloat. Two men we lost overboard, both pressed like me, and a dozen others too badly injured from falling from the rigging to do more than lie idle in their hammocks.

It was not until the twenty-first day of October that the admiral was able to make an observation, and the following day we took soundings at ninety fathoms. At about noon that day we brought to and lay by and he summoned the sailing masters of the other ships to *Association* to confer on the fleet's position. Until this time, I had kept my counsel, but I was as sure as I could be that we were not far distant from Scilly. I could not explain my certainty but put it down to the instinct of a fisherman for his own waters. These were not French waters, they were the waters in which I was brought up. My father called it 'the fisherman's nose'.

By this time I had become friendly with Plank and it was to him I turned. But when I told him what I knew he cautioned me to hold my tongue. 'Wait and see what the masters decide,' he advised. 'If they agree with you, there's no harm done. If not, well, we'll catch that wind if it gets up.' Plank's advice was, I suppose, sound enough, although I wish now that I had ignored it and found a way to speak to the admiral or to Captain Loades before the meeting of the masters.

The masters came on board *Association* that afternoon, arriving by their ships' barges and disappearing with their charts into the admiral's quarters under the poop deck. We were kept occupied keeping the ship steady and minding the ropes that held the visiting boats fast to our sides. We exchanged few words with their crews, just the odd jest about being nearby the American colonies or the coast of China. It was not the time for me to voice my doubts so I kept quiet.

The captain's steward, Lurch, was on good terms with Plank – this was not their first voyage together – and it was he who passed on word of the masters' meeting. He said that they had pored over their charts, taken more observations, to-ed and fro-ed and dithered and dathered and in the end all agreed that we were not far from Ushant, the island that marks the southernmost point of entry to the channel. All, that is, but one, the master of the *Lenox*, who disagreed. He thought we were nearer Scilly. And I was certain he was right.

'Right or wrong, lad,' said Plank, 'there's little to be done but pray.' I protested that he had spoken of catching that wind if it got up, and, to my mind, lowly pressed man or not, it had got up. I was reluctant to stand by and accept our fate as if we had no choice. Plank merely shrugged and wished me luck. 'It may be that twenty sailing masters are wrong and you are right, but I doubt it,' he said.

And not only twenty sailing masters but, from what I overheard among the crew, the ship's company as well. I could not find one to agree with me, or, at least, not one who admitted he did.

By the evening of the day of the masters' meeting, when they had boarded their barges and returned to their ships, I had made up my mind. Better dead at the yardarm than on the rocks or at the bottom of the sea. I approached Midshipman Alexander.

At first he looked down his long nose at me as if I were a rat which had come up from the hold and lost its way on deck. He did not appreciate being spoken to, unbidden, by a pressed man, and made his opinion of me plain. But I perservered and told him just as plain that I knew these waters and that we were much closer to the rocks of Scilly than to Ushant. When the toad scoffed, I could have struck him for his high and mighty manner, but that would have been the yardarm for sure, so I clenched my fists and tried again.

From his look it was clear that I was wasting my breath until, when I pressed on about speaking to the admiral, his eyes narrowed and a sly smile touched the corners of his mean mouth. 'Very well, Jones,' he said, 'I shall inquire of the captain if he or Admiral Shovell will do you the honour of listening to your twaddle. Be assured, however, that neither will take kindly to being contradicted by a pressed fisherman. If that is your wish, however, so be it and I shall look forward to seeing you at the grating or, better still, swinging at a yardarm.'

'I will take my chances,' I replied, 'and trust to God.' Although in truth I did not expect either Captain Loades or Admiral Shovell to agree to listen to me, so my efforts would doubtless prove to be in vain.

I was wrong. I do not know what Alexander said or how he said it, but somehow he convinced the admiral and the captain to hear me out. I was summoned to the quarter deck and there stood before them. Behind and a little to one side, were two lieutenants and Midshipman Alexander. Under his arm, the admiral held the little greyhound. He looked at me not unkindly and said, 'Mr Alexander has asked us to listen to what you have to say, Jones.' He turned to Alexander. 'It is Jones, is it not?'

'Daniel Jones, Admiral,' I replied before Alexander could.

'Well, Jones, what is it that brings you to my quarter deck?' His tone was calm, kindly even, and I recalled Plank saying that among the admiral's qualities was a willingness to deal fairly with any man, whatever his station. I daresay it came from his being a tarpaulin.

I took a deep breath. 'Before being pressed, I was a fisherman from Falmouth, sir,' I began, 'and I know these waters like I know my own face.'

'Rather the waters than the face,' snorted one of the lieutenants. The admiral signalled to the man to keep quiet and I continued.

'We are near the Scilly rocks. I can smell them.'

At this, the admiral's eyebrows rose. 'Can you now? Yet I for one cannot. How do you account for that, Jones?'

'I cannot, sir,' I spluttered, trying to hold his gaze. 'I know only that we are nearer Scilly than Ushant and if we continue on our present course, we shall come upon the islands.'

'And your opinion is based on smell, Jones? Do I understand you correctly?'

'Instinct, sir, I should rather say,' I replied, knowing how foolish I must look and sound to the officers assembled, the looks on their faces saying more than any words.

But the admiral did not immediately dismiss my instinct as worthless. Rather he gave the impression of considering it carefully. He said something to Captain Loades which I could not hear and nodded at the captain's reply. I was beginning to wonder if it would indeed be the grating for me when he spoke again.

'I admire your honesty and your nerve in coming forward, Jones, and I like to think that I would have done the same in your place. However, twenty sailing masters disagree with you and I cannot ignore their opinions and heed yours. Did you expect otherwise?'

The sailing masters were wrong and that was an end to it as far as I was concerned. 'I expected nothing, sir, and only wished to inform you of the fact.'

When the admiral stroked the greyhound's head, a shaft of light caught his emerald ring. 'Fact? Opinion, I should rather say, would you not agree, gentlemen?' The officers grinned and nodded dutifully. When the admiral spoke again his voice had taken on a harsher tone. 'Another man might have you lashed, Jones, for your impertinence, or even worse. But that is not my way and I am told that you did not shirk your duties at Toulon. I have already given orders for three of our fleet to make for Falmouth and the remainder will continue on our present course.' A tiny smile played around his mouth and eyes. 'And I advise you not to make a habit of contradicting Her Majesty's officers. Some there are who would not take kindly to such impertinence. Now be about your duties.' With that, he turned his back, leaving me to return to the main deck. As I climbed down the ladder, I heard laughter, but did not look back.

It was not long before Alexander appeared below. 'You are fortunate, Jones,' he said. 'A lashing is the least you deserve and if I were captain of *Association* that is what you would get.' I stared at him and understood the truth of it. The toad had persuaded the admiral to hear what I had to say only because he hoped to see me suffer.

The wind picked up again that night and continued strong through the following day. The light frigates having been despatched to Falmouth, *Association* was in the van of the fleet. It was with a heavy foreboding that I went about my duties, expecting at any time to hear the crash of breakers on rocks or the blast of a warning cannon.

Alexander made sure that the crew knew of my impertinence and I was forced to endure their taunts. I was called 'admiral' and 'master' and asked my opinion on all manner of matters from the trim of the sails to the nature of the men of Scilly and their reputation for killing and eating shipwrecked sailors. Half of me longed to be proved right, the other half hoped that they were right and I was wrong and that we would not be dashed to pieces on the rocks that surround the islands.

By nightfall, the wind was stronger still and heavy rain lashed the deck. Only fleetingly did we see the lights of the other vessels just as they would have caught only glimpses of our own. In such a storm, in a ship large or small, a man can do little but offer up a prayer and resign himself to his fate.

I cannot say exactly at what time we first heard the waves breaking on rocks but the watch had not long changed and, by the grace of God, I was among those on deck. The marines and half our crew – the starboard watch – were below, although few would have been asleep.

With a little more time we might have been able to change our course and avoid disaster. All but four of the fleet did so. But *Association* was in the van, and was doomed. Within minutes we struck rocks, our hull was holed and we were sinking. Those below were trapped and drowned first. On deck we were hurled about, most into the sea, the rest hanging in vain on to a mast or a timber, as if that might save them. Other than that I can say little of the moments between our ship striking the rocks and its breaking apart and sinking, because the events are disordered in my mind. Only a man who has suffered for himself a shipwreck as violent as was that of *Association* can truly know the terror and confusion of the experience and no man will be able to recall it exactly.

How I was thrown into the sea I do not know, only that I found myself, dazed but unhurt, at the mercy of the waves breaking over the rocks. Around me others struggled and screamed for help. Of course no help could come and few of them would have been able to swim as I could, their feeble efforts soon dragging them down to the depths.

With one stroke of my arm, my hand hit a piece of debris, which I found was a small anker, probably from the ship's kitchen, and to which I was able to cling. For some time I was swept back and forth with the anker as the waves struck the rocks before being washed back out to sea again. I do not know whether I expected to be dashed against the rocks myself or swept away into the darkness but I held fast, knowing that as long as I did so I was at least alive.

Whether by a shift in the wind or the current, still clinging to the anker, I was suddenly borne forward as if on a mill race, and dumped like a sack of corn on to land. It was too dark to know where I was but I was lying on sand while the waves continued either side of me to thunder against rocks. I lay trying to catch my breath until I was able to heave myself forward and beyond the reach of the waves, until I could do no more, and there I lay, sodden, frozen to the bones and exhausted while the storm raged on.

I must have lost consciousness because I remember next the first glimmers of dawn and the screech of gulls. The wind was still strong although the storm had abated. And the rain had ceased. I raised my head and tried to focus my eyes. At first I saw only shapes lying on the sand or moving about. Gradually I made out bodies and a number of women moving from one to another. It had not taken long for the islanders to come in search of booty.

Making my presence known to the scavengers would risk one of them sticking a knife under my ribs or smashing my head against a rock but I was shivering and as likely to die of cold. I struggled to my feet, called out so as not to alarm them by coming too close, and watched for their reaction. I counted six of them, all carrying sacks and wrapped up against the cold. They stared as if I were a ghost or some evil creature from the sea until one of them approached me. She spoke in the strange manner of the Scilly islanders but I could just about understand her. She asked if I had been on board one of the wrecked ships and if I knew of other survivors. I said that I had but knew of no others. She seemed to accept that and, pulling off her shawl, held it out to me. I took it gratefully.

We were on a small, sandy cove between outcrops of rocks. At one end the admiral's barge lay on its side and on the sand the bodies of marines and crewmen. Among them were the jackets of officers and midshipmen. One, larger than the rest, I knew at once to be Admiral Shovell. I stumbled over to it. Beside the admiral was the little greyhound, quite dead, and the admiral lay with arms outstretched as if asking God's mercy. I noticed that both his rings, one gold, the other an emerald, had gone. The scavengers had found treasure.

Among the other officers were Captain Loades, stripped of his jacket and shirt, and Midshipman Alexander, no longer a grinning toad. It was my good fortune to be a crew man in ragged shirt and trousers and without a penny to be killed for.

I asked one of the women where I was and learnt that the cove was Porthellick Bay on St Mary's, which is the largest of the Isles of Scilly. She said that three other ships had been wrecked in the storm but she did not know their names. Only later did I discover that they were *Eagle, Romney* and the fireship *Firebrand*. The four ships together would have held some two thousand men.

When they had completed their gruesome work, the women took me back to their village – little more than a few hovels sheltering under the lee of a cliff – and led me to a tiny cottage where I was given a thin soup and left to warm myself before a fire. Later, covered by a coarse blanket, I lay down in a corner and slept. The woman who had taken me in appeared to live alone and did not trouble me.

It took me a week to travel from St Mary's to Falmouth, at first by fishing yawl to Penzance and thence on foot to Falmouth. I lacked money for a horse or a coach. News of the disaster had reached the town days before I did and it was with some surprise that I was greeted. I said simply that I had been on *Royal Ann*, flagship of Sir George Byng, which had narrowly escaped the rocks by dint of the skilful seamanship of its captain, James Moneypenny, and that I had been permitted to go ashore before the ship sailed on to Southampton. Whether I was believed, I cannot say, but certainly I was never questioned.

Why, you may ask, did I not tell the truth? That is a difficult question to answer, except that I did not wish to be known as the sole survivor of the crews of four of Her Majesty's warships, nor did I wish to undergo the questioning that would surely follow at an inquiry. The disaster itself was painful enough without having to relive it in public. In any event, what would I tell the officers at an inquiry? That I was right and the admiral and twenty of his sailing masters were wrong and those masters who survived should be held to account? If I did would I be believed? Almost certainly not. So I lied, and hoped that the truth would never emerge. In the event there has been neither inquiry nor inquest.

Among the tales that have been told about the wreck is that Admiral Shovell ordered a seaman be flogged for daring to suggest that the navigation of the masters was in error, and that, as a result, grass in the dunes where the admiral was temporarily buried will not grow. As I myself was that seaman I can attest that this was not so. The admiral listened courteously to my opinion and certainly did not order me punished. If the grass does not grow where he lay, it is for another reason.

Nor, I believe, was there drunkenness among the officers on that fateful night, nor was our vessel overcome by a giant sea monster with many arms. Both stories, absurd though they are, have gained currency in the inns of Cornwall. I cannot refute them without revealing my deception so I set down here, for future eyes to see, the truth of the matter.

With less certainty but some confidence I can also state that Admiral Shovell's rings were removed by one or more of the women who found us on Porthellick Bay. Perhaps one day they will appear and be restored to his widow, who, on learning of his death, immediately instituted inquiries into their whereabouts.

I spoke but once to Admiral Sir Cloudesley Shovell and have no reason to think other than well and respectfully of him. The wrecks of *Association*, *Eagle*, *Romney* and *Firebrand*, and the deaths of all but one of their crew were due to the capricious weather, grave errors of navigation and a little misfortune. No single man should be held accountable for that, especially one who had served his country bravely.

This account I shall place in a wooden box under my bed in the hope that it will not be found until after my death.

THE TREE

1651

John had climbed taller trees, but this one was his favourite. It stood alone on the edge of the wood, at the top of a rise in the ground above fields and hedgerows which stretched as far as he could see. The tree had long ago been pollarded so that new branches had grown strong from the trunk, creating a dense blanket of foliage behind which he could hide.

When the tree was in leaf, he spent hours sitting in a fork halfway up the trunk, watching the shepherd and his dog at work with their flock, listening to the distant chatter of the milkmaids who came every day to milk the cows, and whittling sticks into figures. He had a good knife, made for him by his father, which he sharpened on the grinding stone outside the forge. He kept the figures in a hole in the trunk, where they would be safe. He never took them home.

If he was in the tree early enough in the morning he might see deer emerging from the wood to graze, and, in the evening, a fox creeping along a hedgerow. In the fields there were rabbits and hares, pheasants and pigeons. Sitting silent and unseen in the fork, looking out at the world from his hiding place, he was happy and safe. In his tree, he was never told to go and do something he did not want to do, like cleaning out the hen house, or slapped for not doing it properly, he was never hit by his sister, and he never had to listen to his mother and father shouting at each other.

When there was nothing much to watch, and he had tired of whittling, he pulled small pieces of bark off the tree. Underneath the bark, he found beetles and ants, centipedes and spiders, and other insects which he did not recognise. In the spring he watched birds building their nests, and in the autumn squirrels collecting acorns. Once he had climbed along a branch to a blackbird's nest. He had stolen an egg from the nest and taken it home. He had put it under one of the hens to see if it would hatch, but when it was still in the nesting box a week later, he had thrown it on to the dung heap.

It took John about ten minutes to get home from the tree. He had to make his way around the wood and over the low stone wall that enclosed the Boscobel Estate, before walking along the lane to the village. He took care not to be seen inside the wall. He would get into trouble if he were.

He always hoped his father would be too busy in the forge to notice him coming home. If he were seen, he would be questioned about where he had been, whether he had done his chores, or if he had been in any trouble. His father suspected that he climbed over the wall into the estate and worried that he would be caught. 'If they catch you in there,' he had warned, 'you'll be in trouble. They might think you're poaching.'

'I'm not poaching,' the boy had replied. 'I just like to be in the woods.'

'Maybe so, but it's Boscobel land, and the Giffards won't want you on it. Catholics or not, they are important people around here.'

The boy had never mentioned his tree. If he had, it would not have been his anymore.

Their cottage stood beside the forge. It was a good cottage, with a thatched roof, stone walls, and glazed windows. Inside, there were two bedrooms, a parlour, and a kitchen. The family ate in the kitchen and, in winter, sat around the fire in the parlour. The boy shared a bedroom with his sister.

'Your father works hard so that we have enough to eat and a roof over our heads,' the boy's mother was fond of saying. 'I expect both of you to do the same.'

So his sister milked the cow and helped with cleaning, washing and baking, while he fed the hens, collected the eggs every morning, and chopped firewood with a small axe. She was a year older than him, taller, and stronger, and forever complaining that he was lazy.

'John's forgotten to feed the hens, again,' she would tell their mother, sometimes even when he had. If he tried to defend himself, she would clip him on the ear and tell him not to tell lies.

When his father was very busy in the forge, he might have to help. He had learnt to brush and polish the ironwork, and to use the grinding stone to give knives and spades a sharp edge. The forge still turned out swords and pike-ends as it had during the worst of the fighting, but mostly now it was horseshoes, ploughshares, hand tools, and cooking pots. It was a hot, dirty place, and when he was in it, John longed to be out in the fields, or better still, in his tree.

John's father sometimes walked down to the Fox and Hounds after finishing work for the day. He said that when his throat was dry from the smoke of the forge he needed a tankard or two of ale before he could eat his supper. When he came back he passed on whatever news there was. John sat and listened although he did not understand all of it. He knew that the fighting had started before he was born, and he knew that the king's army had been beaten, and the king's head cut off by his enemies. He had never quite grasped who the king's enemies were or what they had been fighting about, and he had not asked his father to explain. His father did not take kindly to questions when he returned from the inn.

Recently there had been talk of another king. At least John assumed it was another king, unless someone had stuck the other one's head back on. It seemed that this king had marched with his army from Scotland far away to the north to the town of Worcester, which was not far away, and that there was going to be another battle with the man who had chopped off the previous king's head. He supposed that the loser of this battle would also have his head chopped off, just like when the winner of a conker fight smashed the loser's conker into pieces. You needed a very hard conker to smash another one, and you would need a very sharp axe to chop off a head. Perhaps his father would be asked to make a special axe for the occasion.

John's mother was upset at the news of another battle. 'We're sick of fighting,' she said. 'Men die, wives are widowed and children orphaned, and for what? Why can't we live in peace?'

His father agreed. 'I supported the king and I still do. But there's nothing to be gained from this. Even if the royalists win, they'll still have to take London, and they're not going to do that easily. And if Cromwell wins, what then? Another execution? There won't be a king on the throne of England again until Cromwell's dead, and then only if the people demand it.'

John thought Cromwell must be the man who had cut off the king's head. One evening when they were in their beds, he asked his sister. 'Daisy, is the man who cut off the king's head called Cromwell?'

'I think so,' she replied. 'Father doesn't like him, so it must have been him.'

In August and September John spent as much time as he could in the tree. It would soon be autumn, when its leaves would turn brown and fall off, and he would not be able to hide behind them again until spring. He dared not climb the tree when it had no leaves in case he were seen. So every day in late summer, whenever he could slip away from the forge, he climbed up to the fork in the branches to watch the corn being harvested and to whittle more figures to put in the hole in the trunk.

One evening he went home to find his mother in tears. She told him that there had been a battle at Worcester. Cromwell had won, the king had lost, and had run off with his friends to Wales. 'I dread to think what we're in for now,' she said, wiping her eyes on her sleeve. 'If they catch him, they'll do what they did to his father. If they don't, they'll go on searching until they find him. He should have stayed in France.'

John knew that Wales lay to the west. If the king thought he would be safe there, it must be different from England. The people in Wales must like kings.

The next day he had to help his father in the forge, and could not go to the tree until late in the afternoon. There had been an order for a new pair of iron gates from Boscobel House, and they had to be ready the next day. All morning and for most of the afternoon, he brushed and polished the iron pieces that his father had shaped in the forge and hardened in the cooling tub, until his father was happy with them. 'Every visitor to Boscobel will pass through these gates,' said his father proudly, 'so they must be perfect. Polish them until you can see your face in them, John.'

By the time the church clock struck four, John's arms were aching and his hands sore. 'Can I go now please, Father?' he asked, fearing that the answer would be no. But his father saw that the boy could do no more that day.

'Off you go, John. Tell your mother I'll be going down to the Fox and Hounds when I've finished the gates. And don't go wandering off. There are soldiers all about looking for the king.'

John gave his mother the message and ran off down the lane to the place where he climbed over the wall. He saw no soldiers, and was over the wall and around the wood as easily as ever. Using the handholds and footholds he always used, he climbed quickly up the trunk towards the fork. Standing on a thick branch and holding tight to another smaller one, he looked out over the fields. In the distance he could see a group of men standing in a circle. He had seen his father standing outside the Fox and Hounds in a circle like this one. It was how men stood when they had important business to discuss. The men were too far away for him to see their faces or what they were wearing, so he thought they must be farm workers. Perhaps they were talking about the harvest or the sheep. Or even about the battle his mother had spoken of.

Hearing a rustle of leaves above him, he glanced up, and almost lost his footing on the branch. Two men were sitting on a higher branch, looking down at him. He put his hand against the trunk to steady himself and looked again. Two woodsmen were sitting in his tree. Not knowing whether to climb up to them or climb down and run off, he stayed where he was. What were two woodsmen doing in his tree? If they had they seen him in it and come here to catch him, he'd better climb down and make himself scarce. But neither of them had moved or spoken, so perhaps they were just sitting in the tree as he did, peering out at the fields from behind the leaves.

Eventually, one of the men spoke. He had a dark look about him and his skin was brown from the sun. John watched carefully for any sign that he should jump down and run off. But when the man spoke his voice was quiet and not at all frightening. His companion continued to look out towards the circle of men in the field.

'Good afternoon, young man,' he said. 'Are we sitting in your tree?'

John stared at him, unsure how to answer. He knew it was not really his tree and it might be a mistake to say that it was. On the other hand, he thought of it as his tree and he did not like these men being in it.

'Well, is it your tree or is it not?'

John nodded.

'I'm afraid we didn't know it was yours. Do you mind if we sit in it for a while?'

'No,' he replied, finding his tongue. 'I don't mind, as long as you don't steal my figures.'

The man held up one of the sticks John had whittled into the shape of a man. 'Is this one of yours?' he asked. 'I found it in the hole.'

'It is. I made it and it's mine.'

'Indeed it is. And it's very good. I'll put it back with the others.' He put the figure back in the hole. 'There. He's back with his friends. Why don't you climb up and sit with us for a while? We could do with some company, could we not, William?'

'As you wish, sire,' replied the other man without taking his eyes from the field.

'Come on, young man,' said the man with the deep voice. 'Come up here and tell us your name.'

John hesitated. Then he climbed up. He liked the man's voice and he had a kind smile. It would be rude to run away. He reached the men and found himself a place to sit.

'There we are,' said the man, patting him on the shoulder. 'And what is your name?' He had black hair which reached down below his shoulders and very dark eyes. John wondered if he had been born to gypsies. His mother had told him to keep away from the gypsies who sometimes came to the village selling lucky charms and reading fortunes. She said they were dirty folk and would steal what they could not pay for.

'John. Is your name Sire?'

The man laughed quietly. 'No, not really. It's just what people call me.'

'Like a pet name?'

'I suppose so. My real name is Charles, and this is my friend William.' William was smaller than Charles, with reddish hair and a beard. 'Where do you live, John?'

'I live in the village.'

'How old are you?' This Charles was full of questions.

'Seven.'

'Have you a family?'

'My father and mother and my sister. She's called Daisy.'

'A pretty name. And what does your father do?'

'He's a blacksmith. He's making new gates for Boscobel House. I've been helping him.'

'Have you now? Are they good gates?'

'Very good. My father is the best blacksmith in England. My mother says that there has been another battle not far from here and that the king's enemies won. If they need a special axe to cut off the king's head, I expect they'll ask him to make it.'

For a long time, Charles said nothing. Then he asked quietly, 'Why do you think anyone wants to cut off the king's head?'

'My father said so. He said a man called Cromwell will cut it off just like he cut off the other king's head.'

'What does your father think of that?'

'I don't know.'

'What would you think if someone cut off your father's head?'

'I wouldn't like it. I'd cry.'

'Yes, I expect you would. And what would you do about the men who had cut it off?'

'I'd catch them and cut off their heads.'

'Yes, John. So would I.'

'I don't think they'll catch the king though. He's run off to Wales.'

'Run off? Kings don't run off, do they?'

'This one did. He lost a battle and ran away. That's what my father says.'

'Perhaps your father is wrong. Perhaps the king will come back with a new army and fight another battle and this time win it.'

John looked doubtful. If the king planned to fight another battle why had he run away from this one? 'Do you know what the king looks like?' he asked.

All the time, William had said nothing and kept his eyes on the circle of men in the field. Now it was he who answered. 'The king is tall and handsome, with black hair and a noble face.' He paused. 'At least, that's what I've heard.'

John stared at Charles. 'You're tall, and you've got black hair. Is he like you?'

'Oh no,' laughed Charles. 'I expect the king's much more handsome than me.'

'Are you woodsmen?'

'We are,' replied William.

'Why are you in my tree?'

'Probably for just the same reason that you are. We like it here. We can see what's happening in the fields without being seen ourselves. It's a comfortable way to be, don't you think?'

'It is. Have you been here before?'

'No. This is our first time. It's a fine tree and I am sorry we did not know that it is yours. If we had known, we would have asked your permission before climbing it.'

'It's not really mine. It's just my favourite tree in the wood.'

'Why is it your favourite?'

'Because I can see all around without anyone seeing me. Just like you said.'

'Yes, that's exactly why we like it. And you can tell from the thickness of the trunk that it is an old tree. Oaks can live for hundreds of years. Did you know that, John?'

'I did. I know about trees.'

'That's good. Trees are a fine thing to know about. I expect this one has been here for more than two hundred years and it might still be here in another two hundred years.'

John took out his knife. 'This is my whittling knife. I sharpen it on my father's grinding stone. Have you got knives?'

'We haven't,' replied William.

'But you said you were woodsmen. Woodsmen always have knives. And axes.'

'We didn't bring ours today because we're not working.'

That was an odd thing. John always carried his knife just in case he might need it. He broke off a thin branch and started shaping it with his knife. He soon had the outline of a head and a body. The two men watched carefully. 'The next bit is the most difficult.' he said, 'making the arms and legs. You have to be careful or the stick might break.' Deftly, he cut a long notch to define the legs, and two smaller ones for the arms. He held it up for inspection. 'There. It's finished.'

Charles took it from him 'It's very good, John. May I have it as a keepsake?'

John did not know what a keepsake was, but he was happy for Charles to have the figure. 'You can have it, if you like. I can make another.'

'Thank you, John. Have you ever carved your name on the tree?'

John shook his head. 'I don't know the letters.'

'Have you never been to school?'

'No. The school closed when the fighting started.'

'I see. Would you like me to carve your name on the trunk? I can carve William's and mine as well.'

'If you want.' John handed him the knife.

Charles took the knife and used the point to carve letters out of the bark. 'That's John,' he said, spelling the letters out. 'And this is William.' Again, he carved out the letters. 'And this is Charles.' The three names were carved in a line. He gave the knife back to John. 'Did you know that all three of our names are the names of kings of England?' John shook his head. 'King John lived more than four hundred years ago; there have been two King Williams, who lived even longer ago, about six hundred years ago; and one King Charles, who was our last king.'

'Was he the king whose head was chopped off?'

'He was.'

William tapped John on the shoulder and put his finger to his lips. He pointed through the leaves to three men who were approaching the tree. They wore round helmets and leather jackets and carried swords and muskets. They were soldiers. He watched them come nearer. When they reached the tree, they stopped and leant against its trunk.

'We'll never find him, even if he is still hereabouts,' said one of the soldiers. 'There's a hundred places for him to hide.'

'You're right, Jethro. He could be anywhere. Even in this wood.'

'Well, I'm not going in there to look,' said the third man, taking a small flask out of his pocket and holding it to his mouth. 'That's better.' He belched loudly and passed the flask to one of the others who drank from it and passed it on to the third man. John glanced at William, who motioned to him to be quiet.

The three soldiers rested their muskets against the trunk of the tree and stood there, passing the flask to each other and taking sips from it. From no more than the height of the forge above them, it was easy to make out what they were saying.

'They put up a good fight, the Scots,' said one.

'They did, but it didn't last long,' replied another. 'Once we turned their guns on to the town, it was as good as over.'

'The townsfolk didn't seem to care who won as long as it was quick,' said the third. 'They're sick of fighting, like the rest of us.'

'Well then, we'd best find Charles Stuart and lock him in the Tower, so we can all go home. There's much to do before winter.'

'Or, better still, cut his head off like his father. Then there'll be no more kings to keep us from our families.' The soldier picked up his flintlock. 'Come on, we'd best get back or we'll be missed. We'll say we searched the wood but there was no sign of him.'

'Who were they looking for?' whispered John, as they watched the soldiers walk off.

'The king,' replied William.

'But the king's run off to Wales. He's not here. Why are they looking here?' Neither of the men answered. 'He's not here, is he?'

'May I see your knife again, John?' asked William. John handed it to him. William looked very sad. The soldiers must have upset him. He took the knife and tested its point on his thumb. Then he began to speak very quietly under his breath in words that John did not know. The words had the rhythm of the prayers they said in church on Sundays, a sort of up and down sound like wind rustling grass. John watched William, wondering what he was doing.

While William was speaking quietly, Charles put his hands over his friend's hands and shook his head. 'No, William.'

'Sire,' replied William, 'the risk is great.'

'The risk of damnation is greater. And John is our friend, aren't you, John?' John did not know what they were talking about. 'John will tell no-one about finding us in his tree because, if he did, other people would know about the tree and it wouldn't be his anymore. Is that not right, John?'

John thought about what Charles had said. He was right. If he told his father about William and Charles, he might want to see the tree, and read the names carved on the trunk. He did not want his father to do that. 'I shan't tell anyone,' he said. 'Can I have my knife back?'

'Not even your mother or father or your sister?' asked William.

'No. Especially not my sister.'

William passed him the knife and they sat in silence – the two men on the thick branch which formed half of the fork, John on a thinner one. Soon Charles's eyes closed and he leant his head against the trunk of the tree. John thought he was asleep, and a sleeping man might easily fall out of a tree. He whispered to William. 'Should we wake him?'

William shook his head. 'No, leave him to rest. He has travelled a long way and is tired. He will wake up soon enough.'

John wondered where Charles had travelled from but did not ask. He cut another slim branch and began to whittle it. He had nearly finished when Charles's eyes opened. He rubbed them with his sleeve and grinned at John. 'I must have fallen asleep for a moment.'

'You did,' replied John, putting his figure in the hole with the others. 'I must go home now or my mother will be cross. She doesn't like me out too long.'

'Goodbye then, John,' said Charles. 'Perhaps we'll meet again one day. Be sure to keep our secret.'

John nodded. 'I will. Goodbye.' He climbed down the tree, waved up into the branches, and made his way round the wood. He jumped over the stone wall and ran down the lane. He passed another group of soldiers, but they took no notice of him.

When John reached the cottage, his father had returned from the Fox and Hounds and was sitting at the table in the kitchen. 'There's talk of him turning back at the border and making for these parts. He's plenty of supporters around here who might hide him.'

'There are soldiers all over the place,' said John's mother. 'They must have reason to think he's here.'

'Is it the king you're talking about? asked John.

His father eyed him sharply. 'Best not to know, John. What you don't know can't hurt you.'

John ate his dinner in silence, thinking about the two men he had found hiding in his tree. William and Charles, they said their names were. Woodsmen, they said, but they had no knives. Two woodsmen without knives in his tree. It was a strange thing.

Just before he went to bed, John asked his father, 'What is the king's name?'

'The same as his father's,' replied his father. 'Charles.'

'Has he got a friend called William?'

'That's an odd question. I expect so. It's a common enough name.'

John smiled. Now he had a new secret.

THE CASTLE

On the south wall of the chancel in St Martin's Church in Ruislip, there is a monument with this inscription:

To the memory of Mary, Lady Bankes, the only daughter of Ralph Hawtery, of Riselip, in the county of Middlesex, esq., the wife and widow of Sir John Bankes, knight, late Lord Chief Justice of His Majesty's court of Common Pleas, and of the Privy Council of His Majesty King Charles I of blessed memory, who having had the honour to have borne with a constancy and courage above her sex, a noble proportion of the late calamities, and the restitution of the government, with great peace of mind laid down her most desired life the 11th day of April 1661. Sir Ralph Bankes her son and heir hath dedicated this.

June 1645

By the flickering light of a wax candle – she could not abide the foul smell of tallow and even in these harsh times would not allow it to be burned in the castle – Mary Bankes looked into the dark eyes of the diminutive Queen Henrietta Maria and saw unshakeable determination. It was no wonder that the four thousand men the

149

queen had recruited on her way from Hull to join the king in Oxford had christened her the '*Generalissimo*'.

Sir Anthony Van Dyck's portrait of the queen – resplendent in blue satin, her hair in lustrous ringlets – had been given to Mary's husband by the king and now hung between the packed bookshelves in his library. From his days as a young barrister at Gray's Inn, Sir John had been an avid collector of books and had loved nothing more than to spend an evening by the fire reading quietly or, sometimes, aloud to his children. Now he had gone, but the shelves were still filled with rows of fine leatherbound volumes which would pass in due course to their eldest son, named, as was the family custom, after his father.

Not for Sir John the crossed swords, shields and coats-of-arms that adorned other castles. For the Bankes family, Corfe Castle in Dorset, grand as it was, was home, and they had furnished it with books, paintings, embroideries and furniture of the highest quality, as befitted their station and that of a home with a distinguished, royal history.

Begun by William the Conqueror, improved and extended by King John and King Edward I, it had been sold by Queen Elizabeth – a woman, thought Lady Mary, cut from the very same cloth as Henrietta Maria – to her courtier, Sir Christopher Hatton, and from him had passed through his nephew to the Lord Chief Justice, Sir Edward Coke, and thence to Sir John Bankes. Mary had studied the history of the castle and could recount all its stories. To her, Corfe's history mirrored that of England itself. And now, like England, it was under siege.

John Bankes, the son of a wealthy Keswick merchant, had become a Member of Parliament at the age of twenty-six and had subsequently held the offices of Attorney General, Chief Justice of the Common

Pleas and Privy Councillor. Mary had been proud not only of her husband's rise to a position at the king's side but also of his reputation for even-handedness and the dispensation of justice to all.

When, in August of 1642, news had arrived that the king had raised his standard at Nottingham, John and Mary had been in no doubt as to the legitimacy of the king's actions or of his ultimate victory over John Pym's rebels. In Parliament he had argued against both Pym and Hampden, not least in support of the king's unpopular ship-money tax.

In November John had returned to his *alma mater*, Oxford, where the king had set up his parliament, and had spent much of the last two years there, leaving the defence of Corfe in Mary's hands. For all his loyalty to the king, Mary knew that her husband would not have done so without being sure of her steadfastness.

She had prayed daily for the strength that Queen Henrietta Maria had shown in support of her husband and had promised John that she would not let the castle fall into unworthy hands. So far, that promise had been kept. Under her direction, a troop of fewer than eighty men had survived a long siege and beaten off every attack on the castle by the Parliamentarians. Gunpowder, scaling ladders, cannon – all had failed. But since John's death at Christmas she had begun to have the first glimmerings of doubt.

The library door creaked opened and Mary turned sharply. 'Ah, Robert, what news do you bring?' she asked, seeing who it was. Robert Lawrence, captain of the castle guard, was a tall young man, fair complexioned and clean shaven. She had relied heavily upon him during the darkest days of the war.

Robert bowed. 'My apologies, madam, I had not meant to startle you. Patrick has returned with intelligence. I thought you would wish to see him.' Patrick Flavin – a farrier with an Irish name but the soft voice of a man of Dorset, who had remained at the castle during lulls in the fighting when he might easily have slipped away – had volunteered to fetch intelligence from the village. On dark nights, he climbed down a knotted rope from a sally-port on the west wall, made his way to the cottage of the village sexton, a Royalist sympathiser, and brought back whatever news there was. Young and nimble, climbing back up the rope presented no great problem, but the risk of capture was great and Mary was grateful to him for his service. But for the brave farrier, their isolation would have been all the more burdensome. She pretended not to know that the sexton's daughter was a comely young lady, much admired by the youth of the town.

'Yes, Robert, bring him in. I would know what is happening in the country, whether it be good news or bad.'

Robert opened the door and Flavin entered carrying another candle. He had been waiting outside to be summoned. 'So, Patrick,' said Mary, 'you are returned unharmed and I thank God for it. What have you to tell us?'

'The news is not good, my lady,' replied the farrier quietly. 'The rebels are reinforcing their garrison at Wareham with troops from Weymouth and Poole.' The ancient town of Wareham, which guarded the road into Purbeck, had been surrendered to Parliamentary forces in August the previous year, leaving Corfe the only Dorset town still in Royalist hands. Lady Mary had been outraged at news of the capitulation and had sent an angry message to the governor, Colonel Henry O'Brien, berating him for not fighting on. 'I fear we must expect more attacks on the castle, madam.'

'I fear we must, unless there is better news from elsewhere. What of the negotiations?'

'The king has rejected the rebels' demands and remains in Oxford.'

Lady Mary sighed. 'How long I wonder before Oxford University and Corfe Castle are the only places still loyal to the crown?'

'We still hold Bristol,' said Robert, with a smile. 'And Prince Rupert still leads his troops in the Midlands. All is not lost.'

'I pray you are right. Any other word, Patrick?' asked Mary.

'I think they might be preparing to try their siege engines again. I heard a whisper.'

Mary and Robert laughed as one. 'Those things!' she exclaimed. 'King Arthur could have done better. Do you recall how pitiful they were, Robert?'

'I do. The boar and the sow. How they thought they could approach the walls protected by little more than sheepskins, I do not know. It was a job to stop the men laughing long enough to fire their muskets.'

The engines, named by the defenders 'the boar' and 'the sow', one large, the other smaller, had been fashioned from wheeled mining covers, their sides covered in sheepskins. The wretches trying to push them into place under the wall to lay explosive charges had been sent tumbling back down the slope with musket balls in their feet and legs and all manner of noxious waste dripping from the covers. It had been, for the defenders, one of the lighter moments of the last two years.

'Let us hope that their design has not improved,' said Mary. 'Thank you, Patrick. Again, you have done well.' When Patrick had bowed and taken his leave, she lit another candle and invited Robert to sit. 'I would offer you wine, Robert, but you know the store is empty.'

'No matter. I will ask Patrick to bring back a bottle or two next time.'

For a moment they were silent. Mary sat with her hands clasped on her lap. When she spoke her voice held a hint of tears. 'How I miss John and the boys. I think of them every day.'

'The boys are safer with their sister. You were right to send them there.' Alice, the eldest of the Bankes children, was married to Sir John Borlase and lived in Oxford. The five boys had been sent there at the beginning of the war and had remained there as it dragged on. At least their father had been close by.

'I know, yet their absence is hard to bear. Sometimes I wonder if the time has not come to seek terms and for us all to join them in Oxford.'

'You vowed to defend the castle, my Lady, and you have done so with great courage. What is weakening your resolve?'

'John is dead and the tide of the war has been turning against us. One heavy defeat and we will surely be beaten. What then of England, I wonder?'

'But your vow, your family, this castle. What of them?'

'I vowed not to let the castle fall into undeserving hands, but much has changed since then. Would it not be better now to hand it over voluntarily than to see it taken from us or, worse, reduced to rubble? And there are the girls and our servants to think of. Should I not do what is necessary to protect them?'

'On that I cannot advise you. King or family? It is a choice that many have had to make. What would Sir John advise if he were here?'

For a moment or two, Mary considered. 'I believe he would expect me to fight on.'

'Then fight on you must.'

* * *

Colonel Robert Butler, governor of Wareham, was in a foul mood. Yet another letter had arrived from London demanding to know why Corfe Castle was still in Royalist hands when Wareham, Weymouth, Dorchester and Poole were safely under the control of Parliament. Lord Fairfax – 'Black Tom' – who had taken over from the Earl of Essex as overall commander of the Parliamentary Army, would brook no more delay. He had even suggested that now that Sir John Bankes was dead, his widow could be persuaded to surrender.

The colonel threw down the letter and thumped his fist on the inn table. 'The noble lord has never faced that woman. She has held the castle for more than two years without her husband. How the devil does he think I am going to persuade her to surrender now?'

Guy Foster, captain of horse, had seen the colonel in such a mood before and kept his voice calm. 'We must think of something, Colonel, or Lord Fairfax will send Cromwell or Waller to do the job for us.'

Butler stood up. 'Such a humiliation cannot be allowed. You and I will travel this afternoon to Corfe. Prepare a troop to accompany us.'

After an easy six-mile ride across the Dorset countryside, the troop cantered into Corfe while the sun was still high. On one of two huge hills stood the castle, dominating the town and the fields around it. King William had chosen the site well and even from a distance the strength of its defences was evident. It was no wonder that the castle garrison had laughed when thirty-two-pound balls fired from demi-cannon had bounced harmlessly off the walls.

Three of the castle's outer walls rose from steep, rocky banks, making a successful attack on them well-nigh impossible. Attackers would find themselves pelted with stones, timbers and burning embers while being fired at from behind the crenellations or from the towers placed around the walls. It did not take a trained musketeer to throw missiles down on to heads, so every woman and child in the castle would be put to work if necessary. The defenders were safe as long as they had food and water and held the gatehouse at the southern end of the castle grounds. That was protected by two huge oak gates with towers on either side and was guarded day and night. Every attempt on the gates had failed.

The castle keep stood at the north end of the enclosure, surrounded by an inner wall as thick as the outer. Between the keep and the outer wall was a wide ditch with grazing for sheep and cattle. Within the inner wall a deep well provided unlimited fresh water. Corfe Castle, strengthened and re-strengthened over the centuries, had never been taken. Nor, nearly six hundred years after the first stone had been laid, did it show any sign of being taken.

The two officers stood outside a cottage some fifty yards from the gates, shielded their eyes against the sun, peered up at the castle and searched for a weakness. There was none.

'Why we cannot leave the cursed thing in the Lady's hands and find some real fighting to do, I could not say,' grumbled the colonel. In Dorset, everyone knew who 'the Lady' was.

Captain Foster agreed. 'It is not as if she is going to do us any harm, shut up in there. We should leave her and her daughters to their sewing.'

'If we could, we would. But since we are ordered to take it we must try.' He turned on his heel. 'Come, let us find that oaf Kendall and see what he has to say for himself.'

The Parliamentary encampment had been set up in a field on the southern edge of the town. There they found Captain Kendall perched on a stool, a wooden tankard in his hand. When he saw them approaching he put it down hastily, slopping ale on the grass, and struggled to his feet.

Henry Kendall was a man of about thirty with a bloated face and a paunch that already betrayed his liking for ale. He wiped his mouth with his sleeve and belched loudly. 'Colonel Butler, I was not expecting you,' he spluttered.

'So I see, Captain,' replied Butler. 'Captain Foster and I have come to hear how you propose to take this damned castle. Our troop is in the village finding fodder for our horses and we wish to return to Wareham before dusk, so let us waste no time. Lord Fairfax is unhappy that it is still in the hands of a Royalist woman.'

Captain Kendall, unprepared for this, sought to win himself a little time. 'Would you care for a tankard of ale, sir, after your journey?' he asked.

Despite being thirsty, the colonel was in no mood for niceties. 'I would not. I would care for an explanation of how you intend to capture Corfe Castle.'

There was no avoiding the truth. 'We have tried everything, Colonel – scaling ladders, gunpowder, cannon shot, even fire arrows over the walls. Nothing has worked. The castle has its own well and sufficient livestock and grain to last them at least another year. All we can do is guard the town and make sure none of them run off.'

'In another year, the war will be over and the castle and its infernal occupants will be of no concern,' snapped Butler. He slapped the back of one gauntleted hand into the palm of the other. 'We need it now.'

Kendall was sobering up fast. 'And how, Colonel, are we to do this? Use a battering ram to break down the gates while being shot at from the towers? Climb over the wall at the dead of night, find our way to the woman's bedchamber without being seen and threaten to ravish her and her daughters if she does not surrender at once?'

The colonel stared hard at him. 'Your flippancy does you no favours, Captain. We are at war. This is a serious matter and for you will become yet more serious if you do not carry out the wishes of our commander. Do you understand?'

Faced with argument or submission, Kendall chose the latter. 'I understand, sir. It will be done.'

'And without delay, Captain.'

'Without delay, Colonel.'

The colonel turned to Captain Foster. 'Come, Captain, we will be about our business.'

'What do you think he will do, Colonel?' asked Foster as they walked back to the village.

'Very little. I can see no means of taking the castle but the man's a drunken oaf and if we are to be reprimanded by Lord Fairfax, be sure that he will suffer a great deal more. The army of parliament does not need creatures of Kendall's sort.'

'Should you not be rid of him?'

'And replace him with whom? No, he might as well stay here. He would be scant use in battle and perhaps he will surprise us.'

The news arrived in Wareham minutes before Colonel Butler led his troop through the ancient Saxon walls and into the town. A rider from Salisbury was waiting for him with an urgent despatch. Butler took it from him, broke the seal and read it quickly. Then he read it again. 'General Cromwell's army has routed the king in Northamptonshire. A place called Naseby. Do you know it?'

'I do not,' replied Foster. 'Are we told anything more?'

'Over six thousand Royalists killed and their artillery captured.'

'And the king?'

'We are not told. Run back to Oxford, I expect.' He waved the despatch above his head. 'If this is accurate, the war will not last much longer, God be praised.'

* * *

Much as Lady Mary missed her sons – John, Ralph, Jerome, Edward and Charles – she did have the comfort of six of her daughters with her. Elizabeth, Joan and Jane had played their part in the defence of Corfe by tipping pails of excrement collected from the garrison's quarters on to the heads of drunken Parliamentary soldiers attempting to scale the walls on ladders and on to the roof of the 'boar' and the 'sow'. The younger girls, Bridget and Ann, had helped by fetching and carrying. Only Arabella, now three, had been too young to contribute. All had suffered the discomfort and privations brought upon them by the siege and all had supported their mother in her defence of their home without question. Their father, on his brief return to the castle the previous year, had been justly proud of them.

But now, for the first time, with the news of the crushing defeat at Naseby, followed by further defeats in the west and, most distressing of all, the fall of Bristol, and with the prospect of another miserable winter, Elizabeth and Joan had spoken quietly together in the chamber they shared in the King's Tower, the oldest part of the castle.

The Parliamentarians under Captain Kendall had made no effort to take the castle but enough news of what was happening in the country had reached them – most from Patrick, the young farrier, after one of his nocturnal visits to the cottage of the sexton – for them to know in their hearts that the war was lost and there was no longer any hope of King Charles agreeing terms with Parliament. At least their father had been spared having to witness that.

They had watched in admiration as their mother had taken charge of the defence of the castle. She had kept up their spirits by insisting that they practise daily on the harp and the flute, recite the sonnets of William Shakespeare, much beloved of their father, and, until their thread ran out, mend their clothing, and she had done what she could to make life easier for Captain Lawrence's men. While they and their servants had foregone at least one meal a day, she had insisted that their guards receive as close to their full rations as possible and all the fresh meat available. 'Better we are hungry and alive,' she had told them, 'than our guards are too weak to protect us. The men must have what beef there is.'

But now, as another summer turned to autumn, they saw the strain on their mother's face and worried for her. 'No woman could have done more,' said Elizabeth, 'but our father is dead and where is the point in our mother dying too when there is no need? Arabella is too young to lose her mother.'

'As are we all, sister,' agreed Joan. 'But she is driven by loyalty to our father. She cannot surrender.'

'What then are we to do?'

'I know not. Let us think on it.'

'Let us not think for too long. It will soon be winter and there are not many trees left for felling within the wall. We could freeze to death.'

The two sisters thought, came up with nothing and decided that they must make a direct approach. They told the other girls their intention and after prayers one morning gathered around their mother.

'What is this?' asked Mary, taken aback. 'Am I to be hauled off to the gatehouse tower and thrown into the dungeon?' The dungeon was a notorious hole under one of the gatehouse towers into which King John had enjoyed throwing his enemies and then forgetting about them. Sir John was fond of making jokes about it when his children misbehaved.

Elizabeth, as the oldest present, spoke for them all. She told her mother that they had discussed their position and had agreed that it was hopeless. Solemn promise or not, there was nothing to be gained from resisting any longer and they wished her to agree terms with the Parliamentary commander for their safe passage to the house of their aunt and cousins in Essex.

'It will not be capitulation,' said Joan, 'but a sensible arrangement for the benefit of all of us. Our father would have approved.'

'And what of our home?' asked Mary. 'Is it to be stolen by the rebels and taken by Fairfax or Cromwell or another of their ilk? Or will they destroy it as they have destroyed so many English homes?'

'Is it not more important to save our family?' asked Elizabeth. 'After all, the castle has been ours for only ten years.'

Mary's voice rose in indignation. 'Your father purchased this house for his descendants. He commanded me to hold it. I will not act against his wishes.' Frightened by their mother's tone rather than her words, the three youngest girls began to sob. Mary went to comfort them. 'If you and Joan wish to leave I will not prevent you but your sisters will remain here with me.' With that she stormed from the room, leaving her daughters staring after her.

'That did not go as I would have wished,' said Elizabeth quietly. 'I do not care to see Mother so upset.'

'Nor I,' agreed Joan, taking the weeping Amelia by the hand. 'Come, all of you, we will find a book in the library and I will read to you.'

Later, alone in their chamber, Elizabeth and Ruth agreed that they would say no more on the subject until after Christmas. Perhaps their mother's view would soften. Until then, they would manage as best they could.

Every evening, by the light of a candle, Mary stood in front of the portrait in the library and asked Queen Henrietta Maria for her advice. And every evening the queen's dark eyes stared back at her, unblinking, unchanging, resolute.

Fires were lit only on the coldest days, the grain store was nearly empty and only two cows remained. The rest had been slaughtered and eaten by the soldiers. The horses would be next. Not a hint of her doubts did Mary ever give although she knew that they could not hold out much into the new year.

When the next attack did come, frost lay on the ground and a layer of ice covering the horse trough had to be broken to enable the animals to drink. Mary was at her morning prayers when Robert Lawrence came to tell her that a troop of soldiers had managed to reach the gatehouse under cover of darkness and were setting fires at the base of the gates. He was not unduly alarmed but thought that Mary should know.

'We are firing down on them and will douse the fires without difficulty,' he said. 'It seems to me no more than a gesture. Perhaps they have been ordered to do something and could think of nothing else.'

The huge gates were held by drawbars and reinforced by an iron-faced portcullis. They would not yield easily to fire and the attackers must know that their task was hopeless.

Mary nodded. 'I daresay you are right, Robert, but let us take no chances. Such a seemingly futile attempt could be a deception. Have you sent men from the towers down to the gates?'

'I have.'

'Then let us inspect the towers. If there is trickery afoot, we will discover it.'

Of the nine towers around the wall, two protected the gate, the other seven having been placed at points from where the natural contours of the hill afforded advantageous lines of fire. They went from one to the next, starting with the Butavant Tower on the west wall and ending at the south tower. Nowhere did they see signs of an imminent attack. Finally, they returned to the gates to find that the fire had been extinguished and the attackers had returned to the town.

Robert Lawrence shook his head. 'I cannot guess at their objective, or even if they had one. Their fire, such as it was, has achieved nothing.'

'It must have been as you suggested,' replied Mary. 'To keep them occupied and to remind us that they are still here.'

'Then let us be grateful that they have nothing better to do. Idle soldiers make bad soldiers.'

At Christmas Henry Kendall had left the camp and, by turfing out the existing occupant, an ageing whore, had found himself a billet in a room above the Black Hound Inn. It was small and dirty but a good deal warmer than a tent. And the landlord brewed decent ale.

Since the visit of Colonel Butler and Captain Foster he had racked his brains for a plan. Not a plan actually to take the castle – that he knew to be impossible – but a plan that he could reasonably claim was meant to do so. He had lost six men in another attempt with scaling ladders, having first filled the scalers with ale to steady their nerves, and was reluctant to risk his men in another futile assault. Eventually he had come up with the idea of a fire. It was absurd, of course, but when the colonel next came calling, he would be able at least to say that they had tried. And now that winter was here, they would not be expected to do more than prevent supplies getting into the castle. With luck, cold and starvation would do their job for them.

According to the sexton, they were not far from that point. The young farrier, Flavin, who visited the sexton's daughter and thought he was taking back useful intelligence to the castle had no idea that everything he said was reported to the captain. For a few crowns and a guarantee of his daughter's protection, the sexton had proved obliging. From him, Kendall knew that the last two cows inside the walls would soon be slaughtered and that there were but a few sackfuls of grain left in the store. And he had made sure that reports, suitably embellished, of all Parliamentary victories were taken back to the castle. The captain had every reason to believe that the castle would soon be theirs without the need to risk more men.

The king was still skulking in Oxford, while in Scotland the loyalist Marquess of Montrose had been defeated by an army of Covenanters who had allied themselves to the cause of Parliament. Fairfax and Cromwell had swept all before them and the war would be over by the summer.

For Lady Mary Bankes, the woman who had refused to give up Corfe Castle, he held a grudging respect. She could so easily have surrendered with honour, citing the safety of her daughters, but had chosen to fight on. In his cups in the tap room of the Black Hound, Kendall had been heard to say that, if 'the Lady' was an example of Royalist womanhood, it was as well for Parliament that it had not faced an army of them. Not only had she held the castle but there had been not a single defection from the ranks of the garrison. All had remained loyal to her. Captain Kendall hoped that one day he would meet 'Brave Dame Bankes'.

On a bitingly cold morning in February, a troop of sixty cavalrymen in red woollen jackets and grey breeches, armed with swords and calivers, rode up to the walls of Wareham. At their head was Colonel James Cromwell who announced himself to the guards and informed them that they had been sent by Sir Thomas Fairfax and were on their way to Corfe to relieve the garrison there. Whether because of his name or the colours the cavalrymen wore, the guards accepted this and allowed them to pass.

Once inside the town walls, the new arrivals split themselves into two groups. One, led by Colonel Cromwell, galloped through the streets to the main camp where the Parliamentary soldiers, taken entirely by surprise, immediately surrendered their weapons and were herded into a barn where they were locked in. The other, meanwhile, began setting fires in the town square and outside the weapons store and powder magazine. The guards at the town gate, realising their mistake, dashed back into the town but were easily overcome and put in the barn with the others.

Colonel Butler, alerted by the commotion and wearing only his undergarments, ran out of the house he was occupying to find out what was afoot. Realising that the town was in the hands of the enemy, he returned at once to the house and barred himself in.

Cromwell's men went from house to house, collecting provisions and loading them together with all the captured weapons on to carts. By the time they had finished, Colonel Butler had been trapped inside his house for two hours.

Cromwell stood outside the house and shouted. 'Colonel Butler, the town is in the hands of the army of the king, your men have surrendered, and I am about to give orders for fires to be lit and the powder magazine to be blown up. You can prevent this only by giving yourself into my charge. You have one minute to make your decision.'

Twenty seconds later, Colonel Butler, now fully dressed, emerged unarmed from the house. He was bound at the wrists and bundled on to a cart laden with sacks of flour. A cavalryman rode either side of the cart.

Leaving the men locked in the barn, Colonel Cromwell led his men out of the town and on to the road to Corfe. His plan had so far gone well but there was no jubilation. They still had work to do.

The colonel hoped that they would be permitted to enter Corfe as they had entered Wareham but on the outskirts of the town they were met by a strong picket line. Word, it seemed, had already reached Corfe of the successful attack on Wareham.

When Cromwell demanded that the captain of the garrison be summoned to speak with him, a soldier hurried off, returning within a few minutes with Captain Kendall. Cromwell signalled for Colonel Butler to be brought forward, a pistol held to his head.

'Your colonel is our prisoner, Captain,' he announced loudly enough for all to hear. 'If you do not permit us to pass through your lines and into the castle unharmed, he will be shot. Do I make myself clear?'

'Clear enough,' grunted Kendall, who realised that he had no choice in the matter. Colonel Butler's death would not much trouble him but there were dozens of witnesses who might later speak against him if he did not comply. He turned to his men and bellowed. 'Let them pass.'

The troop and the carts trundled into the town and up to the castle gates, where they were admitted without hindrance. Butler was escorted to the north tower and locked into a guard room, while James Cromwell and Robert Lawrence directed the distribution of the food and weapons. The castle was now equipped for several months and its guard reinforced by sixty men.

From within the inner wall, Mary Bankes had watched the arrival of Colonel Cromwell and his troop and thanked God for it. Queen Henrietta Maria had been right – honour the memory of your husband; do not give up; there is always hope.

It did not take long for Captain Kendall to act. Suddenly, not only had the castle been provisioned and reinforced but Colonel Butler, the governor of Wareham, was held prisoner within it. It was a situation that could not be allowed to continue. He found pen and ink and sat down to draft a letter. His hand was untutored but the proposal was clear enough. In return for the governor's release, Lady Bankes and her children would be allowed to leave the castle unmolested and would be given an escort to a place of their choosing. The castle would not be damaged and its garrison would be permitted to disperse.

The letter was delivered by a guard at the gatehouse while Mary was dining with Robert Lawrence and James Cromwell. It was the first time she had tasted meat since before Christmas and Colonel Cromwell had even brought with him a few bottles of good claret. She took the letter and read it aloud. 'So, our besiegers offer us a bargain. Our safety for their colonel. Do you suppose it is an honest offer?'

Robert Lawrence stroked his chin. 'There is risk attached to it, certainly. Once you leave the castle and Colonel Butler is released, we shall be at their mercy.' He grinned at Colonel Cromwell. 'And as the colonel has gulled them so splendidly, they may feel entitled to repay the favour.'

'Nor do I trust them not to strip the castle bare and blow it up.' said Mary, 'Then all we have fought for would have been in vain.'

Unlike his more celebrated namesake, James Cromwell was a handsome man, his black hair long and wavy, his beard neat and his eyes a bright blue. He spoke quietly but with conviction. 'Is there not as much risk in refusing the offer? We did not bring a widow's crucible and the provisions will not last forever. Our enemies will be desperate to release their colonel. When Fairfax hears of his capture he will order reprisals in the town and the castle attacked and attacked again until it is taken. That is the nature of the man. Would it not be wiser – less risky – to discuss the proposal further with them?'

Robert Lawrence laid his hand upon Mary's. 'Whatever the outcome of the war and of this siege, your fight will never have been in vain. You have shown that you will not be cowed into submission and your loyalty to the king has been an example to all. And you have kept five hundred soldiers of the Parliamentary Army occupied while they might have been fighting elsewhere.'

'Do you too suggest that I should accept this proposal, Robert, after all we have suffered together?'

Robert Lawrence knew Mary Bankes too well to battle her head on. 'I suggest only that you give it consideration. Colonel Cromwell and I will put our minds to possible safeguards.'

Mary stood up. 'Very well, gentlemen, I shall do so. We will meet again tomorrow morning at seven.'

Elizabeth and Joan were adamant. 'Is this not an opportunity we must take, Mother?' asked Joan. 'Colonel Cromwell has brought us the means to end our imprisonment. We would be foolish to ignore it.'

'Imprisonment? Is that what you think, child?' Mary's eyes blazed.

'For us all it has become such. We have supported you willingly but now surely the time has come to live our lives elsewhere.'

Elizabeth agreed. 'Are our sisters never to walk in the fields or pick flowers or catch a fish in the river? You have done enough, Mother. Let us leave Corfe and join our cousins in Ruislip.'

A tear ran down Mary's cheek. 'I cannot bear the thought of losing our home.'

Joan took her mother's hand. 'We are a family, Mother. The boys will join us and wherever we are will be our home.'

Mary nodded and dabbed at her cheek with a handkerchief. 'Perhaps so. Perhaps the time has come. I will think on it overnight.'

In the library, Queen Henrietta Maria stared back at her. In those dark eyes there was still no hint of weakness. The *Generalissimo*, French princess of the House of Bourbon, queen consort of the king of England, Scotland and Ireland, would never act against her husband's wishes and would not understand any wife who did so. But Sir John Bankes was dead. Should it not be his children's wishes that came first?

Mary slept little that night and was awake before dawn when Robert Lawrence knocked on her chamber door. 'Robert? It is not yet morning,' she said, seeing him outside. 'What is the matter?'

'The prisoner, Colonel Butler, has escaped. I know not how but the guard house is empty. I have ordered a search of the castle and the grounds but I doubt we'll find him.'

'Was he not locked in?'

'He was but had no guard. He must have had help.'

'Then there is a traitor in the castle.'

'I fear there is. One who arrived with Colonel Cromwell, perhaps.'

Mary sighed. 'So now there can be no bargain. Find the traitor if you can, Robert, and let it be known that any of the servants who wish to leave may do so. Your men, of course, I leave to you. My daughters and I will remain here.'

'Mary, I cannot but think that would be foolish. After the attack on Wareham, who knows what the Parliamentarians might do? Your daughters will be in grave danger, as will you. These are men who have been away from their homes and families for many months. Can I not persuade you otherwise?'

'You cannot. And, Robert, ask Flavin to visit the sexton tonight.'

Colonel Butler sat in the taproom of the Black Hound with a blackjack of ale and a plate of bread and mutton. Less than a single night in that infernal castle yet the humiliation had been great and his skin crawled at the thought of the rat-infested guard house. Thank God there had been a friend at hand to free him. Climbing down the rope from the sally-port had been simple enough and he would certainly not be climbing back up. Cheered by the ale, he chuckled at the thought. He swallowed the last of his ale and shouted for Captain Kendall.

The captain, who had been skulking outside the inn, appeared at once. 'More meat, Colonel, more ale?'

'Shut up, Kendall, and listen carefully. This has gone on long enough. For two years five hundred men have been occupied doing nothing but sit on their backsides and wait for that woman to surrender. Well, I can tell you that, left to her own designs, she is not going to surrender.' He belched and sat back in his chair. 'Fortunately, however, we have a sympathiser in the castle, one who will help us remove the woman once and for all. Is that farrier still calling on the sexton's daughter?'

'He is, Colonel.'

'Good. Send the sexton to me.'

In the small hours of the following morning the farrier climbed back up the knotted rope and through the sally-port. He reported at once to Captain Lawrence.

'Colonel Butler has requested a hundred men to be sent from Chichester,' he said. 'They are expected within a few days.'

'How does the sexton know this?' asked the captain.

'His daughter has taken to serving in the Black Hound. She overheard Colonel Butler speaking with Captain Kendall.'

'I see. Then we must expect a fight.'

Captain Lawrence waited until Mary was risen and had breakfasted before giving her the news. 'It can only mean one thing,' he said. 'We will come under attack by a force six or seven times the size of our own.'

'I do not doubt it, Robert,' replied Mary. 'But still we have the castle walls around us. Even if they attack in ten places at once, they will not be able to breach them.'

'Mary, there is a traitor amongst us. Perhaps more than one.'

'That will make no difference. The traitor will reveal himself and will be rendered harmless.'

'Your daughters…'

'Will be at my side, come what may.'

Robert Lawrence had tried every argument he could think of. And he had failed. Mary Bankes would not be moved. But he had prepared

171

himself for this. 'Then I propose that I slip out of the castle and ride to Taunton. Sir Richard Grenville will surely allow me a hundred men from his besieging force. It should take no more than three days to bring them here.'

'Why have you not suggested this before, Robert?'

'Until now I had not thought it necessary.'

Mary considered. 'It will be hazardous. Much of Somerset is in the hands of our enemies.'

'It is a necessary risk. I will leave tonight. If the gates are opened just long enough for me to gallop through, I will be away before they realise what has happened.'

'Robert, I am unsure about this. I need you here.'

'You have Colonel Cromwell and his men. And I will return swiftly. It is the best way.'

'Very well. I can hardly prevent you if your mind is made up. Go tonight and tell no-one lest the traitor hears of it.'

The captain took her hand. 'It is for the best.'

Two days later, the gatehouse guards reported that a troop of infantrymen had arrived from Chichester. They estimated its strength at one hundred. In the castle library, Mary consulted with James Cromwell.

'They will not find it easy,' he said. 'The towers are our greatest advantage so they will attack those first. I will double the number of men at each one. The remainder I will hold in reserve until we see where the attacks are made. Let us hope Captain Lawrence returns before it starts and can force his way through the town. We will need every man he brings.'

That night Mary was woken by what she thought must be an

attack under cover of darkness. She dressed hurriedly and hastened down to the gates, from where the sounds of a disturbance were coming. There she found the gates open and a troop of perhaps one hundred and fifty men filing through into the castle grounds. At their head was Robert Lawrence. He saw her and shouted to her to return to her chamber. Thinking that an enemy attack was imminent, she did so.

With most of his men inside the gates, Captain Lawrence gave an order which was passed on through the ranks. Each man stripped off his coat, turned it inside out and put it back on again. Suddenly, blue-coated Royalists had become grey-coated Parliamentarians.

Taking six men with him, Captain Lawrence ran into the keep and up to Mary's chamber. He hammered on her door and entered without being bidden, to find Mary standing by her bed, her daughters in their night attire around her. The commotion had woken them all. The youngest, Arabella, was crying. Holding the child to her breast, Mary stared at Robert, at the jackets of his men, and again at Robert. She spoke quietly. '*Et tu, Brute?*'

'It was necessary, Mary,' he said, 'to save you and your family. These men will stand guard and ensure that you are unharmed.' With that he turned on his heel and marched out of the room.

The turncoats spread out and quickly took the King's Keep and four of the towers. Outside, Colonel Butler's infantry, who had been awaiting their opportunity, charged the gates and forced their way in. The defenders, taken entirely by surprise, put up little resistance. Even Colonel Cromwell's men, billeted in the keep and the towers and dazed from sleep, laid down their arms. In short order, at the cost of one man killed and six lightly injured, the Parliamentarians had control of the castle to which they had laid siege for three years. Just two of its defenders were killed.

Not wishing them to witness what would inevitably follow the capture of the castle, Robert Lawrence had arranged for immediate safe passage for the Bankes family to travel under guard to London and thence to Ruislip, taking with them what could be carried in two coaches. Most of their clothes, jewellery and personal possessions were left behind. So too the furniture, books and paintings with which Sir John had filled their home. Mary was permitted to take with her only Van Dyck's portrait of Queen Henrietta Maria.

In June the army of parliament took Oxford, King Charles surrendered to the Scottish Covenanters, and the bloody fighting that had rent the country from Montrose to Cornwall and from London to Bristol at last ended. Parliament ordered Corfe Castle destroyed.

A year later, Mary Bankes successfully petitioned for the return of the family's possessions and her son Ralph attempted to trace the whereabouts of the most valuable items. He met with little success.

Her life, however, and the lives of her children were spared. In recognition of her bravery she was permitted to keep the keys and seals of the castle and was able in due course to buy back her estates. She lived to see her son Ralph knighted for his loyal service to the crown and King Charles II returned to the throne. She died in Blandford a few days before his coronation in Westminster Abbey on St George's Day 1661.

A WITCH AND A BITCH

1730

It was a miserable day for it. A vicious east wind whipped across the fields, bending the elms to its whim; dead leaves danced over the graves and lowering black clouds threatened freezing rain. But for the pathetic burial party, the graveyard was deserted. Ancient, moss-covered gravestones, long illegible, marked the resting places of nameless men, women and children of the parish. The two mourners made an odd pair – old Earl Cowper, bent and shivering under his cloak and, from time to time, wiping his rheumy eyes with a white pocket handkerchief, and me.

Mr Ford, the parson, had little to say. He had never met my grandmother and confined himself to a few words about a long and difficult life on earth to be followed by eternal peace somewhere else. We said the Lord's Prayer and each threw a handful of earth on to the coffin – plain pine, iron handles, no inscription – and left the rest to the parson and the sexton. The whole affair was over within fifteen minutes. We shook hands, nodded and smiled, and went our separate ways.

The grave would be unmarked but I knew where it was. In the

north corner of Hertingfordbury churchyard beside an old yew tree, we had buried Jane Wenham, the Witch of Walkern.

I first met my grandmother on my seventh birthday, which was in the year 1707. At about five o'clock in the afternoon while my mother was preparing our supper, I answered a knock on our cottage door. Even then, although she was less than sixty, the woman outside looked terribly old, with a bent back and a face so pinched and wrinkled that I could barely see her eyes. Her hair was matted, she was dirty and she smelt like a midden. She wore an ancient shawl over her rags and she was barefoot.

Seeing this old woman at the door and taking her for one of the gypsies who were camped in a field outside the village, and to whom I had been told never to speak, I stepped back and made to shut the door.

'Emily?' she croaked, before I could close the door. I nodded. 'This is for your birthday.' And she handed me a small cake wrapped in a chestnut leaf. Then she was gone. I took the cake into the kitchen.

'Who was at the door?' asked my mother.

'An old woman. She gave me this.'

Mother looked up sharply from her cooking. 'What is it?'

'It's a cake.'

'Give it to me at once, Emily. It must be burnt.'

'Why must it be burnt?'

'Never mind why. Give it to me.'

I handed her the cake. 'Was she a gypsy woman?'

'I expect so.'

'But she knew it's my birthday. How did she know that?'

Mother shook her head. 'The gypsies are strange people. They know things. Some of them cast spells to lure children from their homes. Keep away from them. And don't tell your father. He'd be furious if he knew you'd taken a cake from a gypsy.'

Mother turned her back and bent over the cooking pot. There was to be no more discussion, although it did seem odd – a dirty old gypsy woman bringing me a piece of cake on my birthday.

In our cottage sounds had an odd way of travelling around and in my bedroom, with the door open, I could hear my parents talking in the parlour. Later that evening I heard them talking about the old woman.

'I didn't see her,' said Mother, 'but from what Emily said, it must have been her.'

'Why did she come?' asked Father.

'She brought a piece of cake for Emily's birthday. I burnt it.'

'Good.'

'She's an evil old woman and Emily must have nothing to do with her. And where did she get the money for cake? It must have been stolen. She's a thief as well as everything else.'

'That she is.'

The next morning I plucked up the courage to ask my mother again about the old woman.

'She's a poor woman who lives in Walkern. She begs and steals. We want nothing to do with her.'

'Not a gypsy then?'

'No, not a gypsy.'

'But you said she was.'

'I was wrong.'

'Why did she bring me cake on my birthday?'

'I really couldn't say, child. It's best you forget about her.'

I gave up. But I knew now that an old woman who lived in the next village knew the day of my birthday. Perhaps she would visit me again.

At that time our village, Ardeley, was a small place with no more than two hundred inhabitants. It was unremarkable except for the church which was more than four hundred years old. We lived in one of the thatched cottages that surrounded the village green and duck pond. The cottage had two bedrooms upstairs and a parlour and kitchen downstairs. We had a fire in the parlour in front of which we each took a weekly bath in a big iron tub.

My father had been born in the village. He was a man of few words, a ploughman and farrier who, like the fathers of most of my friends, worked on one of the farms outside the village. My mother took in washing and mending. As I was their only child, we lived comfortably enough. I attended the village school, we went each Sunday to church, and Father went on Tuesday and Friday evenings to the Ardeley Arms.

We also went occasionally to Walkern. Until I was old enough to walk the three miles there and back, Father carried me on his shoulders. Walkern was a larger village, with perhaps twice as many inhabitants, and businesses making bricks and hats. We went there when Mother wanted a new bonnet or Father needed new tools.

You might have thought that being the larger and more prosperous village, Walkern would have been the more likely to manage its affairs well, such as the school and relief for the poor. But that was not the way of it. The poor were better served in Ardeley, where our local squire and Justice, Sir Henry Chauncy, made sure that they were taken care of and that our school had the books and teachers it needed. Perhaps the wealthy merchants of Walkern were too busy making money to concern themselves with such matters.

When I finished school at the age of eleven I was put to helping my mother with her cleaning and mending. Many of our customers liked to gossip when they called with their bundles of clothes. Old Miss Handforth did not even bring clothes. She came just to gossip. She enjoyed misfortune and the greater the misfortune the more she enjoyed it. The loss of a cat made her smile and the loss of a cow had her chuckling for days. It was from her that we first heard the news from Walkern.

An old woman, unpopular in the village for her begging and stealing and for her sharp tongue, had accused a young man of calling her 'a witch and a bitch' and had tried to persuade Sir Henry Chauncy to bring an action against him. Sir Henry, protesting that he had more important matters to attend to, had sent both of them off to the vicar of Walkern, Mr Gardiner. The vicar had fined the young man a shilling and told them both to stop arguing and live peacefully. The old woman, furious at getting only a shilling for the slander, had gone off muttering about 'having justice elsewhere'. That might have been an end to it but for what happened next.

The day after the old woman had come before the vicar, his young servant, Anne Thorn, started behaving strangely. The vicar and his wife found her partially undressed and shouting wildly that 'she was ruined and undone'. Despite having a painful knee, she had rushed about gathering twigs, had climbed over a fence and fallen into a ditch and had set upon the old woman, accusing her of being a witch. Then the young man who had called her 'a witch and a bitch' claimed that she had compelled him to collect straw from a dung heap and that several horses and cattle in his care had mysteriously died.

When the news got round, the old woman was dragged from her home and arrested. She was being held in the Walkern lock-up and was to be questioned by Sir Henry and examined for signs of being a witch. The woman's name was Jane Wenham.

At the mention of the woman's name, the colour drained from my mother's face and she leant against the wall to steady herself. I fetched her a chair and a cup of water. Miss Handforth did not appear to notice and prattled on about the woman and what she had done. Eventually I told her that my mother was feeling unwell and suggested that she return another day.

When she had gone, I asked Mother what had so upset her. She took a sip of water and looked down at her hands. 'Jane Wenham is my mother, Emily. She's a shameful woman, a beggar and a thief and we haven't spoken for years. I had hoped you would never find out. Now you have.'

I remembered the dirty old woman who had called on my birthday. 'It was her who once came here with a cake for me, wasn't it?'

'Yes, it was.'

'Is it true what they're saying, that she's a witch?'

'Some people say so. She's a thief, to be sure, and perhaps she's a witch. Still, it's a terrible thing to say about anyone.'

'Then why would they say it?'

'Wait until your father comes home, Emily, and then I'll tell you about your grandmother."

When Father came back from the farm and had eaten his dinner, we sat in the kitchen. Mother told him about the news from Walkern and that she was going to tell me about my grandmother. Father nodded and said, 'It's better that Emily knows the truth. She's old enough now.'

This is what my mother told me.

'I do not know exactly how old your grandmother is, nor where she was born, except that she was not born in Walkern. She never spoke of her family. When she arrived in Walkern, she was about eighteen years old. She had no money, no learning and no trade. She could not find regular work and survived by begging and stealing.

'Then a man named Phillip Cooke asked her to marry him. He was my father. I don't know why he married her. My father was a kind man, hard-working and honest. That's when the talk began. Some folk said that she'd put a spell on him to make him marry her. Despite that, they lived together happily enough until he died. That was fourteen years ago.

'I loved my father and took his death hard. One day he suddenly started coughing and retching as if he had eaten something rotten and within a few hours he was dead. I couldn't understand it. We had all eaten the same food, yet my mother and I were quite well. Tongues in the village started wagging again and some said that she had poisoned him. Remember that she had no friends.

'She had always been harsh with me. Once, when I was three or four, I fell into a patch of nettles. She told me that if I didn't stop crying, she'd make me sleep in a nettle bed. I was eight when she beat me for breaking an egg, and ten when she said I was too plain ever to find a husband. I was teased by the other children for having a witch as a mother and often went home in tears. She just laughed and said that if she was a witch, they'd better mind their tongues or she'd turn them into toads. I remember these things because they were painful. When my father died, I grieved for myself but I could not grieve for her. She had made me hate her.

'No more than a year after Father's death, she married again. His name was Edward Wenham, one of the Wenhams who had owned the smithy in Walkern before they had to sell it. He was younger than her, he drank too much and I didn't care for him. We were living in my father's cottage and when Edward moved in, I left and came to Ardeley. That same year, your father and I were married.

'It wasn't long before Edward Wenham left too. My mother had been borrowing money on the promise that he would pay it back, and buying food on credit. When he found out he had the town crier announce publicly that he disowned his wife and would not be responsible for her debts. Thank God we were living here and few people knew that Sarah Porter, who had been Sarah Cooke, was the daughter of Jane Wenham. It would have been too shaming if we'd been in Walkern. I haven't spoken to her since I left and I never shall again. She may be my mother and your grandmother but she's a nasty old woman with a vicious tongue and a thieving eye.'

'But is she a witch?'

'I fear she may be,' said my mother, sadly. 'It wasn't so long ago that witches were common in the county. When people saw a cat with a woman's face or children taking fits or animals dying for no reason, they looked for a witch. When they found her, those things stopped.'

'Some folk don't believe in witches any more,' said my father. 'But I say if there were witches then, why wouldn't there be witches now?'

'How do you know if someone's a witch?' I asked.

'Witches talk with the devil and suckle his creatures. They're called familiars. Witches have teats where the familiars suckle.'

'And if you scratch a witch's face, you won't see blood,' added Father.

'There's another thing,' said Mother. 'Churchmen say there are witches because the Bible speaks of them.'

'If she is a witch, what will happen to her?'

'She'll be examined for the signs. If there is evidence against her, she'll go for trial at the Assizes. If she's found guilty, she'll be hanged.'

'They used to burn witches,' said Father. 'I even heard of two who were half-hanged, then burnt while still alive. I don't think that's necessary. Hang them and be done with it. When the witch is dead, she's dead.'

'So my grandmother might be hanged?'

'It's years since the last witch hanging. There hasn't even been a witch trial in the county for a long time. But if she's found to be a witch, she will be hanged. It's the law.'

My mother must have guessed what I was thinking. 'It's not in the blood, Emily,' she said gently. 'I'm not a witch and neither are you.'

'Can I visit her?' I asked. She was my grandmother, she had brought me a cake on my seventh birthday and I wanted to meet her.

'I don't think it would be wise,' said my mother.

'Why not? I'm her granddaughter. Even if she is a witch, she won't harm me and I want to speak to her. She may tell me things I should know.'

'You're not yet thirteen, Emily. There's no reason for you to know such things.'

'Better I should know the truth for myself than hear lies from others.'

'We're not well known in Walkern and your grandmother is not known in Ardeley. It would be best to keep it that way. We don't want tongues wagging and fingers pointing.'

Disappointed, I went to bed. Later, however, I heard my parents arguing. I could not hear exactly what was being said but I knew it was about my grandmother. The thought of her being dragged into a court and accused of being a witch kept me awake for hours.

Next morning, before he went off to work, Father told me that he would take me to Walkern on Saturday. I could visit my grandmother once and that would be an end to it. We would not talk about her again.

The lock-up in Walkern was known as the 'White House', on account of its white walls. When Father and I arrived there on Saturday afternoon, we were let in by the officer in charge and shown into a small guard room to which two cells were attached. One was empty and the officer was astonished that anyone would want to visit the filthy old woman in the other.

'Have a care, mind, or she'll give you the fits.'

Father went off to the market. The officer let me into the cell and locked the door. 'Knock on the door when you're done,' he told me, 'and I'll let you out. And no flying away on broomsticks.' He went off chuckling.

She was sitting on a low stool in the corner of the cell, a small hunched figure, huddled under her shawl. The shawl was so dirty and ragged that it could have been the same one she had been wearing when she had brought me the cake six years before. She looked up sharply when I came in. She was even more pinched and wrinkled than I remembered, her hair and face were streaked with dirt and she had a livid scar on her cheek.

'Who are you?' she croaked. It was an ugly voice, rough and suspicious.

'I'm Emily, your granddaughter.'

She peered at me. 'You don't favour your mother. You've got blue eyes and brown hair. You're pretty too. Tell you to come, did she?'

'No. I wanted to come.'

'Told you stories about me, has she?'

'She's told me a little about you. Not much. I wanted to meet you. You brought me a cake on my birthday.'

She nodded. 'I remember. Did you eat it?'

'Yes. It was good. I've brought one for you.' I handed her a small cake I had made that morning. She took it and ate it without a word.

'Why have you come?' she asked, wiping crumbs from her mouth with her hand.

'I said. I wanted to.'

'Well, now you have.'

'Yes, I have. Can I sit down?'

'You'll have to sit on the floor.'

The floor was cold but I was uncomfortable standing. I was too far above her. 'How long have you been here?' I asked.

'Must be a week since.' She scratched at her head with a filthy finger.

'My mother says you're a thief.'

'Does she? Well, could be she's right. I took turnips from a field and straw to sell to the hatmakers. And so would she with an empty pocket and an aching belly.'

'Why did they put you here?'

'They say I am a witch.'

'Are you a witch?'

'Too many questions, child,' she hissed. 'If they want to hang me, they will. An old woman on her own, they'll find reasons enough if they choose.'

'What will happen to you now?'

'If the Justice decides it, they'll send me to the Assizes.'

'Would you like me to come?'

'To the Assizes?'

'Yes.'

'If you want. Won't make no difference, though. Go now, child. I've talked enough.'

Father was waiting outside the lock-up. He did not ask me about my grandmother and I did not ask him about the market. We walked home with barely a word exchanged. And when we got home, my mother asked me nothing about my visit or about her mother. As far as both my parents were concerned, from then on the case of Jane Wenham was nothing to do with us and we would not talk about her again.

I am not sure how the thought came to me or when, but it must have been within a day or two of my visit to Walkern. I went to call on Mr Strutt, the vicar of Ardeley. As we were regular worshippers at his church, he knew me well enough and did not seem surprised to see me. I thought he must be used to young girls seeking advice at the rectory. He ushered me into his study, where we sat by the fire, an enormous Bible on the low table between us, and asked me what he could do for me.

'Jane Wenham is my grandmother,' I replied.

'Yes. It is not commonly known but I have known for some time,' he said. 'It cannot be easy for you.'

'I don't understand why she has been arrested.'

'There were complaints. Mr Gardiner and I have questioned her. There is evidence of witchcraft.'

'Do you believe she's a witch, sir?'

For a minute, Mr Strutt stared into the fire. Then he said quietly, 'I have discussed this at length with Mr Gardiner. We were both present when Jane Wenham failed correctly to say the Lord's Prayer and then confessed that she had been a witch for more than sixteen years, using curses and imprecations against any who vexed her. I witnessed Mr Gardiner's servant, Anne Thorn, behaving as if such a curse had been put on her and have since heard of cats with Jane Wenham's face being seen in the village, children falling ill and animals dying without apparent cause. It is hard not to believe that your grandmother is a witch.'

'Why would God allow witches?'

'God moves in mysterious ways. The answer lies in his wish to test us and for us to show our faith in him. He permits witches because they are proof of the devil's existence and therefore of his own. He wishes us to reject one and rejoice in the other.'

'So God wishes us to discover witches and destroy them?'

'He does. In the book of Exodus, chapter twenty-two, verse five, we are told "Thou shalt not suffer a witch to live". Witches speak with the devil and have the power to make trouble. They must be destroyed.' I felt tears on my cheeks. Mr Strutt ignored them. 'You must put the fact that she is your grandmother out of your mind, child. If she is found to be a witch, she will hang. There is no alternative.'

I was sobbing. 'What will happen to her now?'

'If Sir Henry Chauncy decides there is sufficient evidence, she will be tried at the Assizes.'

'When will that be?'

'In about a month, I believe.'

I was still crying when I left the rectory, although whether for my grandmother or myself I would have been hard put to say. No-one liked Jane Wenham. She was a thief who had treated her own daughter badly and whose husband had publicly disowned her. I had not much liked her when I visited her in the lock-up, but she was my grandmother, she had no-one else to support her and I did not want to believe that she was a witch, whatever Mr Strutt, Mr Gardiner, and Sir Henry Chauncy might think. Nor did I want to be the granddaughter of a witch.

A few days after my visit to Mr Strutt, I was delivering a bundle of clean clothes to a family who lived on the other side of the green when two girls jumped out from behind a wall and blocked my way. I knew them both – Alice Brewer and Mary Lott, both daughters of farmworkers.

'Well now,' sneered Mary, 'if it isn't Emily Porter. Mind what you say, Alice, or we'll be running about collecting twigs and falling into ditches.'

'Have you seen any cats with her ugly face, Mary?' asked Alice, with a foul grin.

'I haven't, but I've got a pin.' She held up a bent pin. 'Shall we prick her to see if there's any blood?'

Alice grabbed my wrist, making me drop the bundle, and held it out for Mary to prick with the pin. Three times she stuck the pin into me before I was able to pull my arm away. Blood welled up from the wounds and tears came to my eyes. I shouted at them to leave me alone and mind their own business.

'If you're a witch, Emily Porter,' said one of them, 'it is our business.'

'You'll be on the ducking stool when the old woman hangs, and your mother with you.'

'We don't want witches in Ardeley. They've got enough in Walkern.'

I picked up a handful of mud and threw it at them. Some of it splattered Alice's face. Then I took the bundle and ran home.

When my mother asked why I had not delivered the washing I told her about Alice and Mary. 'You must have been seen in Walkern,' she said. 'I feared as much. I knew your father shouldn't have taken you.'

'Now the whole village will know, won't it?'

'It will. We'd better pray for God's help and hope he doesn't hold it against us.'

'Hold what against us?'

'Emily, people believe your grandmother is a witch. She speaks to the devil. She causes trouble. She's evil. It will do us no good.'

She was right. Within days you would have thought that there was no more important matter in the entire world than the forthcoming trial of Jane Wenham of Walkern. Mr Strutt's flock were happy to take their lead from him, news sheets dwelt at length on the evidence and pamphlets printed in London started appearing in the village.

Worst of all, by then everyone knew that my mother was the daughter of 'the witch'. Our customers – those of them who had not taken their business elsewhere – pointedly avoided the subject but in the village the name of Jane Wenham was on everyone's lips. I dreaded leaving home. Conversations in the street ended abruptly as I approached and I overheard whispered remarks about 'that poor child'. I suffered jokes about dead cows and crying babies, I was called 'the witch's spawn' and 'Wenham's heir' and I was spat at and pelted with stones. I was the granddaughter of a witch.

At home, my parents simply refused to talk about it. My accounts of being attacked and abused were met with no more than 'Ignore them, Emily. It'll pass.'

Some of the pamphlets and news sheets used passages from the Bible, including the one from Exodus that Mr Strutt had quoted, to prove that witches existed, and set out a quantity of theological arguments. The most popular of them suggested that God's twin purposes in allowing witches was to test our faith and to punish sinners. And, as Mr Strutt had claimed, the existence of witches proved the existence of the devil and therefore the existence of God himself. This I found very odd. Why would God need witches to prove his existence to us and why would he permit them to carry out foul acts on innocent people? Or were their victims all sinners?

Others dismissed the notion of witchcraft as no more than a relic of heathen beliefs. Much of the blame for them was laid at the feet of the Danes, who had brought with them stories of witches and wizards being sent by their gods to wreak havoc on earth. Papal inquisitors and ill-informed translators of the Bible also came in for criticism.

One pamphlet from London spoke of the foolishness of believing in witchcraft. It described those who did as 'vulgar country folk'; I wondered what Mr Strutt and Sir Henry Chauncy might make of that. It pointed out that women accused of being a witch were always 'old hags, with wrinkled faces, hairy lips, gobber teeth and squint eyes'. It claimed that there were no beautiful witches and asked why. It also asked how it was that women accused of being witches did not immediately use their powers to silence their accusers, fly off on their broomsticks or make themselves invisible. I put a copy of the pamphlet on Alice's doorstep.

Both sides unearthed cases of witchcraft from old records and recounted them in support of their arguments. It was nearly seventy years since Matthew Hopkins and John Stearne had travelled the countryside searching out women accused of being witches and subjecting them to trial by pricking or by ducking in water, but we had all heard of them. Hopkins was known to have denied suspects sleep for several days and nights in order to help them confess and he and Stearne were thought to have been responsible for over two hundred executions for witchcraft. Angry mothers were still known to threaten a misbehaving child with a 'visit from Mr Hopkins'.

We read of the case of Mary Hall of Little Gadsden who was said to be possessed by two devils and spoke in strange voices and made the sounds of animals; of Jane Stretton of Ware who was seized by fits after her husband had been rude to a 'cunning man'; and of three sisters in Tring whose possession by the devil led them to suffer great pain, fits and visions of strange apparitions. All three girls were eventually cured by prayer meetings in their house. Some commentators took this to be proof of the existence of the devil and of his handmaidens, the witches, others explained the sisters' misfortunes as illnesses which ran their course and disappeared naturally.

Three women had been found guilty of being witches in Exeter about thirty years earlier, but since then most witches must have flown away because incidents of suspected witchcraft had become very rare. Strange happenings which might previously have been put down to magic were now explained in more worldly ways.

Yet some still held to their old beliefs. There were certainly those of my grandmother's age who took witchcraft for granted and others, including my parents, who had not abandoned the idea. If my mother could entertain the possibility of her mother being found guilty and hanged for the crime, its existence was real enough. Whatever I thought was unlikely to make much difference.

My grandmother was made to appear in front of Sir Henry Chauncy. Before a large crowd of onlookers, Sir Henry heard evidence from Mr and Mrs Gardiner, from their servant Anne Thorn and from his own son, Arthur Chauncy.

Anne Thorn claimed to have seen cats with Jane Wenham's face which instructed her to do away with herself and Arthur Chauncy said that he had seen no blood when he stuck the pin into her arm.

When she was asked to recite the Lord's Prayer, she could not do so. Most damning of all, the two vicars, Mr Gardiner and Mr Strutt, reported that in front of a relative of hers, a Mr Archer, Jane Wenham had admitted to having been a witch for sixteen years.

Despite the absence of the devil's marks on her body – two women had searched in vain for four hours – Sir Henry sent Jane Wenham to Hertford to stand trial at the Assizes. My grandmother had been right. If they wanted her to stand trial, she would. And if they wanted her to hang, she would.

While she was in Hertford gaol awaiting trial, more old incidents were suddenly remembered. There had been cats with her face, cattle belonging to the farmer from whom she had stolen turnips dying of the staggers, a child dying after being touched by her and a poor girl named Ann Street, who suffered convulsions and ran about collecting twigs, much like the servant girl, Anne Thorn. All this added weight to the evidence against her.

One news sheet offered advice on remedies for witchcraft. It recommended burning thatch from the witch's roof, or a bunch of her hair, drawing blood from her, or making a cake of her victim's urine mixed with grain and burning that. It also urged us to be wary of 'the Sabbat', the day on which witches met the devil, danced naked and ate children. Someone, probably Alice Brewer or Mary Lott, left a copy on our doorstep, underneath a dead cat and a pile of twigs. My mother got rid of them.

And there was talk of legal matters. One concerned the charge. Jane Wenham had been charged with 'conversing familiarly with the devil in the shape of a cat'. She had not been charged, as was expected, with bewitching Anne Thorn. I could see no difference. If found guilty on either charge, she would hang. Another matter concerned the appointment of a judge. There was much speculation about this. The names of Sir Matthew Hale and Sir John Holt were mentioned. One had always convicted witches, the other had always acquitted them. I remember thinking that judges, of all people, ought to agree with each other.

By then, the case of Jane Wenham of Walkern was one upon which everyone held an opinion. Everyone, that is, but me. I did not know if witches existed and, if they did, whether my grandmother was one of them or whether the idea was simply nonsense – no more than a way of explaining odd things and of disposing of unwanted old women. What I did know was that my grandmother, old, sharp-tongued and difficult as she was, was in Hertford gaol with every chance of being found guilty and hanged. Witch or not, she was my grandmother and she had brought me a cake on my birthday. I wanted to be at her trial.

Towards the end of February, we heard that the trial had been set for the fourth of March. All of Hertfordshire and a good deal of London were awaiting the day with an eagerness normally reserved for Christmas and Easter. Yet more pamphlets, some demanding the execution of Jane Wenham, others calling for her immediate release, were by then appearing daily and I heard someone observe that, even if war were declared on China, that would not arouse more public interest than the trial of the Witch of Walkern.

Even if I had had the fare, I could not have travelled on any of the coaches going to Hertford for the trial. They would be full of people who knew me, most of whom had already found my grandmother guilty. It was too far to walk there and back in a day and I had neither a horse nor a broomstick. I had all but given up hope of attending.

On its eve, however, my father took me to one side and said quietly, 'Your mother will not thank me for this so best she doesn't know until she has to, but there's a cart travelling from the farm to Hertford tomorrow to collect barrels and tools. It'll leave first thing and come back in the evening. There's room for us, if you want to go.'

I was astonished. Not a word had been said about the trial in our house and I had no idea that Father knew I wanted to go. He must have guessed. 'It's only a thought, Emily,' he went on, 'if you want to go, that is.'

I reached up and kissed his cheek. 'Thank you, Father,' I said. 'I want to go. She'll have few enough supporters.'

'That's what I thought. I daresay she's guilty of what they say but if you want to be there, I'll take you. We should be at the farm by six. The trial will start at nine. I'll tell your mother before we leave.'

A complete stranger would have had no difficulty in finding his way from Ardeley to Hertford that morning. The road was one long line of coaches and carriages. For us, it was an uncomfortable twelve miles, the cart having been designed to carry farm tools rather than passengers. I sat between my father and the driver, huddled up against the chill of the morning and wishing I had thought to bring a cushion to sit on. After more than two hours of bumping over the hard road,

I was cold and sore. It made me think of my grandmother stealing a turnip. The driver, who had barely opened his mouth the whole way except to spit or swear at the horses, dropped us in the centre of the town and said he would collect us there at four o'clock.

'It shouldn't take them any longer than that,' he said. 'If it does, you'll have to leave them to it. We must be back by nightfall.'

Men and women of every description had converged on the town for the event and, from their mood, were looking forward to a most entertaining day. Coaches had come not only from neighbouring villages but also from Cambridge and London. Spotting an opportunity for easy money, traders had set up their stalls along the streets. They offered food and drink, models of witches, broomsticks, pointed hats and false noses. There were magic potions and feather cakes, cats with human faces and bundles of twigs. There was even a man taking wagers on the outcome of the trial. He was expecting Jane Wenham to be hanged.

I held on to my father's hand as we made our way through the crowds to the Assize Court. There was a queue at the entrance and I thought we might not be allowed in. When we reached the front of the queue, however, my father spoke to the court officer and gave him a coin. We were among the last to get in. Most people were left milling about in the town and having to wait outside for news. I doubted if they cared. They were having a day out.

I am not sure what I had been expecting, having never before been in a court, but it certainly was not what I found. We squeezed into seats at the end of the first row in the public gallery and looked around. The courtroom was small – no larger than my old schoolroom – with dark oak panelling on the walls, a high ceiling and wooden benches for the jury and officials. It was not at all grand.

Father said that the benches to our left were for the jury, the desk on a raised platform in front of us for the judge and the seats below for the lawyers and clerks. My grandmother would have to stand in the dock, which looked very sturdy, perhaps to prevent prisoners leaping up and attacking the judge. I wondered if it had occurred to anyone that if she were a witch Jane Wenham would have no difficulty in flying over the dock or turning herself into a cat and jumping over it.

The first to enter the court were a number of lawyers and clerks in their gowns and wigs, followed by the twelve jurymen and then the judge. The jurymen were ordinary-looking fellows, not working men and certainly not gentry, but somewhere in between. Their expressions betrayed nothing of what they were thinking.

I rather liked the look of the judge in his long wig and flowing gown. He had creases around his eyes as if he smiled a lot, and a twinkle in his eye. By the time he entered the courtroom, it was bursting at the seams and we were so squashed up that I was almost sitting on my father's lap. Everyone was talking at once and taking no notice of anyone else. A court officer shouted for silence and the judge took his seat.

The prisoner, Jane Wenham, was brought into the courtroom and told to stand in the dock. Two more officers stood on either side of her. She had been cleaned up and given new clothes, but looked very small and very frightened, resting her hands on the dock for support. She did not look up to the gallery and did not see my smile or my wave.

We were told by a clerk with a very loud voice that the case would be heard by the Honourable Sir John Powell and that the defendant was charged with 'conversing familiarly with the devil in the shape of a cat', at which the judge's eyebrows disappeared under his wig and he coughed loudly. Sir John Powell was the judge who had never presided over a successful prosecution for witchcraft and it must have been clear to every person in the court what he thought of the matter. I found my father's hand and held tight.

In answer to the charge, the defendant said nothing. The first witness called against her was the Reverend Gardiner. He said that his servant, Anne Thorn, had been compelled by the defendant to run off to gather twigs and leaves and had brought them back to his house wrapped in her apron. He described her fits and her great fear of Jane Wenham. Mr Gardiner's story was then confirmed by his wife and by Mr Strutt, who also reported that the defendant had admitted to having been a witch for sixteen years.

The Reverend Francis Bragge – a pompous little man to whom I took an instant dislike and who I later discovered to be Sir Henry Chauncy's grandson – told his story of finding the cakes of feathers. When the judge asked to see one of these cakes, Mr Bragge replied that he had thought it best to destroy them.

Anne Thorn gave her version of events, confirming that she had heard Jane Wenham say 'If I cannot get justice here, I will have it elsewhere' as she left the house, and that she had been 'bewitched' and consequently could not control her actions. Despite her knee, she had run to a place half a mile away where she had met an old woman in a hood who had made her collect the twigs and leaves and who had actually given her a pin for the bundle. No sooner had the bundle, at Mrs Gardiner's insistence, been thrown on the fire, but Jane Wenham appeared again, claiming to have forgotten to mention some washing that had to be done. As it was well known that a witch would appear if one of her charms was burnt, this was strong evidence of her guilt.

The jury members nodded their heads solemnly and whispered to each other. Some of the spectators around us shook their fists at the defendant and called out for her to be hanged. The judge rapped on his desk again and told them sternly to be quiet. 'I will have order in my court,' he thundered, 'or the gallery will be cleared.' Despite his twinkle, Sir John Powell could sound very fierce.

The same thing had happened twice more, said Anne Thorn. After seeing Jane Wenham, she had been compelled to run off to collect wigs and leaves, and despite her knee to jump over streams and gates. So disturbed by this was she that she started having fits and tried to drown herself.

Matthew Gilston, a servant of Mr John Chapman, was asked about the events which had caused Jane Wenham to be at the Gardiners' house. He said that after he had refused her straw to sell to the hatmakers, he had felt compelled to run off to collect some from a dung heap and put it under his shirt.

Then some of his master's cattle and horses had mysteriously died. Suspecting that it was her doing, he had called her 'a witch and a bitch'. She had complained about this to Sir Henry Chauncy who had sent them to Mr Gardiner. The jury did some more nodding and the spectators more fist-waving. I was glad my grandmother was not looking at them. Watching the jury, it seemed to me that they were more impressed by the witnesses themselves than by what they had to say. Three churchmen and one churchman's wife were not to be taken lightly.

More witnesses followed, including Arthur Chauncy who claimed to have witnessed the later instances of Anne Thorn's odd behaviour. He also described his attempts to draw blood from my grandmother's arm. I had seen her arm and knew that he must have stuck his pin into it hard and often.

Among the others who gave evidence was Elizabeth Field who claimed that Jane Wenham had killed her child some nine years earlier. When the judge asked her why she had not brought an action at the time, the woman said that she had been too poor to do so. He asked her how she had suddenly become rich enough. He made everyone laugh and he did so again when another witness said that he had seen the defendant flying. 'There is no law against flying,' said Sir John.

There were sixteen witnesses in all, each one of whom spoke against my grandmother. Not one spoke for her. She herself said only that she was a 'clear woman'.

When Sir John Powell gave a summary of the evidence, he made it plain that he did not believe in witchcraft and that he thought the case absurd. Without explicitly saying so, he invited the jury to acquit the defendant.

I cannot recall exactly when during the trial I realised that he was right but it was at some point during the witnesses' statements. It was as if they had all agreed on what they were going to say and had rehearsed their words as actors do. Not one of them expressed any doubts, there were no contradictions and no hesitations. We were asked to believe their accounts of cats with Jane Wenham's face, bewitchings, dead animals and even dead children, but we were offered no proof of any of these things. The witnesses were not asked any searching questions by the lawyers and the jury was expected to take their good faith for granted. We might as well have been watching a play.

My grandmother, having stood and listened all morning, was taken back to her cell while the court adjourned and the jury considered its verdict.

Outside, the crowd was even larger than it had been when we arrived. The man taking wagers was shouting out the odds he would give against verdicts of guilty and not guilty, the traders were selling their models of witches and broomsticks as fast as they could hand them over and a man with a long beard and dressed all in black stood on an upturned box and railed against the wickedness of the devil and 'his whores', the witches.

Father bought pies from one of the traders and we found a quiet spot by the church gate to eat them.

'What did you make of it?' he asked me.

'I thought the witnesses were making up stories.'

'Even Mr Gardiner and Mr Strutt?'

'Especially Mr Gardiner and Mr Strutt. Just because they are churchmen doesn't make them good or honest. They just want people to believe in witches.'

'What about what the Bible says?'

'I don't know, Father. Perhaps there were witches then. What I do know is that my grandmother is not a witch and nor is anyone else. If they were, Mr Gardiner and Mr Strutt and all those other witnesses would not have to make up stories about her. They could find a real witch.'

'What about her confession?'

'What about it? If people went on wrongly accusing you of something, you might admit it just to be rid of them. And I think she wanted to frighten them.'

'So you're sure she's innocent?'

'Of course she is. Where's the proof? Stories about cats and babies and sticks and spells? It's nonsense. It's the people who tell lies who should be on trial.'

'The judge agrees with you but the jury will decide.'

It was two hours before we were allowed back in to the court room. By then the lawyers and clerks had reassembled and the gallery was filling up again. My grandmother was escorted up to the dock, the judge took his place and the jury filed in. Nothing was said until they were settled.

The judge asked the foreman of the jury if they had reached a verdict. I held my breath. The foreman said that they found her guilty. The judge asked whether they found her guilty of 'conversing with the devil in the shape of a cat'. The foreman replied that they did.

All of a sudden the court was in uproar and the gallery emptied. Everyone wanted to be the first to carry the news of the first conviction for witchcraft for years, a crime for which there was only one possible sentence. My father put his arm around my shoulders. I was shaking.

My grandmother stood in the dock, an officer on either side of her. She must have sensed me because for the first time she turned and looked up at the gallery. There were tears on her cheeks.

Once again Sir John used his hammer to silence the court. He explained that he had no alternative under the law but to sentence the defendant to death. He was shocked and angry. Not only had the jury ignored his advice but as a result an old woman would be hanged.

He passed sentence and then announced that he was suspending the date of execution while he explored the possibility of a pardon. I did not understand this. My grandmother had been found guilty and sentenced to hang. How could she now be pardoned?

The journey home was much worse than the one there. I sat with my father's arm around me, bumping about on the cart and wiping my eyes with my sleeve. When at last we got home, I went straight to bed. My mother said nothing.

Another stream of pamphlets appeared within days of the trial. Some were vicious. The Reverend Bragge, who had testified against her, described Jane Wenham as having 'the character of a whore', and deserving to die 'on other accounts than witchcraft'. Others set out to prove the existence of witches 'from scripture and reason' and pointed to the plight of Anne Thorn as conclusive evidence of Jane Wenham's guilt.

Only a few poured scorn on the idea of witchcraft and on the reasons for the trial. One described the trial as 'absurd' and the testimony of Anne Thorn as that of a sick woman and a shameless liar. I read them all.

Oddly enough, once the trial was over and the verdict known most of the jibes and taunts stopped. Our customers returned and I could walk down the street without being abused. It was as if a battle had been fought and won and the victors had decided to be merciful. Even Alice and Mary kept their distance.

Meanwhile my grandmother was in Hertford gaol, having been sentenced to hang. I wondered why, if the judge could reprieve her execution, he had not simply quashed the jury's verdict and let her go free. Instead, a week after the trial he let it be known that he would personally apply to the queen for a royal pardon. I wondered if my grandmother knew that or whether she was resigned to being hanged.

In April, four weeks after the trial, I travelled again to Hertford, this time without my father. The coach stopped in the market square from where it was a short walk to the prison in Fore Street. The gaoler told me that I was Jane Wenham's first visitor. If she was surprised to see me, she did not show it. She sat in a low chair, the same shawl around her shoulders, her face and hands filthy again and a look of resignation on her face. I sat beside her on a narrow straw cot.

'Grandmother, it's Emily,' I tried. 'I came by coach from Ardeley.'

She squinted at me but said nothing. I tried again. 'Have you enough food? Here's some bread.' I gave her a loaf which she put on the floor. 'If there's anything else you need, I could bring it for you.' She shook her head. 'Have you heard the news?'

She looked up sharply. 'What news?' It was more of a croak than a voice.

'Sir John Powell, the judge, is to ask the queen for a royal pardon for you.'

'Won't do no good. They want me dead.'

'I don't want you dead, nor does the judge.'

'Won't make no difference.'

'Of course it will. The queen will grant a pardon and you'll be free again.'

'Free? Free to do what? Starve? Might as well be hanged and be done with it.'

'I'll take care of you. Find you somewhere to live in peace. Bring you food.'

For perhaps ten minutes, she was silent. Then she said, 'You don't think I'm a witch then?'

'Of course I don't. There are no witches and there's no witchcraft. It's just nonsense.'

'Sometimes I wonder myself.'

'Do you?'

'I do. They said it so often, I began to believe it.'

'They said you were a whore, too. You didn't believe that, did you?'

'That was that bastard Bragge. He's a liar.'

We talked about the trial for a while, agreeing that all the witnesses were either liars or idiots, until she said she was tired. When I asked her if I could come again, she nodded.

I took the coach home. Although my parents knew where I had been, they still said nothing.

It was another three weeks before I was able to go again to Hertford. This time, my grandmother smiled when she saw me and thanked me for the cake I had baked for her.

'How are you being treated?' I asked her.

She laughed. 'It's better in here than outside. I've got a roof over me, a bed, enough food and no-one to stick pins in me or call me names.'

'That's good. Aren't you lonely, though?'

'I'm used to being on my own. I don't mind it.'

'There's no news of the pardon. There should be some soon.'

My grandmother's voice took on a new tone – not bitter, but determined. 'I want to tell you about my life. If they hang me, someone ought to know about it. There's no-one else. Won't take long.'

I was astonished. Until then she had said so little and that begrudgingly. Now she wanted to tell me about her life. 'I'll listen if you want to tell me.'

Including breaks for her to rest and for us to share the cake, it took about an hour. Where she was hard to understand, especially when she jumped from one time to another and back again and when her words became muddled, I have tried to make sense out of it. She spoke quietly, stopping often to catch her breath. I sat on her bed and listened.

'My mother told me I was born on the day King Charles lost his head, so that would make me sixty-three years old now. My name was Jane

Smith. I didn't know my father. My mother was a serving woman in Hertford. We lived in a room above the inn where she worked. When she brought a man to the room, I had to hide under the bed. Later, when I was older, I went downstairs until they were done. I helped out in the inn until my mother died. Then I came to Walkern. I was about eighteen. I hadn't more than a few pence and went looking for work. I tried the hatmakers and the brewers but they didn't want me. I tried the inn and the shopkeepers. Nor did they. No-one did. They said local people should have the work, not strangers. I don't think it was that. They didn't like me because I couldn't find the right words to say. My words came out wrong and I got confused. That made me angry and it got worse. Swearing and shouting and such like. I got no work.

'There was no help for the poor in Walkern so I took to begging. It was that or starve. I stole a bit too, when I had to, food and straw mostly. I slept where I could. Then I met your grandfather. Philip Cooke was his name. He let me sleep on his floor. After a bit, I moved upstairs and then I married him. That's when tongues started wagging. They said I must have used a spell to make him marry me. If I'd known how, perhaps I would have. He was a good man. He got me work in the brewery where he worked. Two babies were stillborn before your mother but things weren't too bad.

'Then he died. Sarah would have been about fifteen. It was something he ate. Could have been anything. Tongues wagged again. Said it was me that poisoned him. Why would I do that? I asked them. They said there was no telling what a witch might do. Cruel, it was. Lost my husband, lost my work in the brewery and called a witch. So I let them think I was a witch. Thought it might frighten them enough to give me money and food.

'The year after Phillip died, I married Edward Wenham and your mother moved to Ardeley. We'd never got on. She was a wilful child. Daresay I wasn't much of a mother, having never had much of one of my own. She didn't like Edward. Nor did I. He was a drunk, like his father and his brothers. They drank away the smithy and had to sell it. That's why he married me. He'd no money and nowhere to live after they lost the forge. He came to live in the cottage. I took him in because I thought things'd be easier with a husband. I was wrong. I still couldn't find work. He earned a few shillings here and there but he drank them away. Gave me nothing. I had to get food somehow, so I said he'd pay. When he found out, he had the town crier say that he wouldn't. I had to start begging again and I went to those meetings of the Dissenters. They gave me a little money. That's why I went. Didn't care what they were talking about.

'One day I asked Matthew Gilston for straw to sell to the hatmakers but he wouldn't give it me. I called him a filthy miser and a stinking bastard. He didn't like that. So when his cows died he blamed me. Called me a witch. A witch and a bitch, he said. I wanted to teach him a lesson, so I went to Chauncy. Thought I might get a guinea or two for the slander. Chauncy sent us to Gardiner. He only gave me a shilling. It wasn't enough. I was starving. I told them I'd have justice somehow. Then that bitch Anne Thorn started playing up, pretending I'd put a spell on her, and Gilston did the same.

'All of sudden everyone had a story. Gardiner joined in and so did Strutt. They said I'd poisoned Phillip, killed my own babies, put a spell on Edward and a lot else besides. It was a chance to be rid of me. I had not been born in their village and they didn't like the way I spoke nor when I had to beg and steal. They took me from my cottage and made me go in front of Chauncy. They searched me for marks and made me say the prayer. I never could say the bit about trespasses right. I got confused with the words. When they asked if I was a witch I told them I'd been one for years, just for the devilment. They believed it and Chauncy sent me to the Assizes. And now here I am. Waiting to be hanged for a witch.'

When she had finished I asked her if she thought Chauncy and Gardiner and the others really thought she was a witch or whether they were just lying to be rid of her. 'Some really think it. Gardiner and Strutt do. Gilston too. Bragge's a liar and so's the Thorn girl. Don't know about Chauncy. Doesn't matter now.'

The story had exhausted her. I left her to rest and took the coach back to Ardeley. I would not read any more pamphlets. I knew the truth of the matter.

Waiting for news of Sir John Powell's attempt to obtain a royal pardon was bad enough. Having no-one with whom to share the waiting made it worse. My parents would still not talk about the case and it was no good expecting anyone else in the village to do so. I thought of going to see the Reverend Strutt again but quickly abandoned the idea. I even considered writing a letter to Sir John Powell. I never did though. I did not have the words for it.

I travelled twice more to Hertford during May and June. On both occasions I found my grandmother cheerful and pleased to see me. The roughness in her voice had disappeared and she stumbled over her words only now and then. Speaking calmly and clearly, she asked about my work and my friends and what schooling I had had. She remembered what I told her and smiled when I told her stories that I thought might amuse her. It was as if a great weight had been lifted from her, although whether that was due to her being resigned to her fate or having unburdened herself of her story to me, I do not know. She did not ask about a pardon or what people were saying about her and I am sure she did not care.

I had no idea how long it would take for Sir John Powell to apply to the queen for a pardon or what the queen herself thought about witchcraft. For all I knew, Queen Anne had been brought up to believe in witches and wizards and imps and familiars. She might agree with the verdict of the jury and send Sir John packing. Or she might not wish to interfere. The longer we waited for news, the less likely a pardon seemed, and by the end of June there had been no word.

Eventually, at the end of July the news arrived and was reported in newspapers all over the country. Sir John Powell had secured from the queen a royal pardon for Jane Wenham. There was another rush of pamphlets but I ignored them. I was relieved and happy but concerned about what would happen to my grandmother now. She could hardly go back to Walkern and she had no money and no means of getting any, except her old ways of begging and stealing. My mother would certainly not take her in and, as far as I knew, there was no-one else to turn to.

Happily, we soon learnt that Sir John had thought of this and had arranged for my grandmother to live in a cottage on the estate of his friend, Captain John Plummer. I think Sir John felt responsible for the outcome of the trial and wanted to make amends.

Over the next five years I made many visits to see her there. She was comfortable in her cottage, bothered by no-one and quite happy to sit and talk. Had she but known it, her case was still talked about, although the pamphlets did eventually stop. Anne Thorn and Ann

Street both married men who had testified against my grandmother. Sir Henry Chauncy admitted to having been much troubled by his part in the affair. His son Arthur, who had stuck pins in her arm, turned out to be a scoundrel and it was commonly agreed that most of the witnesses were liars. The others, especially the Reverends Strutt, Gardiner and Bragge, believed that Jane Wenham was a witch because they wanted to believe it.

When Captain Plummer died, my grandmother moved to another cottage, this one on the estate of the Lord Cowper. In the same year, I was married and moved to Cambridge. Then I could only visit her rarely. When she died, I travelled to Hertingfordbury for her funeral. Only the parson, the Lord Cowper and I were there.

THE BUTTON SELLER AND
THE DRUMMER BOY

1815

The Button Seller

The button seller's horse had gone lame just outside Waterloo and he had had the devil of a job finding a replacement – every charger, shire, Belgian draft pony and rundown old nag having been bought or appropriated by the regimental quartermasters. He was beginning to think that if he was to see the battle, he would have to walk.

He had left Brussels a week earlier and ridden to the town of Enghien where the First Infantry Division under Major General Sir George Cooke was garrisoned. There he had managed to take orders for pewter buttons from the Second Foot Guards and the Coldstream Guards and would have stayed longer in the hope of more business had the news of Napoleon's advance over the border at Charleroi not arrived by galloper in the early hours of Friday morning. By dawn the streets of Enghien were jammed with men and horses and carts and wagons hastening to block Napoleon's road to Brussels. There would be no more business to be done in Enghien, so he had joined the throng of camp followers and artisans and ridden with them as far as the little town of Waterloo.

It had occurred to him to ride back to Brussels and from there to Antwerp or Ostend to find a passage home, but something – the fear of being thought cowardly perhaps – had made him stay. A civilian he might be, but he was also a proud Englishman, who would not take kindly to being accused of fleeing in the face of the French. In any case, Napoleon had already been defeated once and would certainly be defeated again. And the button seller wanted to be there to see it.

At the village of Braine-le-Comte his resolve had been tested by a procession of miserable, battered, wounded men heading north, some using their muskets as crutches, others leaning on the shoulders of comrades. Arms and legs and heads were swathed in blood-soaked rags. Few had the strength to speak other than to beg for water. It was the first time the button seller had seen for himself the terrible consequences of battle.

He had dismounted and sat at the side of the road for a while beside a private wearing the badge of the Third Infantry Division. The young man had taken a sword cut to his shoulder. The wound had been roughly bound with a blood-soaked shirt and the button seller doubted he would last the day. From the private he learnt that the troops now retreating northwards had met the French at a crossroads known as Quatre Bras, from where, having suffered heavy casualties and spent a miserable cold, wet night with little to eat, they had been ordered to retreat. The button seller gave the wounded man the bread and cheese he had intended for his own lunch and wished him luck.

In the town that evening the stories became more alarming with every telling. In the foul inn in which he spent an uncomfortable night on a narrow straw cot – beds, like horses, being in short supply – he heard that to the east Napoleon had routed old Blucher's Germans, that Marshall Né, the one they called the 'bravest of the brave', having won a decisive victory at Quatre Bras, was now marching north with his invincible Imperial Guard, that Wellington's army was hopelessly inexperienced and outnumbered and that the French would be in Brussels within a day. The button seller began to think that he might have made a mistake in travelling south.

The reputation of the Imperial Guard preceded them. Napoleon's habit of allowing them free rein after a victory had led to rape and plunder on a monstrous scale. Ask any Hanoverian or Brunswicker what he thought of the French Imperial Guard and he would spit and curse and call them defilers of wives and daughters and murderers of innocent civilians and vow revenge for what they had done. If Wellington could not halt the French, the women of Waterloo and of all the towns on the road to Brussels would be at their mercy.

But, unlike Napoleon, the Iron Duke had never been defeated in battle, would have chosen his ground well and would have devised a plan to halt the oncoming French and send them scurrying, cowed and beaten, back to Paris. The button seller, despite what he had seen and heard, put aside his doubts.

He did not much relish the thought of walking on a morning already sweltering after the thunderstorms of the day before, so it was with relief that he at last found a stable with a single horse remaining and an owner willing to sell it. The sale was quickly agreed at about twice the usual rate; he loaded his bags, mounted, and set off.

The horse was a stout cob, more accustomed to pulling carts than carrying men, and it plodded along not much more quickly than the procession of local townsfolk that snaked southwards along the road. Some of them pushed carts laden with barrels of ale and cuts of meat and huge round cheeses, others carried wicker baskets on their arms. Whether the baskets were also laden or were to carry souvenirs after the battle, he could not tell, but he supposed that after any battle there would be plunder aplenty, including silver and gold buttons taken from the uniforms of fallen officers. He tried not to think of that. His job was simply to sell the buttons, not to worry himself about what happened to them.

Passing small groups of women and children heading north – no doubt ordered to leave their husbands and fathers and return to the town – the button seller made his way slowly down the road, wondering, as every other man and woman must have been wondering, what that day would bring.

The firm of Blinks and Blinks, established in the thriving jewellery quarter of the city of Birmingham, had been manufacturing and supplying buttons of excellent quality to military and naval officers and to the tailors who made their uniforms, for many years. The war in Spain and Admiral Nelson's campaigns at sea had been undeniably good for business and the partners, two brothers, were keen further to enrich themselves by taking advantage of the unexpected opportunity presented by Napoleon's escape from exile on Elba and his subsequent march to Paris, building his strength as he went. It was not that they had wished for this to happen, merely that it had done so and no businessman worth the name would ignore it. Belgium was awash with British officers who would not countenance a missing button on their uniform or that of a soldier under their command. Every colonel set great store by the appearance of his regiment. A ready supply of replacement buttons, obtainable from the regimental store, was essential if proper standards were to be maintained.

Blinks and Blinks manufactured buttons in pewter and brass plate and, for officers, in silver and gold plate. Every button was made with a wire shank to facilitate its hanging correctly and carried the insignia of the wearer's regiment. The button seller's own favourite was not military but the crown and anchor on the gold-plated button of a naval captain. He sometimes wondered what life would have brought him had he followed the advice of his father and joined the navy. He had not done so because he could not see himself as a fighting man.

The profit to be had from a single set of buttons was not great. There were other manufacturers and competition for the best customers was strong. He had been despatched to London and thence to Brussels with clear instructions from the brothers Blinks. 'Make yourself known to the quartermasters and officers, speak to their adjutants, speak to anyone in authority. Many regiments are already our customers, some are not. Acquire them if you can. Reduce prices if you must, but do not let a competitor steal a customer from us.' The brothers would not be happy to learn, for example, that an order from the First Foot Guards had gone elsewhere. The uniform of an officer in that regiment was incomplete without twelve large gold-plated buttons.

From Brussels he had been able to send back to Birmingham orders not only for the Guards regiments but also for the Light Dragoons, the Grenadiers, the King's Own German Legion and smaller orders for other regiments. His book of illustrations and the samples he carried had made his task easier but he felt nevertheless that he had done well and hoped for suitable recognition when he returned. Although you never knew with the Blinks. They might be pleased or they might look down their noses at the orders and demand to know why they were not larger. He supposed that was the way of successful businessmen.

His samples – one for each officer and each private in every British regiment, over fifty in all – he guarded closely. His wife had carefully sewn each one through its shank on to a roll of soft calfskin spaced so that, when it was rolled up, no button touched another. He polished the buttons once every week and more often if needs be. He knew every regimental insignia – and of every naval rank, although he had not brought his naval samples with him on this trip – and could converse knowledgably about the history and honours of each regiment. The gold-plated buttons of an officer of the 19th Regiment of Light Dragoons, for example, were decorated with an elephant and the word 'Assaye', while an officer of the 6th Regiment of Foot now wore silver-plated buttons, decorated with an antelope, the regiment's insignia having been changed a year earlier. And he knew that the way to tell a Third Foot Guard from a Coldstream was by the pattern of buttons on his tunic. There was very little the button seller from Blinks and Blinks did not know about military and naval insignia, most particularly the buttons. It was his job to do so.

Although he was used to travelling, it was the first time that he had set foot outside England or Wales. His predecessor had travelled in Scotland and Ireland but, as yet, he had not. He had crossed the Channel with mixed feelings. It was a feather in his cap to have been entrusted with the task and he looked forward to seeing a new country, learning its ways, sampling its food and wine and seeing its sights, but he was heading towards the threat of gunfire and had little idea of how long he would be away. Most of all, he had left behind his wife and infant daughter.

They had been married five years earlier when they were both in their twenty-first year, he a junior clerk in the factory of Blinks and Blinks, she a seamstress. Their daughter had been born two years later. It had been his wife who had urged him to apply for the position of salesman when the elderly incumbent could no longer manage, and had given him the confidence to do so. Without her he would have remained a clerk. 'If you do not take the opportunity when it presents itself,' she said, 'it might never come again. If you put your mind to it, you will be good at it and who knows where it might lead.'

Thus encouraged, he had presented his application to the partners, although deep down he did not expect it to be successful. But she had coached him well and when the time came he so impressed them with his knowledge of the economics of the manufacturing process and of the requirements of their customers, that they offered him a trial period in the position. Within two years, he had doubled the business of his predecessor.

Yet despite this, he lacked the ebullient self-confidence of many successful salesmen. He succeeded through diligence and perseverance, never made a promise he could not keep and never let a customer down. Others might blow their trumpets and bang their drums, but his was a quiet way, efficient and, he liked to think, business-like.

It was a way that reflected both his character and his appearance. At only five and a half feet tall, narrow in the shoulder, bespectacled, his hair already receding, he knew that he could never cut a dashing figure. Nor did he seek to. When on business he wore a tall hat, a black tail coat and a white stock. It had not occurred to him until he had seen him in Brussels that it was much the same manner of dress as that favoured by the Duke of Wellington himself. He had made a mental note to ask his wife's opinion on the adoption of a different style. He would not want to be accused of copying the duke, nor would he relish being teased for doing so.

A little north of the hamlet of Mont St Jean, the sights and sounds of an army preparing for battle reached him. At first, smoke from camp fires spiralling into the sky, the crash of iron upon iron and the deep thunder of hooves as the cavalry regiments took up their positions; then, as he approached, voices raised in command or complaint and the squelching of boots on ground still wet from the unseasonal rain.

Soon the road was a mass of troops and their paraphernalia converging on a crossroads from west and east as well as from the north. Carefully, fearful of getting in the way, the button seller dismounted and led his cob to the side of the road, away from the wagons and artillery pieces that were still hurrying south, and picked his way along a narrow strip of grass between the road and the mud of the fields to his left.

He reached a farm which was being prepared as a hospital. A line of ambulances waited in the farmyard while medics bustled about with bundles of linen, heaps of bandages and wooden stretchers. Among the medics were a number of women – wives and daughters and locals with their strange dog-eared caps, pressed into service. From there he caught his first sight of the allied lines. Stretched out along a ridge, partly protected by its slope, was Wellington's army. He halted the cob and checked his pocket watch. It was ten o'clock.

As he came closer, he was able to make out some of the uniforms.

To his left, the plumed helmets and red tunics of Inniskilling Dragoons, to his right the bearskins and blue jackets of the Royal Horse Artillery. Before long he had picked out Hussars, Grenadiers and the green-jacketed Riflemen.

When he reached a second crossroads, he remounted. Below the high ridge on which he stood, the French army had taken up its positions. Its front line was perhaps half a mile away. To east and west, line after line of blue waited for the order to advance. Before them lay undulating fields, rising sharply nearest the ridge. Even to his unmilitary eye, the duke had chosen his ground well. To gain the road north to Brussels, the French would have to march down into the floor of the valley before climbing up to the ridge, and they would be bombarded by cannon every step of the way. At least that was how it looked to him.

An ancient elm tree stood at the crossroads. Its canopy offered a little shelter from the sun and an excellent view of what would be the battlefield. Mounted on the little cob, he chose it as his vantage point. To left and right Wellington's army were getting ready for battle. Camp fires were doused, artillery crews heaved their pieces into position, Horse Guards and Hussars struggled to keep their mounts steady, infantrymen checked their weapons and stood in lines abreast ready to fire down upon the advancing waves of blue. At the first threat of attack by cavalry they would form squares to present bristling lines of bayonets from which cavalry horses would shy away. He had never seen the manoeuvre carried out but he had heard it described by a cousin who had fought with Wellington in Spain. When properly formed the squares were a certain defence against cavalry but an easy target for artillery. The cousin had spoken of the terror of standing in square while the men around you were ripped to pieces by artillery shells. But it had to be done. If the square broke, the cavalry would be amongst them in a trice. Shell or sabre – take your pick.

The button seller let his eye wander over the lines. This was not an army fresh from the parade ground. Boots were splattered with mud, uniforms torn and bloodstained. After the bloody engagement at Quatre Bras there would have been no opportunity for mending or cleaning. Nor would there have been much for sleeping or eating. He could hope only that the French had fared no better.

From his right a party of riders trotted towards him along the ridge. One he recognised instantly as the duke, in white breeches, white stock, dark blue coat and cloak and cocked hat, and mounted on his favourite chestnut, Copenhagen. Behind the duke rode ten others – eight officers, his aides, and two others in civilian dress, one of whom could not have been more than fifteen years old and carried his arm in a sling. As the party came closer, he could see that the duke had a writing slope attached to his saddle. Was it this, he wondered, upon which the man who commanded the entire army would write orders that might bring victory or – he hardly dared think the word – defeat? The party rode passed him without a glance, crossed the Brussels road and proceeded on down the lane on the other side.

The button seller looked again at his pocket watch. It was fifteen minutes before eleven o'clock. Suddenly, a cheer went up along the lines. He looked about but could see no reason for it. He nudged the cob with his knees and trotted along the ridge to the nearest troop. 'May I know what has occasioned the cheer, sir?' he asked a young lieutenant.

The lieutenant grinned. 'You may, sir. A galloper has arrived. Old Blucher and his Prussians will be here by midday.' So the Prussians had not been entirely routed by Napoleon and their arrival would surely ensure victory. The button seller sighed with relief.

He thanked the lieutenant and turned to resume his vantage point under the elm. But the vantage point was no longer his. The duke and his party had returned from their inspection and had stationed themselves exactly where he had sat not five minutes earlier. He smiled. Better the commander-in-chief and his aides than an unarmed civilian should have the best seats in the house. He would have to find another spot. Seeking cover behind the lines or returning to the safety of the farmhouse they had passed did not occur to him. He had come this far and he was going to observe the battle for himself. And if the Prussians were close, victory would surely be theirs.

The first shells exploded away to the right, from somewhere near a farm partly hidden from view by woods and about mid-way between the French and the allied lines. The roar of the guns ripped through the valley and along the ridge, soon followed by plumes of smoke rising into the morning sky and the whiff of gunpowder borne on a fluke of wind. The battle had started.

The French cannon were answered by the allied artillery – crash after crash of heavy shells smashing into the wood, uprooting trees and sending up great sprays of earth. In no time, the button seller's head was throbbing. He held his hands to his ears and marvelled at the stoicism of the men along the ridge, quietly awaiting their turn to be targets for the French gunners.

They had a long wait. It was at least an hour before the French gunners turned their attention to the centre of the allied lines and the first shells began to fall amongst them. Half-deafened, the button seller instinctively ducked when a volley landed nearby. The terrified cob did its best to unseat him but he held on with hands and knees and managed to calm it. He had found a place on the other side of the crossroads from the elm tree, where the duke and his entourage were still watching through telescopes. His view was not quite as good as it had been from under the elm but it was good enough. He could see the battle raging at the farm away to his right and, when it was not wholly obscured by smoke, almost all the battlefield. Beyond it, the lines of blue still stood awaiting the order to advance.

Twenty yards away a French shell exploded against an allied cannon. The cannon disintegrated in a storm of metal shards which scythed through its crew and left heads and limbs detached from bodies and strewn across the mud. He was close enough to feel the air move and the heat of the explosion. His stomach heaved and voided itself of his half-digested breakfast.

To his right, back from the ridge, artillery crews scrambled to load and fire their guns, slipping about in the mud and struggling to keep their feet. Behind them, cavalry horses, terrified by the noise, bucked and shrieked and tried to unseat their riders. In front, infantrymen lay flat on the ground, allowing the shells to scream over their heads. Everywhere the wounded lay unattended among the dead. In his bag he carried a small flask of brandy. He pulled it out and swallowed a mouthful.

Very soon the air was filled with smoke and the stench of gunpowder and he could see little. He edged closer to the elm tree, hoping that he would see more from there. The duke and six of his party were still there, telescopes to their eyes, looking over the valley towards the French lines. They appeared unmoved by the shells exploding around them.

As if sensing the presence of a stranger, the duke lowered his telescope and turned his head towards the button seller. 'You, sir,' he called out, using the telescope as a pointer, 'I do not know who you are, but you are in grave danger.'

The button seller touched his hat. 'No more so than your Grace.' The duke nodded and returned his gaze to the French lines.

The bombardment went on and on. Heavy balls of iron crashed into the allied ranks, severing limbs and slicing bodies in two. Through fleeting gaps in the smoke, he watched the carnage, horrified and unable to move or to think clearly.

And then, at last, it stopped and a strange silence descended upon the field. But not for long. From down in the valley came the sound of drums beating out the rhythm of the charge, at first far off, but soon close and getting closer. The drums were joined by voices raised in the joy of battle. The French were singing. The button seller's skin crawled and he had to force himself to raise his head to look. When he did, he saw line after line, column after column of blue jackets advancing through the valley and up the slope. In the allied lines, barely a man moved or spoke, but waited silently, muskets at the ready for the order to fire.

When the order came, the leading French troops were almost at the base of the slope up to the ridge. The British infantry rose from their crouched positions and sent a volley of musket balls crashing into them. The French fell in a mass of screaming, writhing bodies. There was a second volley and a third, each of them cutting bloody swathes through the blue columns.

The button seller closed his eyes and mouthed a prayer. What in the name of God had induced him to come here? Why had he not returned to Brussels? Even the Blinks brothers could hardly complain if he had chosen to go home when the French crossed the Sambre. Buttons would be the very last thing on any soldier's mind; there would be no more orders and he might as well take ship for England. At that moment, had he been asked why he was mounted on an elderly cob on the ridge at Mont St Jean while all around him was bloodshed and death, he would not have been able to offer a single reason. Yet here he was.

He glanced over to the elm tree. There was no-one under it. Wellington and his aides must have ridden off to take stock of the battle from some other vantage point. It crossed his mind – fleetingly – that he might do the same, but he decided to stay where he was. If he rode along the ridge, he would only get in the way.

The French guns had fallen silent for fear of their shots landing short and killing their own men, but the allied artillery were still pounding away, sending their eight- and ten-pound balls into the thick of the French infantry and beyond them to where their cavalry waited.

Then the allied guns also went quiet, the smoke cleared and, on both sides of the road, the cavalry charged over the crest of the ridge and straight at the French infantry. The button seller watched in awe as they galloped headlong into the enemy ranks, sabres slicing and thrusting into defenceless flesh.

Not a Frenchman, he thought, would have been left alive had their cavalry not galloped up to join the fray. Then it became a battle of sabre against lance and lance against pistol. Infantrymen used their muskets as clubs, cavalrymen crushed wounded bodies under the hooves of their horses. Away to the right, the farmhouse was burning, straight ahead another farm was being attacked by French cavalry. It was quite impossible to detect any pattern or to judge which side, if any, had the advantage. The button seller, scarcely able to comprehend the slaughter, simply sat, motionless, and watched.

Three or four times, the French riders turned back towards their own artillery lines, only to regroup and charge again up the slope. For perhaps two hours this went on, the number of dead and wounded mounting with each charge. By mid-afternoon, the ridge and the valley were strewn with the bodies of men and horses. When the French cavalry came too close, the British infantry formed their squares and waited for them to lose patience and go away. From near the elm tree, the button seller saw it all.

Each time he saw the duke, he was accompanied by fewer aides. And when he next appeared from the direction of the burning farmhouse, he was alone. He halted his chestnut under the tree and peered down into the melee below, then looked about as if surprised that he had not a single aide with him. Catching sight of the button seller, he beckoned him closer. 'You, sir,' he shouted above the roar of the battle, 'who are you?'

The button seller took a calling card from his pocket and handed it to the duke, who peered at it. 'Blinks and Blinks, eh? Well, I fear there's no order for you today, but do you see that man down there?' The button seller followed the direction of the duke's arm to where, about two hundred yards away, a troop of cavalry stood in line, ready to receive an enemy charge. Their commander, easily identifiable by his uniform and bearing, stood at their front. 'That is Marshal Kempt, Commander of the British 8th Brigade. Would you be so good as to ride down there and tell him to refuse his right?' The button seller looked again. A troop of French cavalry, hidden from the British by a fold in the land, were approaching Marshal Kempt's line from his right. If the brigade did not turn to face them, they would be taken by surprise and cut to pieces.

If the button seller was surprised he did not show it. 'Certainly, your Grace,' he replied without a moment's pause, and set off on the little cob down the slope into the valley across which the battle was raging.

The cob was nimble enough and managed to pick its way through and around bodies and debris while musket fire whistled about over their heads. They were no more than ten yards from the line of cavalry when the cob fell, blood pouring from its flank. The button seller was thrown off, landed on grass and picked himself up. Other than a bruise on his shoulder he fancied himself unhurt. Unarmed and unable to put the cob out of its misery, he half-ran, half-stumbled to the cavalry line. The cavalrymen were too intent on their business to pay him heed and he reached Marshal Kempt without being impeded.

He explained his business and delivered the duke's message. The marshal peered at him and asked him to repeat what he had said. He did so. The marshal glanced back up to the ridge to where Wellington sat, tipped his hat, thanked the messenger, and immediately passed on an order to an aide.

His task completed, the button seller ran back to the dying cob, retrieved his leather roll of samples and flask of brandy and set off to climb back up the slope. He had gone only a few paces when he felt a tug at his trousers. Startled, he looked down. A soldier lying face up had reached out and grabbed him as he passed. The fallen man had lost an eye and his tunic was so ripped and splattered with blood and mud that the button seller could not identify it. He dripped a few drops of brandy on to the wretch's lips and went on.

His legs were heavy and his mind numb from the unceasing noise. Several times he slipped and fell but each time he managed to get back to his feet, the thought of a French sabre at his neck driving him on.

Holding tight to the samples, he bent forwards against the incline and kept his head low. Behind him were the enemy, whose cavalry might at any moment launch another attack, and in front British sharpshooters who could not know that the man in the black coat scrambling up towards them was there on the orders of the Duke of Wellington. For all they knew, he was a up to some French trickery and should be shot.

With a grunt of relief he reached the top unscathed and with his samples intact, intending to report to the duke that he had carried out his task successfully. But the vantage point under the elm tree was deserted. No duke and no aides. And, now, no cob. Just what he stood up in, his flask and his leather roll. Still, other than a bruised shoulder, he was intact. He tucked the flask and the sample roll under his shirt and made his way around behind the lines, not knowing where he was going or with what purpose, but knowing that he was no longer merely a spectator.

The Drummer Boy

The boy would never forget the day that the news reached Paris. As it usually was in the evenings, his father's inn near the Porte St Denis was crowded with noisy drinkers, many of them old comrades in the emperor's army who like nothing better than to share a bottle or two of wine and talk about victories they had shared in his service.

As long as he was not needed to wipe tables or collect glasses and carry them out to be washed by his mother, the boy liked to sit quietly in a corner and listen to the old soldiers telling their stories. He heard them speak of great victories in Bavaria and Spain and Austria and in a place called Borodino. At times they argued – perhaps about who had done what – but they never spoke of defeats. One day he plucked up the courage to ask his father if the emperor's army had ever been defeated. 'Never!' his father had replied, thumping his fist on a table. 'The emperor's army has never been defeated. We suffered setbacks, as all armies do, but never defeat. And do not let any man tell you otherwise.' The boy did not ask why then the emperor lived not in Paris but on a small island in the Mediterranean Sea. There would be a good reason, and he did not want to upset his father by asking what it was.

He was wiping tables when the inn door was thrown open and a man he knew by sight but not by name burst in. 'Napoleon has escaped!' he bellowed. 'The emperor has returned to us!'

Immediately, every man in the inn was on his feet, waving a glass or a bottle in the air and shouting '*Vive l'Empereur!*' at the top of his voice. Bottles rattled on the tables, a glass or two was knocked off and broken. No-one bothered to sweep up the glass.

When the noise eventually died down, the bringer of the news was given a glass of wine and told to report everything he knew. The inn went quiet while the messenger collected himself, squaring his shoulders, clearing his throat and evidently enjoying the attention of his audience. He drained his glass and held it out to be refilled. Then he began.

'Gallopers arrived this afternoon from Orléans. The emperor landed near the town of Cannes on the first day of this month, with a thousand loyal men. Already they have been joined by the fifth and seventh infantry regiments. Men are flocking to his service. He will be in Paris within the week!' At this, the inn erupted. Bearded old men hugged each other, the fat butcher from next door grabbed a serving girl and insisted she dance with him, and the apothecary climbed on to a table and tried to sing. His voice was not strong enough to be heard over the din and soon he gave up.

The news was certainly good for business, or it would have been if his father had collected payment for every bottle drunk. By midnight, however, he was too drunk to care and was sloshing wine into glasses without bothering to ask for money. Every few minutes one or other of the drinkers would raise his glass and shout '*Vive l'Empereur*' or '*Vive la France*' and call for more wine.

In his bedroom above the inn, the boy lay awake listening to the celebrations until dawn. He was not sure what the news meant but he was too excited to sleep.

Despite the quantity of wine he had drunk, his father was still in high spirits the next morning. Together they set about clearing up the mess and getting the inn ready for another day, while his mother washed glasses and counted the money they had taken. 'They drank a lot but paid little,' she complained, gathering up coins into a canvas bag. 'At this rate we will soon be penniless.'

'Nonsense,' replied the innkeeper. 'The emperor is returned to us. Mark my words, glory and prosperity lie ahead.'

Almost every day for the next two weeks more news arrived. Napoleon's army was growing apace, King Louis and the royal family had left Paris and fled to England, Marshal Né, the one known as 'the bravest of the brave', had joined the emperor with six thousand veterans of the invincible Imperial Guard. Flag-waving supporters thronged the streets of every town, officials read out declarations of loyalty in the squares and markets. Very soon France would be at war again.

On the evening of the day that Napoleon finally arrived at the city gates, the boy heard his parents arguing. 'You cannot join the army,' shrieked his mother, in a voice he had never heard before. 'How will we cope without you? I cannot look after the inn and our son alone.'

'The boy will come with me. I will leave the inn in your care.'

'Come with you? For the love of God, he is only twelve years old. How will he defend himself against the English? With his sling-shot? Every son of France knows that the scum of England are cruel and merciless. They will carve him up and roast him over their fires.'

The innkeeper laughed. 'That I doubt. And he will carry no weapon. We march to the sound of the drums. He will be a boy drummer. There will be many others like him.'

'It is monstrous,' wailed his mother, 'Twelve-year-old boys should be at their lessons, not on a battlefield. What if he is killed? How will I bear the loss?'

'By knowing that your son died gloriously fighting for France, that is how. Now let there be no more talk of this. Tomorrow I will take him to a recruiting station and we will join the emperor's army.'

The boy heard all of this and was happy that his father had prevailed in the argument. He did not want to stay at home and wipe tables. He wanted to go with his father and join the emperor's army. He too wanted victories and glory.

The queue outside St Agnes's Church, which was being used as a recruiting station, stretched down the street and around the corner. The boy and his father joined the end of it and for three hours shuffled slowly forward until at last they reached the church doors.

The innkeeper had taken his old uniform from the chest in which it had lain for nearly five years, brushed it down and proudly put it on. The jacket bulged a little over his stomach but otherwise it still fitted well enough. It was the uniform of the infantry regiment in which he had chased the British through the mountains of northern Spain to Corunna and routed the Spanish at Medellin. The recruiting sergeant recognised the uniform and shook the innkeeper by the hand. 'An old soldier, I see,' he said. 'And a brave one.' He looked at the boy. 'Is this your son?'

'It is, sir. He wishes to serve as a drummer.'

The sergeant beamed. 'Then he shall do so.' He made a note of their names and told them to be at the training depot set up outside the Porte de la Chapelle at seven o'clock the next morning. '*Bonne chance et vive la France.*'

'*Vive l'Empereur.*' The boy and his father had replied as one.

That evening the family did not open the inn but dined together on a chicken roasted with carrots and garlic, fresh bread baked by the boy's mother, and an apple tart made with last year's crop. They spoke little and later the boy heard his mother sobbing before he went to sleep.

The depot outside the Porte de la Chapelle consisted of rows and rows of tents, lines of wagons loaded with weapons and equipment and dozens of harassed officers trying to bring order to the chaos.

Once again the boy and his father joined a queue and waited to collect their uniform, musket, ammunition and rations. The innkeeper did not expect to be issued with a new uniform, his own being perfectly serviceable, but when they reached the front of the queue, the sergeant looked him up and down and told him that he and his son would be in the Light Regiment of the 1st Brigade of the 6th Division, to be commanded by General Prince Jerome, the emperor's brother, and that the emperor wished every man in his army to have a new uniform whether or not he had served before.

Equipped with their uniforms, cross belts, shakos and haversacks, they were sent to the armoury where the innkeeper was issued with a musket, powder, and sixty rounds of ammunition in a wooden cartridge box. The boy was given a drum with a leather strap to go over his shoulder and two drumsticks. They were told to find a tent in which to sleep and to parade at three o'clock that afternoon for training.

The boy had been too overawed to say anything in the day, but when they found a tent, he put on his new uniform, slipped the drum strap over his shoulder and marched round and round the tent beating out a rhythm until his father told him to stop. 'There will be time enough for that,' he said. 'Now we will eat and rest.'

Over the next two weeks, the boy found that in the army much time was spent eating and resting. Between practices with the other drummers there was little to do but snooze in the tent he shared with his father or sit by the fire they lit outside it. While he practised beating out different marching rhythms his father practised carrying out orders to form columns and squares, to march in time and to load and fire his new musket. The boy was beginning to wonder if he had joined an army that would be trained to perfection but would never fight, when the order came one morning to strike camp and prepare to march. The camp stirred itself, the tents were dismantled and put on wagons, the men collected their marching rations and checked that their equipment was in order, and soon, to the sound of drums and trumpets, they were on their way.

Drummers and trumpeters were placed in the centre of each block of marching men, where they would have some protection from enemy fire and their drums and trumpets could be clearly heard from front to rear of the lines. Head high, shoulders back and unable not to grin with pride, the boy stepped out on his way to war. Somewhere in the ranks around him, his father did the same. What finer thing, the innkeeper thought as they set off, than for a soldier of France to march to battle with his son? He had thought that his military days were over yet here they both were in the emperor's Armée du Nord and destined for victory and glory in his service.

For two more weeks they marched through villages and towns, by rivers and woods, cheered by the crowds lining the roads, and were joined as each day passed by more troops and horses and artillery, until the army that had set off from Paris had doubled in size. They pitched their tents each evening, ate whatever rations they had and helped themselves to whatever they could find in the farms and villages along the way. The emperor, the boy was told, expected his soldiers to live off the land. His task was usually to find fresh water from a well or a stream and to carry it in buckets back to the camp. Now and again he was sent in search of food from a nearby farm and came back with a chicken or two or some eggs. He was quick and nimble and was shouted at by angry farmers but never caught.

As they travelled north, rumours reached them of a huge army led by the British gathering in the towns of Belgium and preparing for war. His father told him to ignore everything he heard because rumours were just rumours, they could not know for certain what the strength of their enemies was and in any event they would find out soon enough. With each day, the boy's legs grew stronger from marching and the weight of his drum lessened as he became used to it.

When they reached the river Sambre, which marked the border between France and Belgium, they pitched camp. Across the river stood the small town of Charleroi. The boy's father told him to be ready for a long wait because crossing the river would be an act of war which the emperor would not want to carry out until all his forces were assembled and he could be certain of victory.

The boy and his new friends among the drummers spent the days fishing in the river and trapping rabbits in the fields. They stole from the farmers and from the kitchens of local cottages. It was what the emperor expected his soldiers to do. In the evenings they sat with the soldiers smoking their pipes around their fires and listened to their stories.

On a hot summer's day in the middle of June, his soldiers, many for the first time, saw the emperor in person. Mounted on a fine grey mare, the man who had been appointed a general at the age of twenty-four and had led his army to victory after victory, rode into the camp. Word of his arrival sped through the rows of tents and every man hurried to catch a glimpse of him. The boy's father hoisted him on to his shoulders so that he could see over the heads of the men in front. The emperor, his bicorne hat worn side-to-side as was his custom, in a blue jacket and white trousers, waved to his men as they raised their hats and cheered. No wonder Napoleon was confident of victory, thought the boy, with such devotion from his army. He waved and cheered as loudly as he could without falling from his vantage point.

The order soon came to assemble in marching order. The boy took up his place like the other drummers in the centre of the columns of infantry and prepared to beat out the march. Three lines abreast, they crossed a narrow bridge over the river and entered Charleroi. As they did so, another huge cheer went up. They were at war.

Ahead of the infantry, a regiment of green-jacketed lancers had galloped over the bridge and into the town. The boy saw them go and felt a flash of pity for any man who stood in the way of the needle-points of their lances. He had seen them training in the fields outside the camp and knew how easily a lancer at full tilt could thrust the point into a leather bag of straw, use his wrist to twist it so that straw flew out of the bag, and ride on, barely checking his pace. An enemy's stomach would be no more difficult a target than a bag of straw. It did not occur to him that the enemy might have cavalrymen and weapons just as fearsome.

From the other side of the river, they had waited and listened to the sound of gunfire. It did not last long and by the time their regiment entered the town, its defenders had been routed. They halted only long enough to take whatever they could find from the shops and houses in the town and were soon on their way again, marching north on the road to Brussels, their enemies fleeing before them. Soldiering was just as the boy had imagined it would be.

But the enemy had not been entirely routed and soon the thunder of heavy cannon reached them and flat carts carrying the wounded trundled past them drawn by ponies and cobs back down the road towards Charleroi. The boy tried not to turn his head to look at the blood-soaked heads and stumps of arms and legs but he could not avoid hearing the cries of the suffering.

That night the rain came and it was all they could do to keep their guns and powder dry. They had only their meagre rations to eat, there being no farms or villages nearby, and for the first time the boy missed home. It was cold in their sodden tent and he found himself thinking of his bed and his mother's cooking and wondering if he and his father would see Paris again.

'Tomorrow,' said his father, 'we will fight. Be ready.'

His father was right. They marched at dawn, solid columns of infantry, flanked by curaissers and lancers, the artillery at their rear.

All that day the battle raged in the fields and hills and woods through which ran the road. The boys were put to helping the wounded where they could and scavenging from the bodies, both friend and foe, which lay everywhere. British bullets could not be used in French muskets but enemy powder and rations were as good as their own. The boys went from body to body, taking what they could find and carrying it to the wagons while shells whistled over their heads and smashed into the woods on either side. Without having to be told, they knew that the fighting ahead was fierce.

When darkness fell, they found themselves bivouacing in much the same place as they had pitched their tents on the night before. Having fought all day, the boy's father was exhausted. He lay down under the branches of an elm and went to sleep with his pack as a pillow and his coat as a blanket. Relieved that his father was unhurt, the boy lay beside him.

All that night it rained and by morning the emperor's army was cold and sodden. The boy watched his father heave himself to his feet and try to stretch the stiffness from his legs. They drank rainwater caught in a cooking pot and ate hard biscuit taken from the pack of a dead Netherlander. All around them, men were doing the same. 'Today we will crush the British and their allies and march on Brussels,' said the innkeeper, wiping his mouth with his sleeve. 'Today we will prevail for the emperor.' The boy grinned. 'He has marched east to destroy the Prussians, leaving us under the command of Marshal Né, the finest of his generals. We will join forces again today or tomorrow and together send the British scurrying back to their miserable little island.'

By noon, it seemed certain that his father was right. They had advanced as far as a village named Quatre Bras, for the four arms of its crossroads. From there the enemy had retreated without much of a fight and were still retreating, harassed by French cavalry and bombarded by French shells. All afternoon they marched on in their columns, the drummers and trumpeters encouraging them on, forcing the enemy back and back. And from the east came news that the emperor, true to his word, had routed the Prussians and was marching to join them.

In the evening they arrived at a low ridge which stretched from east to west. Before them was a shallow valley, rising to a higher ridge well within cannon range. Along that ridge the enemy had halted their retreat and were waiting for them. The emperor's army had already arrived from their victory over the Prussians and were encamped along the lower ridge. Tomorrow the final battle would be joined and the road to Brussels would lie open before them.

The boy was preparing food when the order came to move on. To their left, about halfway between the two lines, there was a wood, to one side of which they could make out walls and hedges, which suggested that a farm lay behind it. The Light Regiment of the 1st Brigade was to deploy to their left, taking up position on the south side of the wood. He put out the fire he had painstakingly made with twigs damp from the rain, collected his things together and joined the regiment making its way to the wood.

As they approached, they caught glimpses of the farm and of a chateau beside it and heard the voices of the men defending them. They heard also the sounds of timber being sawn and nails being hammered into wood. Finding what cover they could from the rain which had started again, they settled down for another wet night. There was no hope of lighting a fire so they dined once more on hard biscuit and a few morsels of cheese. The boy sat with his father and half-a-dozen comrades under a makeshift roof of coats draped over branches stuck into the soft ground. The men kept their cartridge pouches under their shirts and the barrels of their muskets pointing downwards to prevent water dripping into them. The boy held his drum against his chest, trying to protect its leather skin from the rain. The roof was better than nothing but only just.

All of the men gathered under the coats had fought before and all had something to say about what the next day would bring. One of them, a lieutenant named Legros, an enormous man – the tallest the boy had ever seen – was known as *L'Enfonceur*. It was he who had the most to say. 'Our enemies are a ramshackle lot, by all accounts,' he growled, between sips from a bottle of brandy. 'The dregs of English prisons, cowardly Dutchmen and dog-eating Brunswickers. We will smash our way through them as if they were sheep waiting to be slaughtered. As they will be.'

'And we outnumber them,' added another of the men. 'Blucher's Prussians have been routed so we won't be seeing them.'

The innkeeper patted his son on the shoulder. 'Tomorrow you will see the Imperial Guard for the first time and it will be a sight you will never forget. Even I, who saw them in action more than once in Spain, feel my hair stand on end when their drums beat out the march and their buglers sound the advance.' Under their dripping roof, there were grunts of agreement. 'It is no wonder that they have never been defeated in battle.'

'What will our task be?' asked the boy.

L'Enfonceur replied. 'Tomorrow is a Sunday. Our task will be to make sure that not one of the rats defending this wood and the farm beyond lives to say his prayers tomorrow or ever again. Our task will be to capture the farm and the chateau, kill every one of them, and open the way for Prince Jerome to attack the enemy's right flank. If we get the job done by noon, we will be enjoying Belgian beer and Belgian women tomorrow night.' He raised his bottle. 'To victory!'

'To victory!'

The boy was too cold and too excited to sleep. He lay awake under the coats, thinking of the victory tomorrow would bring and hoping that he would have a part to play in it. Drummer boys would hardly be needed in an attack on the farm or the chateau and he hoped he would be given more than scavenging to do.

It was dawn before the rain stopped. When it did, they gathered up their coats, checked their cartridges and fired their muskets to clear them of dirt and water. All along the south side of the wood, the men of Prince Jerome's Light Regiments were doing the same. The innkeeper put his arm around the boy's shoulders. 'It won't be long now. Are you ready?'

The boy nodded. 'I am ready, Father.'

But for an hour and then another they waited for the order to advance through the wood and launch their attack on the farm. Away to their right, lines of blue stretched as far as they could see and further back stood the artillery ready to bombard the enemy positions high on the ridge. 'The ground is sodden,' explained the innkeeper. 'It may be that the emperor is waiting for it to dry out a little for the cavalry. They cannot charge through mud.'

For the boy it was a long, long wait and he was beginning to despair of the order ever coming, when from behind them the artillery opened fire. Cannon thundered and shells screamed over their heads. They were soon followed by the artillery all along the lines and in no time the valley between the ridges was filled with the thunder and the smoke of the guns.

For the first time, the boy felt fear. His eyes stung from the smoke and his head throbbed from the noise. His father sensed it, and tried to reassure him. 'It will stop soon,' he shouted over the noise, 'and then we will advance. You will stay here with the other boys until you are told to move forward. It should not be long.'

The boy tried not to let his fear show. He looked his father in the eye and grinned. 'Good luck, Father.'

Abruptly, the guns went quiet, the order to advance came and the boy watched the Light Regiment, his father among them, disappear into the trees. For an hour he could do no more than listen to the crack of musket fire and hope that the English rats were being driven back to the farm. Wounded men – not many at first – were helped back out of the wood by comrades and left in the hands of medical orderlies.

Very soon, all across the valley between the two ridges, the battle was raging, making it impossible to tell what was happening in the wood and beyond. Then one of the men who had sat with them under the roof of coats stumbled out of the trees, one arm hanging limply at his side. The boy went to help him.

The soldier spoke in a hoarse whisper. 'The wood was full of Hanoverians and Nassauers. We cleared them out but there is an open gap between the trees and the walls of the farm. We were driven back when we tried to cross it and now they are trying to regain the wood.'

'My father. Did you see him?'

'I did not. It was so hard to see anything in the wood that we were afraid of shooting at our own men.' The boy left the soldier to wait his turn with the orderlies and went back to wait with the others.

But he found that he could not wait. He could not stand by while his father risked his life. He could not listen to the cries of the wounded and the crack of muskets and do nothing. He edged away from the group of drummer boys and slipped into the wood.

He moved cautiously from tree to tree, straining his eyes to see what lay ahead but unable to make out more than shapes and shadows. But as he grew accustomed to the gloom, he began to see a little more and to his left, protected by the thick trunks of a stand of elms, he saw the backs of a troop of infantry, firing at an enemy somewhere in front of them. One of the men he knew at once from his size was Lieutenant Legros. Beside him was his father. He crept forward until he was right behind them and tapped his father on the shoulder.

The innkeeper started and turned in surprise. 'God in heaven, boy, what are you doing? Did I not tell you to wait for the order to move forward?'

'I waited, Father, but the order did not come.'

Legros was ramming a ball into the barrel of his musket. He spoke without looking up. 'Nor will it until we clear this wood of vermin.' He raised the musket to his shoulder, took careful aim and fired. A man screamed. 'That's one rat less.'

A voice to their right shouted above the noise of the guns. 'General Bauduin has been hit. Our commander is dead.'

Legros swore. '*Merde*. He was a good man.' He turned and sat with his back to the tree.

'What do you think, Lieutenant?' asked the innkeeper. 'Shall we press on without him?'

Legros pushed himself to his feet. 'We shall.' He took a deep breath and bellowed. 'First Light, with me!'

'Go back,' said the innkeeper to the boy. 'You cannot stay here.'

Perhaps fifty men of the 1st Light Regiment appeared from behind trees and bushes and congregated around the lieutenant. He signalled for them to follow him forwards and a little to the left. Taking care not to be seen by his father, the boy followed them. One or two men went down, struck by enemy bullets, but the rest made it to the edge of the wood, where the ground opened up in front of the farm wall. Pursued by musket fire, the retreating rats scuttled across the clearing and through a gate into the farmyard.

Legros did not lead them into the open where they would be easy targets but under cover of the trees around to their left until they reached a narrow track running alongside the farm wall. They charged past a handful of men set to block the path, killing them all with musket and sabre, and followed it around to the rear of the farm. Still, unnoticed, the boy followed.

Outside the north wall they came to another clearing. Two high wooden gates, through which the last of a troop of British infantrymen were hurrying, were almost closed. From the walls on either side and from the roof of a building just inside the gates, riflemen opened fire on them. Ignoring the fire and the wounded, Legros ran forward, threw down his musket and picked up a long-handled axe that had been abandoned in the clearing. Just as the gates were closing he brought the axe down. The timber splintered, he put his shoulder to it and pushed. Ten men rushed to join him and gradually the gates opened under their weight. If they could get into the farm and open the gates on the south side, the farm and chateau would be theirs.

The boy crossed the clearing and stood in the lee of the wall. Perhaps sensing him, his father turned his head. For a moment, just a moment, he stared at his son. The boy grinned and mouthed 'push'.

The gates were open and the lieutenant led the men through them, brandishing his axe and forcing the enemy back into a small yard. It looked as if all of them would get into the farm but some of the defenders must have stood their ground because gradually the gates began to close again. The boy darted forward and squeezed through just before they slammed shut. The British were too intent on heaving two heavy cross-pieces into place and securing the gates to pay him any attention. One unarmed drummer boy was the least of their worries.

In the yard, *L'Enforceur* was smashing his way forward, using his axe like a scythe to clear a path for his comrades. Right behind him, the innkeeper used the butt of his musket to break bones and bloody heads. The others were doing the same. They charged past the chateau, hacking and thrusting, and into a second, larger yard. Keeping his back to a great barn on his right, the boy edged around the yard, still unnoticed or ignored.

About twenty men had reached taken the defenders by surprise and reached the south wall from which the British were firing down on to the attackers in the woods and the open ground in front of them. If they could open the gates, their comrades would flood into the yard. *L'Enforceur* raised his axe to strike at the bricks and timber that had been piled up to reinforce the gates. But before he could bring it down, the axe fell from his grasp and blood spurted from his head. He crumpled on to the ground.

All around musket shots rang out and one by one the French soldiers died. British musketeers, led by their colonel, had reloaded and reformed and surrounded them. The boy saw his father fall and ran to him. He had been hit in the neck by a musket ball. The boy tried to stem the blood with his hand but it was useless. The light faded from his father's eyes and he died.

A hand took hold of the boy's jacket and hoisted him to his feet. All around lay bodies – French and British together. A big man in an officer's uniform – not as tall as *L'Enforceur*, but broad shouldered and muscular – asked him in French what he was doing there. The boy pointed to his father. '*Mon père.*'

The English officer looked surprised. '*Ton père était brave et toi aussi.*' He turned to a fat soldier beside him and said something the boy did not understand. Thinking that he was to be taken off and shot – he had heard that that was what the British often did to their prisoners – he tried not to look afraid. The soldier took him by the shoulder and marched him back towards the gates through which they had entered the farm.

The great barn by the gates was being used for the wounded. The boy was pushed inside. The fat soldier spoke to an orderly tending to a man who had lost a leg. The orderly nodded and pointed to a heap of straw in the corner of the barn. His meaning was clear enough and the boy made his way past rows of silent, bloody men. Some had lost limbs, others eyes. Their blood and muck covered the floor and for the first time in his twelve years the boy smelt death. In the open, even at the crossroads where they had swept the British aside, he had not smelt it. In this barn it was suffocating. He held his hand to his mouth and tried not to vomit.

Shells flew overhead, muskets fired in their hundreds, men and horses screamed. All around the terrible sounds of battle filled the air. The boy could only guess at what was happening outside in the farm, in the orchard, in the woods and away in the valley and on the ridge. He knew only that his father was dead. He curled up on the heap of straw with his hands over his ears and wept.

For hours the battle raged, wounded men were carried into the barn, the pile of severed limbs grew larger. The surgeons and orderlies could not rest. Arm after arm, leg after leg were thrown on to the pile. Those with minor wounds were patched up and sent back out. Those for whom there was no hope were left to die. His tears dry on his cheeks, the boy sat and watched.

And then a shell crashed into the roof of the barn. Timbers and tiles fell and in seconds the barn was on fire. It filled with smoke so thick that the boy could see no more than an arm's length in front of his face but he knew that he could not stay where he was. He got to his feet and stumbled towards where he thought the door was. Those who could walk were doing the same. But the door had been replaced by a wall of fire. Some hesitated. The boy did not. He leapt through the flames and tumbled on to the earth outside. He crawled to the well and sat against its wall. From the barn came the crack of burning timber and the screams of the dying. Very few escaped.

Too numb to move, he sat by the well not knowing what to do. Should he find somewhere to hide or should he stay where he was? Either way, he was as likely as not to die. If the British did not kill him, a French shell would. He stirred himself.

All along the south wall, opposite the wood, the British had built fire steps from which to shoot over it. He dashed past the chateau and the yard in which the bodies of his father and his comrades still lay, jumped up on to an unoccupied fire step and vaulted over the wall into the clearing. Musket fire whistled around but he reached the edge of the wood unhurt.

The trees, now broken and limbless, offered scant protection. French voices shouted at him to keep his head down and run back towards their lines. Weaving between the trunks and ducking under low branches, he ran as fast as he could until he emerged at the other side, where more troops were waiting for the order to advance. They too were too intent upon what lay before them to pay him much heed and he passed between them without being stopped.

Further back he found a medical station. Drummer boys and buglers were fetching and carrying and bringing water to the injured. He took a pail from a row beside an ambulance, followed a boy to a stream which ran behind them into the valley, filled it with water, drank until his stomach was full, and carried what was left back up to the station. He could hear the battle raging in the valley but he could see nothing for the smoke. For all he knew it was almost over and the British were beaten, just as his father and the lieutenant had said they would be.

Pushing all thought of his father to the back of his mind, all that afternoon he filled his pail from the stream and carried it back to the station, expecting each trip to be the last before he heard shouts of victory. But shouts of victory never came and, when word arrived that the Imperial Guard, the invincibles, had been beaten and were in retreat, they knew it was over. As the light began to fade, he and the other drummers joined the remnants of the 1st Regiment trudging back towards the lines of artillery, defeated, exhausted, broken.

Gradually the smoke cleared and they could see the battlefield on which lay countless thousands of dead and wounded. The battle was over.

1820

At seventeen, he was young to be an innkeeper but with his father dead, killed in the service of France at Waterloo, he had been forced to take the inn on. Now he and his mother ran it together, she in the kitchen and he in the taproom.

He never spoke of his own experiences at the battle but alone at night he did think of them. He thought of the noise and the stench and the wounded and the crippled, of the ill-fated attack on the farm at Hougoumont, of his father's bravery and of the many thousands who had died. Most of all, he thought of how lucky he had been to survive.

Veterans of the battle came to the inn to share their memories – sad memories now, of defeat and death, not of triumph and victory, as it once had been. Nor would there be victories to look forward to. The emperor was imprisoned on the island of St Helena in the middle of the Atlantic Ocean, from where even he could not escape, and every Frenchman knew it. The king had returned with his family to Paris, Napoleon's army was no more; in the towns and villages of France women and children starved. There was precious little for the drinkers to celebrate.

Sometimes he wondered if he had been brave or cowardly or just plain foolish. Sometimes a veteran would try to regale him with tales of the battle; then he would excuse himself and leave the man to someone else. He did not wish to speak of it or to hear about it. Even his mother knew only that her husband had died bravely and that her son, a drummer boy, had mercifully survived. In this, she counted herself fortunate. Many others had been left widows and childless.

The boy had made only one concession to his memories. He had asked his mother to clean and mend his uniform and had folded it away neatly in a chest in his bedroom. On the eighteenth day of June in each of the last five years he had taken it out, brushed it down and swore that his son, if he had one, would never wear one like it.

* * *

The button seller was travelling in Ireland when the duke's letter arrived at the Blinks and Blinks offices, and he did not see it until he returned a month later.

Business was harder to come by than it had been during the French wars and in Ireland he had been taking only modest orders from military outfitters and high-quality tailors and, at the age of thirty, was beginning to worry about the future. His salary, even with a small bonus at the end of each year if the Blinks brothers were happy with his work, had been reduced and he was no longer able to put a little aside for the future. Furthermore, he was away from his wife and daughter much of the time. But, unlike many of those who had fought at Waterloo, and the widows of those who had died there, he had a position, albeit a modest one, and he knew that he should be grateful for it.

The first he knew of the letter was when the brothers summoned him into their office. The Duke of Wellington, they said, had recently visited Birmingham and had made contact with them. He had inquired about the button seller who had been at Waterloo, had described him as slightly built, polite and mounted upon a small cob, and had asked if the whereabouts of the man were known. On learning that he was still in the employ of the firm but was presently in Ireland on business, the duke had had a letter delivered to await his return.

One of the brothers handed him the letter. 'We were unaware that you were known to the duke,' he said. The button seller, at a loss as to how to reply, shuffled his feet and kept his eyes on the floor. 'I do not recall your mentioning it.'

He looked up. 'I was able to perform a small service for the duke, although why he would wish to contact me, I could not say.'

'What was the nature of the service?' asked the other brother.

'Merely the delivery of a message. There was no-one else available at the time. I did not think it worth mentioning.'

'His Grace apparently thinks otherwise. Perhaps you should open the letter.'

'Mr Blinks, I would rather read it in private.'

'Nonsense. The letter has been delivered to this office and therefore concerns all of us. Kindly open it and tell us what his Grace has to say. After all, it might be a large order.' He glanced at his brother. 'We could certainly do with one.'

Reluctantly, the button seller broke the seal and opened the letter. It was brief and he read it quickly. Then he read it again. 'His Grace invites me to Apsley House as soon as it is convenient. He does not say why.' Apsley House, looking out over Hyde Park, had been purchased by the duke from his elder brother, Richard. The London news sheets had reported that the duke had employed the celebrated architect Benjamin Dean Wyatt to carry out extensive renovations on the interior.

The eyebrows of both brothers shot up. 'Apsley House, eh?' asked one. 'A great honour.'

'Indeed, and we would wish to know how it is that the duke considers you worthy of it.'

'I really could not say, sir, but I shall be sure to inform you when I return from London.'

'So you will accept the invitation.'

'It would be discourteous not to and, if I decline it, I might never discover what it is the duke wants of me.'

'Does he suggest a date?'

'He does. He proposes an appointment at 10 o'clock on the

morning of next Wednesday. That is in eight days' time. May I be permitted to travel to London, as his Grace requests?'

Again the Blinks brothers exchanged a look. 'We would never wish to incur the duke's displeasure, but your salary will be adjusted accordingly. We cannot afford to pay you for not working.'

It was a price the button seller would have to pay. If the journey to London cost him a little money, so be it. 'Very well, sirs. I will depart for London on Saturday and aim to be back a week later.'

Apsley House, widely known as Number One, London, for its position as the first house travellers came to when arriving from the west, was every bit as imposing as he had expected. Four great columns rose above three arches and three rows of seven windows each looked out over Hyde Park.

When he arrived punctually at ten o'clock, he was met by a servant who escorted him to the library. Books lined the walls from floor to ceiling, six high-backed library chairs were set around the room, beside each one a small table. It was an informal, welcoming room, no doubt where the duke met his less illustrious visitors. The servant announced him and the duke put aside the book he was reading and rose from his chair. Almost a head taller than the button seller, he wore a black coat, white stock and black trousers. He was just as the button seller remembered him – slim, upright, somewhat forbidding.

He held out his hand. 'Here you are, sir, the cob man himself. I doubted we would meet again and I am happy to see you.'

The button seller shook the duke's hand and bowed his head. 'And I you, your Grace. I am flattered that you should remember me. There was much going on when last we met.'

The duke smiled. 'Indeed there was.' He indicated a chair. 'Sit and tell me what happened to you at the battle. I assumed that you had been a casualty.'

The servant returned with two glasses on a silver tray. He put one on the table beside the button seller. The duke raised his glass in a silent toast. 'I am listening.'

The button seller took a sip from his glass and began. He explained that after he had delivered the message to Marshal Kempt, he had managed to get back to the allied lines, but without his cob. While the battle had raged, he had wandered about behind the lines for a while, uncertain as to what to do, until a medical orderly had seen him and asked for his help getting the most badly wounded on to the ambulances ferrying them to the farmhouse at Mont St Jean. He had spent the rest of the day of the battle working with the medics, carrying stretchers and patching up minor wounds, and having very little idea of how the battle was progressing. It had not been until they had heard cheering that he and some of the orderlies had left their posts and ventured to the top of the ridge. There they had seen that the Prussians had at last arrived and the French Imperial Guard were beaten, and had known that the battle was won.

The duke listened in silence, his gaze never leaving the button seller. 'And you managed to find your way back to Birmingham.'

'I did, your Grace. I was fortunate.'

The duke nodded. 'Perhaps you were, but some say I too am fortunate. I believe that fortune is what a man makes of it. And you performed a signal service to your country. At last the Corsican is safely marooned on the island of St Helena, from which not even he will escape, and England is safe again.'

'There were many on that day who gave much more than I did, sir.'

'There were many indeed who gave their lives or suffered terrible wounds, but with very few exceptions, they were soldiers carrying out orders. You were a civilian and need not have taken that message to Kempt.' He laughed. 'I could not have had you shot if you had refused. By doing as I asked, you risked you own life and saved others.' He paused to take a sip from his glass. 'As a civilian, I cannot award you the Waterloo Medal, much as I would like to. I can only thank you and ask if there is anything I can do for you in return for your service.'

The button seller had not expected this. He had not really expected anything at all. A few minutes with the duke, perhaps, certainly no orders for buttons, nor any sort of reward for what he had done. Indeed, he had scarcely thought of the matter in the five years since that day. He thought of his wife and daughter at home in Birmingham and took a deep breath. 'I am looking for a new position, your Grace, one that does not so often take me from my family. If you were able to suggest a suitable opportunity, I would count myself more than amply rewarded.'

The duke scratched his chin. 'It so happens that my brother is Master of the Royal Mint and I believe that he may be able to help. I will speak to him and ask him to contact you at Blinks and Blinks in Birmingham. How would that suit you?'

'I should be most grateful, your Grace. I do hope it was not impertinent of me to ask.'

'Not at all. Leave it with me.' He rose and extended his hand. 'And I thank you for your service.'

The button seller bowed. 'And I thank you, your Grace.'

A month later, the button seller and his family moved to London. They rented a small house in Smithfield, near to the premises of the

Royal Mint, where he had accepted a position at nearly twice the salary he had received at Blinks and Blinks. He never again spoke of the battle or his part in it.

The story of the button seller, or 'the cob man', was one the Duke of Wellington himself liked to tell.

Several contemporary accounts mention the French drummer boy who managed to get into the Hougoumont farm.

The names of neither the button seller nor the drummer boy are known.